FDR'S TREASURE

By

Joel Fox

ISBN 13: 978-0615889399

Library of Congress Control Number 2013917166

Printed in the United States of America
Bronze Circle Press
Los Angeles

DEDICATION

To the men who sailed on the USS Houston (CA-30) in World War II and to all veterans of that war, especially my father, Tec 4 Harry Fox, 328th Infantry Regiment, 26th Yankee Division, U.S. Army.

ACKNOWLEDGMENTS

Thank you to the librarians at the Franklin D. Roosevelt Presidential Library and Museum in Hyde Park, New York for guiding me through the documents of President Roosevelt's travels on the USS Houston.

A salute to Captain Steven B. Frates, United States Navy Reserve (retired) for readily offering advice on Naval operations.

To David Finkel for filling me in on small aircrafts.

Thank you to my editor, Mike Sirota, and to FBI Special Agent, Alonzo Hill, who offered me some key insights.

A big thank you to author, mentor, and friend, Teresa Burrell, without whom this book would not exist.

And, finally to the late Jeff Sherratt who inspired me to keep at it.

Any errors of fact or imaginings are mine alone.

Zane Rigby Series

Lincoln's Hand

FDR'S Treasure

Prologue

"Went on a treasure hunt myself once," the president said, tilting his head back and clamping his teeth onto a yellowish cigarette holder for a quick puff before removing it. "Up to Oak Island in Canada. Didn't find anything. Wish you chaps better luck."

"Thank you, Mr. President, jolly good," replied the taller of the two men sitting in chairs beside the president on the aft deck of the USS *Houston*. The warship rolled ever so lightly over the gentle waves flowing into Wafer Bay off Cocos Island in the Pacific Ocean three hundred miles from Central America.

The man's thick British accent brought a smile to the president's face.

"You sound a bit like Mr. Churchill," Franklin Delano Roosevelt said. "I've listened to his recorded speeches on the happenings in Europe."

"Mr. Churchill says it right. I think you know that, Mr. President. That's why we seek your help with our..." The man lowered his voice for emphasis rather than to be secretive "...treasure hunt."

"We shall see. We shall see. It's important to at least get the ball rolling, as we say in my country." Roosevelt laughed then dragged smoke from the cigarette through the holder and blew it away with the sea breeze.

"Colonel Randolph," Roosevelt called to a Marine officer standing by the rail waiting for the president's attention. "Please join us."

The Marine colonel stepped toward the president and his party. He was a short man but solidly built. The expression, *Built like a fireplug*, came to mind. The colonel saluted the president and when the president gestured with his hand the colonel stood at ease.

"Colonel Randolph, our British treasure hunting friends need help with their plan. I think you're the man for the job."

"Treasure hunting, sir?" The colonel could not hide his surprise.

"Surely you know Cocos Island is famous for hidden treasure. Pirates and mercenaries burying their loot." The president laughed and his guests smiled along with him. The colonel's face did not change expression.

The president let the smile slip from his lips and stared at the Marine. "Our friends here need help with their treasure plans. See what you can cook up, Colonel."

The Marine knew when a superior officer gave an order. He snapped off a strong, "Yes sir!"

The president smiled. "After lunch of course. Ah, I see the steward is on his way."

Roosevelt placed the cigarette holder between his teeth and drew smoke deeply into his lungs.

Chapter 1

"I don't talk to errand boys," the famous writer and political commentator, Paul Mallory, growled. He had the door of his Georgetown townhouse opened wide enough to expose only the width of his fleshy, dough-like face.

In his early days as a Private Investigator Zane Rigby would have responded to such a comment with a right hook to Mallory's jaw. But, the senior FBI agent had mellowed over the years, as had the Bureau with its dictates of politeness in the face of arrogance and just plain idiocy.

Idiot must be Mallory's middle name, Rigby thought. The agent had seen Mallory turn his arrogant streak into a nice paying gig, popping up on the tube to shoot at and shoot down all sorts of personalities in the public arena. He was referred to as that *Son-of-a-Bitch Mallory* so often that some people probably thought it was his given name.

Rigby's jaw remained tight as he tried to calm his voice. "I'm an FBI agent following a lead. That lead was provided by the Speaker of the House of Representatives—"

Mallory cut him off. "That makes you an errand boy, and I don't talk to errand boys."

Rigby ignored the comment and plowed ahead. "The Speaker wants to know what your interest is with President Franklin Roosevelt and a buried treasure."

"Isn't that too bad," Mallory said. He wore a blue cotton sweat suit, the top zippered halfway up exposing a gray t-shirt underneath. It looked like Mallory had just returned from a jog or walk. Maybe he wanted to end the conversation and jump into the shower.

"Scram before I call the cops." Mallory smiled. He apparently enjoyed threatening an officer of the law with arrest.

Rigby had no idea what the Speaker's "special project" was and he couldn't imagine how a treasure hunt by a former president eighty or so years ago could disrupt it, but that's the kind of crap you got involved with when you ran the Bureau's Office for Cases of Historical Significance. For Rigby though, there was only so much guff he was going to take from this guy. TV show moderators and producers might like Mallory's style as a ratings booster, but for Rigby the only thing boosted by Mallory was his blood pressure and he was about to explode all over the sap.

Mallory didn't give him the chance. Without another word he slammed the door in Rigby's face.

Fine!

Rigby didn't want to deal with the jerk anyway. Just being asked to talk to Mallory hurt his pride. The government was on the verge of shutting down with the president and Congress at odds over some funding bill. More partisan squabbling. The Monument Bomber was still out there despite being stopped in his latest attack on a cherished American monument. And, here he was having a door slammed in his face by *Son-of-a-Bitch Mallory,* who was chasing a story that probably wasn't worth spit when it happened decades ago—if it ever happened. Who the hell cares!

Rigby walked down the stairs, through the open wrought-iron gate and out to the sidewalk. His car was a block to his left but storefronts were off to the right. He expected he could find a bar or a coffee shop there.

A coffee house popped up first and he went in, ordered a black coffee—none of the fancy stuff that coffee places pushed out these days—and added the biggest piece of comfort food he could find, a glazed bear claw, before settling in at a corner table.

As irritated as he felt having to put up with Mallory, he was more disgusted with his assignment and what it meant for him. Sure, he had success uncovering the secret in

Lincoln's Tomb, but Rigby wasn't concerned about history. He was concerned with doing the job he'd joined the FBI to do. Chasing down leads on what a dead president did long ago wasn't the job for which he signed up.

It was a crazy job, Rigby recalled, reading about pirate treasure on the document sent over to him by the Speaker of the House of Representatives. Franklin Delano Roosevelt found pirate treasure, said the document. A secret find only now about to be revealed by a big-time investigative journalist who draws the biggest paydays and is a talking head on all the cable news shows. That supposedly made him a credible source. Rigby didn't think so. He had seen Mallory perform on those TV talk shows a number of times. *Perform* was the right word. The guy loved theatrics.

Rigby shook his head again. This time the disgust was minimal. It was the sheer incomprehensible idea that made him doubt.

How did Roosevelt manage to find this treasure on some faraway island and keep it a secret? The man was president of the United States, for goodness sakes. He traveled with Secret Service agents and aides and was on a Navy ship with officers and crew.

And, he was in a wheelchair.

You'd think there would be a record of this treasure somewhere, from someone.

The reason he knew the story was crazy was because the document said Roosevelt found a pirate treasure on his fishing trip—*and left the treasure behind.*

Yet, for whatever reason, the Speaker of the House found this to be important. He personally called the Judge, the head of the FBI, asking for help to find out what Mallory knew, and the Judge ordered Rigby to investigate. It came under his Office for Cases of Historical Significance, she said.

His office. The one-man show in which he had absolutely no interest. But, that was the job he'd been

5

assigned. Do this job, he told himself, and the Judge would put him back on the Monument Bomber Task Force. It was just a matter of time.

Rigby sighed.

Do the job and don't let *Son-of-a-Bitch Mallory* get the best of you. Rigby saw the only way to do the job was to go right through Mallory. That's exactly what he intended to do.

Don't put off till tomorrow who you can beat up today, he remembered his father telling him, or something more gentle than that. Same idea. Rigby wasn't in a gentle mood. He was still in Mallory's neighborhood and he was going to revisit Mallory now and get it over with.

This time he was going to be more PI than FBI.

Rigby downed the rest of his coffee and left the half-eaten bear claw on the table. He didn't need more comfort food.

Rigby made his way through the unlatched wrought-iron gate in front of Mallory's brownstone. He climbed the six stairs to the entrance and reached out to push the front door buzzer.

His finger stopped an inch away from the button when he saw the smear of blood on the doorknob.

The blood sparkled in the midday sun. Rigby saw the door was slightly ajar, caught up on the edge of what appeared to be a throw rug inside. Someone rushing to get out the door must have kicked the rug forward.

Rigby reached inside his jacket and pulled his gun from the shoulder holster. He gently pushed the door back with his free hand and looked down the corridor entrance of the townhouse. The corridor ended at an open double door to a room occupying an oversized roll-top desk against the back wall.

Sprawled on the rug in front of the desk was a body—dressed in a blue sweat suit.

Chapter 2

Rigby walked through the doorway cautiously. He looked to the right into a parlor. Everything in place. A stairway on his right past the parlor entrance led to the second floor. He took a few steps down the corridor to an archway on the left. The dining room, a table and chairs, a hutch against the wall filled with plates, cups and saucers. Nothing broken, nothing disturbed. The door to the kitchen was open. From where he stood in the hallway, Rigby saw nothing out of the ordinary in there.

He moved to the end of the corridor and the double doors that opened into a large office/study, sun pouring in through large bay windows.

Unlike the other rooms on this floor, this room was a mess. Papers scattered about, books on the floor, drawers pulled from the desk and dumped.

Rigby looked at the body lying face down in the sea of papers.

Quickly checking the room, Rigby looked behind the chair and sofa, cautiously approached the room's closet and yanked it open, his gun at the ready. He knew the upstairs needed to be checked but he was comfortable enough to attend to the man on the floor.

He crouched down, put a hand on the man's shoulder and turned him over.

Paul Mallory.

An ugly, crimson wound opened the top of his chest just below his neck. A small trickle of blood rolled from the wound and absorbed into the collar of a gray t-shirt Mallory wore under the sweat suit.

Mallory was not breathing. He would not breathe again.

How long since Mallory had slammed the front door in his face? Twenty minutes? Was there someone in the townhouse with him when Rigby first arrived? Is that why Mallory stopped him at the door? Or had someone showed up right after he left for the coffee shop, did Mallory in and ran off?

If the killer had run off. Rigby couldn't be sure that the killer wasn't on the premises; he would have to inform the cops right away.

Rigby didn't know what this turn of events meant for his current assignment. Mallory was on a search for FDR's treasure. Rigby had no clue about the treasure and could find no reference to it. Without Mallory his investigation would be over before it began.

Nothing could be done for Mallory except find his killer. Rigby pulled out his cell phone and dialed 9-1-1. He would report the murder and wait for the police backup before searching the upstairs.

As he waited for the police to arrive, Rigby stayed in the study. The room at the end of the hallway was a defensible position in case the killer still lurked in another room of the townhouse. However, the blood smear on the front doorknob was a strong indicator that the killer was gone.

Rigby knew better than to touch anything in the room. He glanced at the papers that were turned face up on the hardwood floor and the round carpet in the center of the room. Mostly bills, a couple of invoices for writing assignments Mallory had carried out, a double-spaced page of what appeared to be an article he was writing that mentioned Babe Ruth and a baseball connected to the 1927 Yankees.

Rigby looked about the room more closely. One wall was made up of bookshelves. A number of books on each shelf had been pulled off and were on the floor. Rigby detected a pattern to where the books had been pulled.

Whoever did that was looking for something behind the books. A safe, perhaps?

Rigby walked around the wood-paneled study taking in the framed paintings on the wall. There certainly wasn't a theme. Two cowboys squaring off against each other, hands on the butts of holstered guns, ready to draw; Civil War soldiers, some in blue some in gray, sharing a canteen, all marked by the sweat and dirt acquired at a recent battle; a bucolic valley with deer scampering over a meadow and drinking from a stream.

A large frame included both the citation for a Golden Pen Award as the best magazine article of the year along with the copy of the article. He scanned the article, which had something to do with a letter of peace sent to Adolf Hitler in 1939. A second prize for an article on the Selma civil rights march was framed next to the other prizewinner. A third framed article with a nasty comment handwritten across the text that, judging from the article's title, appeared to be a positive appraisal of former president John F. Kennedy.

Framing the article with the negative comment scrawled across it indicated Mallory took pleasure in getting under people's skin. That was the *Son-of-a Bitch Mallory* Rigby watched on the tube, the guy who had slammed the door in his face.

There was one unframed piece hanging on the wall— a topographical map of an island. It was taped to the wall of the study by the entrance doors on the opposite side of the room from the bay windows. Rigby's back was to the map when he had entered the room.

Rigby walked to the map and looked at it. The island appeared fairly small, perhaps three or four miles by five miles he guessed, just eyeballing the size of the island based on the scale depicted on the map's key. He saw no indications of towns or villages on the map. No *X marks the spot* if, indeed, this map had anything to do with the pirate treasure he was supposed to be trailing.

A squad of police arrived all at once, led by a skinny detective who identified himself as Rory Denver. IDs were exchanged and Denver followed Rigby's advice to send a team of officers on a search mission to the second floor of the townhouse.

Surveying the scene as some of his investigators got to work, Denver said, "The press is gonna be all over this one. Not only a celeb o' sorts 'cause of all them TV appearances, but one of their own. Cops make sure they get the guy who takes down one of their own. Reporters the same. They don't admit it, but reporters go hard when one of their own is gunned down."

Rigby said nothing and Denver turned to focus his attention on the FBI man.

"So tell me, Agent Rigby. Exactly why were you visiting Mr. Mallory?"

"Official business," Rigby said, an automatic response to give him a moment to think through his situation, to decide if there was any reason to play coy with the cop.

"What kind of official business?" Denver said. He spread his feet apart and put his fisted hands on his hips. He was getting comfortable, prepared for a long conversation.

The detective's question wasn't innocent. The cop was exploring a connection between Rigby and the murder. Rigby was not offended. He was found standing over the body. Even a wayward cop or FBI agent occasionally commits murder. The cop was doing his job.

Rigby decided there was nothing to hide about his current assignment. He wasn't trying to prevent leaks of extraordinary activity as when he participated in the opening of Lincoln's Tomb. As strange as this assignment might be, revealing his mission was the best way to quell Denver's suspicion.

"I intended to question Mallory about a story he was working on. Something about Franklin Roosevelt and a buried treasure."

"Franklin Roosevelt?" Denver's eyebrows lifted in surprise. "*The* Franklin Roosevelt? The FBI don't have enough to deal with in our messed up world, you gotta investigate somethin' that happened when my daddy was a pup?"

"When you're in charge of the Office for Cases of Historical Significance you do."

"So what was this article Mallory was writing? Why's it so important now?"

"Wish I knew," Rigby said. "I got a note from a higher up and I came here to talk to the man."

"And did you?"

"What?"

"Talk to the man?"

Rigby paused. He knew his answer would get him in deeper with the cop.

"Tried to. He wasn't interested."

"You mean you saw him alive?"

Rigby nodded.

"When?"

"Half-hour ago."

Denver blinked. Rigby knew this bit of information surprised the cop. He was turning it over in his mind. Denver said, "Did you kill him?"

"He slammed the door in my face. I never got into his house. I went and got a cup of coffee."

"Then why'd you come back?"

"Someone slammed the door in your face and you were on an assignment, what would you do?"

"I wouldn't get no damn cup of coffee first," the cop said in a Humphrey Bogart tough-guy voice.

The medical examiner was working over the body. He said, "Bullet wound. Not long ago. If the killer's on foot you can probably catch him with a bicycle."

"If I knew which way he went," Denver said with a

shrug. "Guy like this got lots of enemies. Anybody and his mother could be out for revenge."

Turning back toward Rigby, Denver continued. "I'm gonna need to talk to that person on the top that gave you the order."

Rigby suppressed a self-satisfied smile. The Judge isn't going to be happy with this inquiry, he thought. "Goes all the way to the top. My mission was authorized by the Director of the FBI."

Denver let out a low whistle. "Hear she's tough," was all he said.

Rigby would be visiting another higher-up—the Speaker of the House. It was his request that the FBI confirm Mallory was on to something with his FDR story. Rigby was convinced this request was more than about treasure. He wanted to know what that something was.

Rigby left the townhouse, pausing for a moment to again look at the blood smear on the door handle.

That's when the outdoor wall light above the door shattered in many pieces a split second before Rigby heard the distinctive report of a gunshot.

Chapter 3

"Fool," the man muttered as he screeched the car around the corner and into a nearby parking garage. Was there ever a bigger fool? He bit his lip and chewed on it, wanting to draw blood, wanting to punish himself.

It was an impulse that made him pull the trigger, an impulse that could ruin months of planning. Revenge is a terrible thing, he learned from the teacher in the one-room mountain school. Yet, he must have his revenge against the FBI man. Rigby denied him his great prize—destroying a cherished American monument.

He was not finished with his one-man war against America. He would destroy another monument. But that was not all he would do in this war inside the belly of the beast. He would finish Rigby.

The man pulled the new Mercedes into a parking stall and turned off the engine. He left the keys in the ignition. It had not been difficult stealing the lady's purse. She left it on a chair beside her in the outdoor seating area of the restaurant. Let them find the car. He left no fingerprints behind.

He knew where Rigby was. He'd been following him. He was building his dossier. He would know the man's every move. Where he spends his weekends; where he eats breakfast. He knew of his mistress, the young Asian woman. She must be a mistress. He spent much time with her at that bar in Cleveland Park.

He had spent months planning his revenge, gathering facts. His benefactors were troubled. They wanted another attack on America. He demanded assistance and equipment, needed to find his prey, to get his revenge. He promised a spectacular destruction would come. He would not tell them what he planned. The truth was, he had nothing planned. He would come up with a target, but destroying Rigby was something he had to do.

He felt he was almost ready. Then something strange came over him this day. Preparing to follow Rigby to his next destination with the stolen Mercedes, he was sitting in the idling car. Rigby emerged from the townhouse with the police cars out front and stood on the top step. He presented such a welcoming target.

Why spend so much time planning when fortune put Rigby in his path, standing still at the doorway at the top of the stairs? He was not worried about the police. He would dump the car quickly. They would search for the car and he would be gone.

He just took the gun off the seat next to him and fired.

And missed!

He swore to himself he would not miss next time.

Chapter 4

"Is that a shard of glass caught in your lapel?" Richard Nolan asked Rigby, pointing to the glass sliver.

Rigby craned his neck to the left so he could check out the portion of his suit jacket's lapel where Nolan pointed.

"I believe it is," Rigby said matter-of-factly and picked the piece of glass off the jacket.

"Have a close encounter with a beer bottle?" Nolan asked with a smile, holding his hand out across his desk in a helpful way to take the piece of glass from Rigby and throw it away.

"Actually had a close encounter with a bullet." Rigby dropped the glass into Nolan's outstretched hand. "One of the reasons I want to see your boss."

Nolan held the piece of glass for a moment as the smile faded from his face. He then tossed it into a trashcan.

Richard Nolan was a well-built man in his late thirties, sporting a crew cut, something not seen very often nowadays. Rigby remembered wearing one as a teen. He never liked it but the cut was in then and he went along. Rigby wondered if Nolan was a former Marine still carrying around the spit and polish. A top aide for the Speaker of the House of Representatives, Nolan had come far in a short time, Rigby thought. However, they just gave him the menial job of blocking back, as in keep the FBI agent away from the boss.

Nolan had ushered Rigby into his office, walls decorated with Nolan shaking hands with every notable personality and elected official in Washington regardless of party from the president on down.

The aide shook his head. "I'm afraid you're going to have to deal with me."

15

"Did you kill Paul Mallory?"

The Mallory killing had hit the cable news cycle and had been worked over thoroughly since it occurred hours earlier. Washington was abuzz with the story of the big-time reporter meeting a murderous end. The bullet that missed Rigby by inches was not revealed to the press corps.

The listing of Mallory's enemies amassed in a lifetime had begun. Rigby assumed an ambitious young political aide had no desire to be added to the list.

"I was working at this desk all day; people know I was here."

"And your boss?"

"Please, Agent Rigby. I know you don't believe that. Why are you going in this direction?"

"Because the Speaker asked my boss, the Director of the FBI, to go have a chat with Mallory about something in FDR's past. Now Mallory's dead. Murdered. Could be for any number of reasons, I suppose. I watch the cable news shows, too. He wasn't a likeable sort. But my connection with this case started with the request from the Speaker. So he has to answer a question or two."

"I don't think he does," Nolan said, pushing his chair back. "I know a little something about your assignment. I prepared that paper for the Speaker. He wanted to know about a treasure hunt in the 1930s."

"That's all?"

"Yes."

"Why?"

Nolan smiled but remained silent.

Rigby knew Nolan was going to protect his boss. To get to see the Speaker, Rigby would have to use Nolan's strength to get past him, a sort of verbal jujitsu move.

Rigby stood. "Thanks for your time, Mr. Nolan. Sorry you won't cooperate."

"Nothing personal." Nolan allowed the smug smile to grow wider across his face. "Enjoy the rest of the day."

"How do you expect me to do that when I have to deal with reporters all day?"

"Reporters?"

"Reporters can be a pain. You know that. Good thing you got all that experience dealing with them."

"What are you going to do, Rigby?"

"Since I can't talk to the Speaker, I'll just tell reporters that the Speaker had me investigating Mallory for some reason. I don't know what was behind it exactly. The Speaker had some dealings with Mallory and now Mallory's dead. Think maybe if I start with a couple of those talking heads on the cable shows I won't have to talk to so many reporters—the word will spread like a prairie fire."

Nolan peered hard at Rigby as if he were warming up some X-ray vision to melt the FBI man on the spot. Finally, he opened his mouth to a narrow slit and hissed, "Wait here!"

The wait was a short one. Nolan returned in less than three minutes and without a word motioned Rigby to follow him. They exited Nolan's office and crossed the reception area of the Speaker's suite of offices. After a rap on the door by Nolan they entered the top man's spacious office.

Speaker of the United States House of Representatives, Marshall Gaines, was working at his desk but he sprang up and circled around, hand extended in greeting to his visitor.

"Welcome, Special Agent. Always good to see a dedicated member of the Bureau," the Speaker said in his Midwest twang.

A little too much politico-type patter for Rigby, but he let it pass with a nod and a handshake.

"I understand you have a question for me. Please take a seat."

Rigby was directed to a set of comfortable, stuffed chairs set around a wide coffee table.

"Maybe a few," Rigby said.

"Few?" the Speaker echoed as he sat down across the table.

"A few questions," Rigby said. He didn't wait for a response but dove into the interview.

"Of course, you know why I'm here. You asked the Director to involve the Office for Cases of Historical Significance in Paul Mallory's investigation of FDR and..." Here, Rigby hesitated a moment and realized he was curious to study the Speaker's expression when he uttered the next words: "...buried treasure."

Gaines didn't flinch. He waited for Rigby to proceed.

"I have to ask you why?"

"This is a sensitive matter," Speaker Gaines began. "At least, the bottom line is. Mallory told me he had uncovered some important information about President Roosevelt and he intended to track down the story and publish it."

"What information?"

Gaines gave a snort and turned his palms up. "I don't know."

It surprised Rigby that the Speaker was so obviously ducking his question.

"With all due respect, Mr. Speaker, you can't expect me to believe that. You involved the FBI. I'm sure you didn't do so lightly. What did Mallory have on FDR and what is this treasure business?"

"Why do you say that, I mean, that he had something on FDR?"

"Because Paul Mallory writes exposés. To my knowledge, every time a subject of his exposé sues him, Mallory wins. So he may be a shark...*was* a shark," Rigby corrected himself, "but he knew where and how to swim. If you got Mallory chasing down something about Roosevelt then I'm guessing he had something on the president. The only thing I can't figure is, who cares? It's ancient history."

"Is it?" was all that Gaines would say.

Rigby leaned forward, his torso extending partway across the table separating the two men. "Mr. Speaker, why don't we stop the dance and you tell me what this is about?"

"The truth is," Gaines began, "I don't know what Mallory was after. He said he had a lead on something meaningful regarding Roosevelt. He knew of a special project I'd cooked up that involved FDR's memory. He told me I might not want to proceed if he could prove his suspicions."

"What suspicions?"

"Good question. I know this sounds foolish but I do have more important things to attend. If he had something damaging on FDR—and remember, this was Paul Mallory we're talking about—he had the reputation that would make me believe him. I would let him play out the string.

"Yes, I asked the Director to assist," the Speaker continued. "I had two reasons. One, if this were research into something of historical significance your office should be there. It's the law. Two, I wanted the FBI to keep an eye on Mallory to see what he was up to."

"Spy on him, you mean."

"You know what the man was like. I didn't want him running off half-cocked but I also knew he's right on what he reports. Given the circumstances, I had to give him a chance. I couldn't afford to make a mistake."

Rigby considered what the Speaker was saying, then asked, "What's this special project Mallory knew about?"

Marshall Gaines blew out a breath and looked across the room to Richard Nolan standing by a window. No words were spoken and Rigby was not sure if facial expressions communicated any thoughts between the men, but when Gaines looked back at Rigby the FBI man saw a determination in the other man's eyes.

Gaines raised his hand extending two fingers and motioned Nolan to the corner of the room. The aide understood and crossed the room to a piece of furniture with bookshelves on top and a set of drawers below. Nolan opened the top drawer and extracted a large folio case. Rigby recognized it as the kind that artists used to hold larger paintings or drawings. The case was fairly flat.

Nolan carried the case to the table between Rigby and Gaines and laid it down. The Speaker pulled the zipper around three sides of the case and pulled back the top cover. Some sort of cardboard-like backing for artwork, if that's what it was, lay face down in the case.

Rigby wondered what incriminating evidence would be revealed when they turned over the drawing or picture, or whatever it was. He allowed his imagination to fly. Was there a picture of a dead body with Franklin Roosevelt sitting in his wheelchair, a shotgun across his lap? Or FDR with a naked woman, not his wife, cavorting in a swimming pool?

The Speaker looked at Rigby again and the agent could see Gaines was weighing his decision to proceed. Then, the Speaker turned over the cardboard backing.

Chapter 5

"**M**ount Rushmore," Rigby said, not hiding his surprise at what was pictured on the board.

The crystal clear photograph of four American presidents sculptured on a South Dakota mountainside filled the other side of the board. White stone faces of Washington, Jefferson, Theodore Roosevelt and Lincoln were backed by an azure sky. The photograph was awe-inspiring, but Rigby didn't understand the significance.

"Nice," Rigby said. "So what's the deal? I saw that *National Treasure* movie. Is FDR's treasure up in the Black Hills like in the movie?"

"If life were only as easy as finding treasure in a movie," the Speaker responded. "Do you know how hard it is to get anything done in Washington, Agent Rigby?"

Rigby had that creepy feeling on the back of his neck whenever politics entered a discussion. He smelled that rat from the beginning of this Roosevelt treasure exercise.

"Ideology, pressure groups that see a solution only one way. You have to be pure to a group's ideal…and, of course, there are many groups with their ideals. It's often like arguing the true religion. There's no room for compromise. What did Bismarck say? 'Politics is the art of the possible.' Not in this day and age. I don't know how close we are to a caning on the Senate floor like the one that occurred in 1856, but this country's political future is actually edging closer to its political past. Polarization is as fierce now as in any era since the Civil War."

"That stuff turns me off to politics," Rigby said as he watched Speaker Gaines put the photograph of Mount Rushmore flat on the table.

"Might be nice to bridge the gap…"

"Get something done," Rigby said, finishing the Speaker's thought.

Gaines nodded. "Right. When we're all in the cloak room or sitting around a bar puffing on cigars or having drinks there's more agreement than the press reports. For many of us, anyway. The press stirs up the conflict. Sells papers, as they used to say."

"Mallory was going to fix all that up for you by discovering a buried treasure? I don't get it, Mr. Speaker."

"Actually, Mallory was trying to disrupt the fix."

Rigby felt like he had wandered off the trail in thick woods and didn't know how he got lost. "What's your fix to this never-ending thing with the president and the senate leader…?"

Rigby fluttered his hands in the air as though he could grab the right word if it floated by.

"Pissing contest," the Speaker said with an easy smile. "Partisan ideology, no give, pissing contest."

Okay, Rigby thought. That works, although he was a bit surprised at the Speaker's choice of words. Rigby was a bit old-fashioned, but he felt there was a certain decorum to maintain inside the walls of the U.S. Capitol.

"What's happening, or what we hoped to happen, is not going to change human nature. But, maybe, just maybe, people will put down their swords. Take a moment to think before making harsh attacks or have pre-determined negative thoughts just because someone is from a different political party. Try to work together knowing at times different attitudes prevail in this great country of ours."

The Speaker finished his speech. Rigby had no doubt Gaines had made this short talk before. The words sounded practiced, the tone polished. What he had to say made sense, although Rigby felt it was pretty naïve coming from the Speaker of the House. Rigby watched as Gaines lifted the next card placed face-down in the folio and looked at his aide… Richard Nolan offered a slight nod. Gaines turned over the card.

An elaborate drawing filled the opposite side of the card. Rigby instantly recognized it as Mount Rushmore— except it wasn't quite right. Washington, Jefferson, TR, and Abe all held their familiar spots on the mountaintop.

They were not alone.

Rigby moved in for a closer look even as the Speaker held the card higher to offer a better view. Two other faces stared out from the mountain in this depiction of Mount Rushmore, and Rigby had no trouble recognizing either one of them. Next to Abraham Lincoln, peering off in the same direction as Jefferson and Teddy Roosevelt was the sculptured head of Franklin Delano Roosevelt. Next to FDR, carved into the rock so that the face looked off in a southwesterly direction, was Ronald Reagan.

Gaines lowered the card. He had a big grin on his face. "I'm going to get the funding to build it," he said.

Given the budget situation, getting the money might be a bigger trick than the carving, Rigby thought. All he could say was, "A huge undertaking."

"An important one, Agent Rigby. America lives by symbols. How symbolic to bring the icons of two political factions together side by side on the memorial. Both Franklin Roosevelt and Ronald Reagan transformed the modern presidency. They're both extremely polarizing figures, yet both enjoyed huge popularity during and after their terms. Think of this: Reagan started out as a Democrat and became a Republican. Roosevelt started as a Republican and became a Democrat. FDR and RR sitting side by side for eternity. I think it will lead to healing and to progress."

Rigby understood the enormity of the project and he could feel the expectation and confidence Gaines exuded for the mission, but he didn't understand the Mallory connection.

"I'm impressed, Mr. Speaker, but why is Paul Mallory dead?"

The smile vanished from Gaines' face as Rigby dragged him back to the reality of the moment and away from fantasyland in South Dakota.

"I don't know why. A burglary gone wrong, I suppose. It couldn't have anything to do with Double R."

"Double R?"

"The code name for the project. Roosevelt and Reagan. Everyone involved in the project was instructed to use the code in correspondence and email. This was not a government secret of national importance, although I firmly believe the goal is extremely important. No security clearance to know about it. We just thought the fewer people that knew, the better. Trouble is, word started to leak. Mallory found out."

"So he was going to write about it and tell the world?"

"As I told you, Agent, he was going to write about it in a way that would stop the project. At least, he thought he was onto something."

Rigby was confused. He saw the enthusiasm the Speaker had for the idea of putting the Double Rs on Mount Rushmore. He heard the hope in his voice that the project might heal the great polarizing divide in the country. Yet, it was the Speaker who authorized the investigation by Mallory into Roosevelt's past that Gaines was now telling him could end the project.

"You're going to have to clear something up for me, Mr. Speaker. What exactly was Paul Mallory after?"

"We've gone over that territory, Agent Rigby. I don't know what he was after. He simply came to me and said he knew about the Mount Rushmore project. He told me I better hold off because he was onto an angle about FDR and if it played out I might not want to put Roosevelt's face on the memorial. What his *angle* was, I don't know. He was a top reporter with plenty of scalps on his belt. I figured I better give him some rope. Asking the FBI to assist made sense so I could know what he was up to."

"All he told you was that there's some buried treasure involved and no more?"

"What he said," Richard Nolan interjected, taking a seat at the coffee table, "was that Roosevelt was onto buried treasure in Cocos Island but he left the impression there was more to it."

"He didn't tell you what more?" Rigby looked at Nolan, then Gaines, and each answered with a shake of the head.

Rigby continued: "I guess the secret died with him unless he wrote something down. Not much for me to do now."

"Not true," said the Speaker emphatically. "You must find out what Mallory was after."

"Excuse me, sir, but Mallory was trying to undercut your project, now Mallory's out of the way."

"Are you accusing the Speaker of putting him out of the way?" Nolan snapped, seemingly ready to explode from the chair.

"You'd know if I was accusing someone." Rigby sent the volley back as hard as he'd received it. "What I'm asking, Mr. Speaker, is if Mallory can't reveal the secret, why don't you just go ahead with your project? You don't need me. I wouldn't know where to begin."

"I do need you, Agent Rigby. I need to know what Mallory knew. I wish I could give you a starting point but I can't. I think this is a momentous venture we have here. Both from a standpoint of the carvings and the political message it will send. As everyone knows, the president and the Senate Majority leader are at each other's throats and the Congress is at a standstill. I want to proceed. But I don't want any surprises. I don't need for FDR's history that Mallory was tracking to take down the project when I try to get it funded. You have to find out what Mallory was after and eliminate the surprise so I can go forward."

25

How would he even begin? Rigby wondered. He doubted there was anyone around from the Roosevelt days who would know anything about a treasure hunt. How could a treasure hunt undercut Roosevelt's reputation? Maybe he didn't have to expend too much energy trying to find a starting point. The Judge wasn't going to permit him to run off looking for buried treasure.

Chapter 6

Rigby's call for an immediate appointment with the FBI Director was routed to her assistant, who informed Rigby that the Director had decided to attend the closing session of the annual meeting of the Society of Former FBI Special Agents. Rigby knew the meeting was taking place. He had attended the opening day to mingle with some of the former agents that he knew. The Judge gave a speech in the opening session and had returned the evening of the last day to make some goodbyes.

Rigby headed to the Washington Hilton. He found the Judge standing outside a meeting room amid a small knot of agents. He knew Walt Adams, who had spent time teaching him the ropes when he was a new agent and recognized the tall African-American, Bill Hightower, who dominated the after-hours baskctball league under the nickname "Higher" Hightower. Hightower looked like he could still play some ball. There were a couple of older retired agents in the group that Rigby didn't recognize. One senior agent had bushy white eyebrows and was also in good shape; the other must have been in the service when J. Edgar was still a young man. He was forced to lean forward with a curved spine, his weight balanced on the head of a cane.

The group was in a merry mood and enjoyed a good laugh at what the Judge was saying. Rigby attached himself to the group with a "hello" and nod to Hightower and a handshake with Adams. The Judge introduced the older men as Agent Jones with the bushy eyebrows and Agent Fillmore, who could not let go of the cane to shake hands.

"Agent Rigby," the Judge said with a bemused smile. "Are you on the program?"

It was her way of asking—*what are you doing here?*

"I need to talk to you."

"It can't wait?"

"About the Mallory case."

Surprisingly, the Judge's response was a wide smile that prompted a laugh from another member of the group. "Yes, we were just talking about that."

Rigby arched an eyebrow in surprise. The Judge talking about a case that required secrecy because of its sensitivity was *not* according to the book. She must feel very comfortable among the former agents.

"Looks like Mallory made life easier for you, Rigby," Agent Jones said. "No need to investigate that Roosevelt thing anymore."

The Judge must have chatted away like a parrot to these guys, Rigby thought with dismay.

"More reason to investigate," Hightower offered. "Mallory's murder makes this newsworthy."

The old man leaning on the cane cupped a hand to his ear and said, "I heard Roosevelt. Talked to him once. I was new to the Bureau. We were tracking some Nazi saboteurs here in the states during the war. He wanted to know all about it."

"Did you get your man?" the Judge asked.

"All eight of 'em. In only two weeks' time. Six were hanged in short order. No waiting around like they do today. We *always* got our man," Fillmore concluded, clenching his fist.

"Sometimes the bad guys survived," Jones said.

"You weren't with the Bureau then, Jones. You don't know. You were in the army during the war."

"I was in the army two decades after the war," Jones corrected with a sympathetic tone toward the old man and his memory. "But I served with some who were in the war."

Rigby interrupted the debate to get back to business. "Director, if I can have a minute."

"All right. You'll excuse me gentlemen." The Judge

led Rigby off into a corner once reserved for telephones now hosting a single house phone, since cell phones eliminated the need for pay phones.

"Two more faces on Mount Rushmore will stop the bickering in Congress? I think the Speaker's been smoking something funny," the Judge said after listening to Rigby relate his conversation with Marshall Gaines. "He told me his idea the other day when he asked me to have your Office for Cases of Historical Significance look into it. I couldn't believe it at the time. I had to run off to give my welcoming speech at the opening of this meeting. Absurd. I told some of the agents during the cocktail reception and we all had a good laugh. Typical politician…thinks this will change the world."

Rigby appreciated the Judge's sense of humor. He hardly saw anything like a sense of humor when she first took over as Director of the FBI. His bubble popped when she sighed and said, "I wish we didn't have to bother with this crap. I've got my hands full without dealing with special requests from the guys with the big brass balls on Capitol Hill."

Rigby wanted to be part of something more important than setting the historical record straight. "Anything new with the MB Task Force?"

The Monument Bomber had been quiet since Rigby had stopped him at the Lincoln Memorial. Rigby had not heard of any of his activity, but the Judge had removed him from the Task Force and, apparently, didn't intend to send him back.

"He's been quiet. Nothing. Maybe he quit. You should forget about him," she said.

"No," Rigby replied sharply. "It's my duty. I take that very seriously. I joined the Bureau to protect people, to make sure they have an equal shot at justice. I was responsible for chasing the Bomber down when I ran the Task Force. I failed. I failed myself; I failed the Bureau, and most of all I failed my fellow citizens who are counting on me. I have to make good on all that. I have to catch this guy before he does any more damage to the country."

The Judge studied his face for a long time before she spoke.

"I know how hard this must be for you. I must follow the law and respond to the wishes of my superiors. Congress created the Office for Cases of Historical Significance within the Bureau and the Speaker of the House demands that the office get behind an investigation.

"Should it matter to me that the end game seems outrageous, even frivolous to try and end partisan gridlock by adding some faces to a mountain? These guys on Capitol Hill have been drinking the happy juice too long. Our friends over there agree…" She pointed at the group of elderly agents. "…and we all had a good laugh when I told them. We're still laughing. It doesn't matter. The Speaker is in position to call the shots.

"It all adds up to one thing. You're going to Central America. Make contact with the legation office in Panama. Their jurisdiction covers Costa Rica. Find out what you can about Roosevelt and this treasure and what Mallory knew."

Rigby had been down this road before. The Judge would stick to her position and there was nothing he could say to change her mind. He told himself he had a job to do, whether it made sense to him or not.

As Rigby started to walk away, the Judge called after him. "One more thing. DC detective Rory Denver contacted the Bureau. Wanted to talk to you about Mallory and why you happened to be there with the murdered man. When you talk to him, don't muck up the Speaker's confidence in us by talking about his project. I'm not returning his calls so he'll go after you."

How could he avoid talking about the project? Rigby thought. That was the reason he'd been sent to talk to Mallory.

Then the Judge answered his question as if he had asked it aloud.

"I think it best that you don't talk to him until some things are cleared up. Best way to avoid him is to leave for the island right away."

Chapter 7

"The Judge said, 'Go.' Never figured it that way." Rigby took a sip from his beer and dug his fingers into the bowl of peanuts in the center of the table. The waitress stood right there to fill it up.

"Costa Rica. Cocos Island. Pretty romantic, don't you think," Smitty said with a wink.

"Not when you're chasing a wild goose."

Smitty dipped into her briefcase and pulled out a short stack of papers. She looked around to see if anyone was looking at her cache. The waitress sat at the next table tabulating numbers in her receipt book. There were few customers in the bar that evening.

"What ya got for me, Smitty?" Rigby asked.

"Veronica," she said sternly, pulling the stack of papers back from him.

"Smitty because you're at the Smithsonian and what you dig up for me."

"Veronica at the Smithsonian and her friends did the digging, Mr. Rigby." She gave him a gentle kick under the table.

"Ouch," he said in mock pain with a smile. "Okay, Veronica, what do you have for me?"

"Everything you could ever imagine if you gave me a chance."

If he were twenty years younger, Smitty's age, he'd love the fact this intelligent woman was chasing him. The age gap made it wrong somehow but it was sure difficult for a hungry man not to eat when a tempting morsel was laid out in front of him.

"I mean about FDR and his buried treasure."

"Of course you do," Smitty muttered. She shuffled

through the papers and settled on one. "It's real."

Rigby starred at her in surprise. "Are you kidding me? Roosevelt found a buried treasure?"

"No, that's not what I mean. Silly me for saying it that way." She winked at him. "I meant there are supposedly three or four buried treasures on Cocos Island and President Roosevelt spent a lot of time there."

"Treasure hunting?"

"Fishing."

Rigby held up a finger to ask for a moment and raised his glass, taking a long drink. When he put it down the waitress was at the table asking him if he would like another.

"Haven't finished this one, yet," he said.

As the waitress walked away, Smitty whispered across the table, "The service certainly has improved around here."

Rigby nodded, took another sip from his beer, placed the glass back on the table and said, "Hit me."

"Sometimes that's all I can think about," she responded with a devilish smile and once again consulted the papers in front of her.

"Roosevelt went fishing off Cocos Island four times when he was president. Three times he was aboard the cruiser, USS *Houston*. The island has been noted throughout history as a haven for buried treasure. Ever hear of Benito of the Bloody Sword?"

"I think that was my last barber," Rigby said.

Smitty smiled her *Isn't he cute* smile before continuing. "Supposedly, in the early 1800s he captured a rich mule train in Acapulco intended for Mexico City. He disguised himself as a muleteer and led the convoy to the coast where he loaded the treasure on ships. Then he buried the gold in a number of spots on Cocos Island, setting off explosives to cover the hiding places."

"Makes it inconvenient to dig up again," Rigby said before quaffing more beer.

33

"Bloody, as I'm sure he was known to his good friends, wasn't the only one who used the island as a bank. There was Captain Edward Davis, a pirate who sailed along the west coast of South America in the late 1600s aboard his ship, *Bachelor's Delight*."

"A man after my own heart." Rigby braced himself for another kick under the table. It came.

"But the big prize," Smitty continued, "was the treasure of Lima, Peru. The treasure came from the cathedral there. In 1820 when Peru revolted against Spain, the governor and clergy entrusted the cathedral's treasure to an English seaman, Captain Thompson."

"And that was a mistake?"

"Big one. Captain Thompson killed off his passengers after escaping Peru and he and the crew sailed to Cocos Island to bury the loot in a cave. Thompson left his secret of the treasure years later with a man named Keating and he—"

"Hold on now," Rigby said. "I get it that this place is loaded down with treasure. Anyone ever find anything?"

"There've been some stories. We discovered that a Belgian treasure hunter in 1931 supposedly found a two-foot gold Madonna statue on the island and sold it in New York for $11,000."

"What about President Roosevelt?"

"I'm getting there."

Rigby downed the rest of his beer and held up his glass. The waitress, standing nearby, responded quickly, grabbing the empty glass and heading for the bar for a refill.

"I dug up a lot for you. I don't know what you'll find important. Maybe the trivia. Did you know that a 1941 Charlie Chan movie called, *Dead Men Tell*, dealing with four pieces of a treasure map and the ghost of a dead pirate, takes place on a treasure cruise headed for Cocos Island?"

"You watch Charlie Chan?"

"Don't believe all the negative stuff you hear about

Chan. The Chinese community doesn't have a uniform attitude about the Charlie Chan character. He was based on a real Honolulu detective who's well respected in our community."

Rigby studied Smitty's pretty Asian features and wondered why she spoiled them with her ugly, wide, black frame glasses. He wondered even more why she dyed her hair blond. He decided not to ask.

"Who knew this treasure hunt would include popular culture," was all he said.

Smitty wriggled her nose at him in a sign of displeasure and looked back at her papers.

"There's no proof the president found any treasure on his fishing trips, but we do know a few things. One, he was in the waters near Cocos Island in July 1934. He returned in October 1935 and actually was on the island. He even met with British treasure hunters on that trip."

"He wasn't there to fish?" Rigby asked.

"That's what he was there to do, *officially*. None of his trips were *officially* treasure hunting trips. In fact, the president reeled in a 110-pound sailfish on that trip. His boat was pulled five miles in heavy seas as he tried to land the fish. Know where that fish is now?"

"Stuffed and mounted over your desk."

"You've been reading my notes," Smitty said in mock indignation, fists on her hips. "You're close. The Smithsonian has it."

The waitress came back to the table and put down the full beer glass. Rigby nodded appreciatively.

Smitty shuffled through her papers. "Listen to this. A *Time* magazine reporter went along on the 1935 trip. He wrote this: *The president's eyes sparkled when he stepped ashore on a treasure island as fabulous as Robert Louis Stevenson's. Like a green peppermint gumdrop ringed with a frost of spun sugar, the densely vegetated peaks of Cocos Island rose 2,000 feet over his head, while all around the*

35

island's steep 13-mile perimeter the Pacific lathered its boiling white waves."

"Descriptive," Rigby said.

"My college English professor would have given the writer an F. Over the top, he would say. There's more. Get this. The article talks about FDR meeting with British treasure hunters. Then the author writes, *The man who has dug up and dispensed 15 billion dollars of the U.S. treasure since March 4, 1933 gave his best advice on how the Britons should go about locating the Cocos cache."*

Smitty gave out a hoot and Rigby smiled.

"FDR went back again in 1938," Smitty went on. "Also went ashore on that trip."

Rigby couldn't understand what any of this had to do with Mallory's quest to besmirch the memory of FDR and scuttle the Mount Rushmore project. That is, unless Roosevelt followed the example of Old Captain Thompson and killed a few witnesses to keep the hiding place of the treasure secret.

"Did you find any references to treasure hunting by the president? Or did he order a search for treasure?" Rigby asked.

"Afraid not. Not on Cocos. He did participate in a treasure hunt when he was younger at Oak Island in Nova Scotia. There's supposed to be a money pit there that no one can get into because it floods with ocean water. Even as president, Roosevelt remembered those years fondly. We have a letter he sent to a friend in New York City recalling the early expedition to Canada. He also mentions the search for gold aboard a ship that was rammed and sunk in 1911 while carrying wealthy refugees from the Mexican Revolution. The ship supposedly was carrying a safe filled with gold and silver."

"Okay, you've convinced me FDR liked the idea of treasure hunting. He went to an island that had a reputation for buried treasure. I still don't see how this adds up to what

I'm looking for?"

"What are you looking for?" Smitty asked.

"You know I can't tell you that."

"How can I help you if you don't tell me? I don't know if *I'm* looking for the right stuff if you don't trust me."

"I trust you," Rigby said. "I got orders. This investigation is tied to a government project that I can't talk about."

"Like the Lincoln tomb thing."

"Like the Lincoln tomb thing," he repeated.

Smitty frowned. "I certainly helped you with that."

"You did."

"I could've helped more if you brought me in earlier. You wouldn't have found Lincoln without me."

Rigby simply nodded his agreement but said nothing.

Suddenly, Smitty brightened. "This doesn't have to do with Mount Rushmore, does it?"

Rigby opened his eyes wide in astonishment. Smitty had a pleased look on her face. Rigby glanced around, for Smitty had blurted out her guess in a loud voice. The waitress was staring at them.

Rigby turned back to Smitty and motioned with his hand, palm down, to lower her voice.

"Why did you say that?" he asked.

"That's it, right?" she said in a whisper coated with excitement.

"I can't tell you. You know why? Because you'd tell the world."

"I would not!"

"You just did."

Smitty realized that her loud voice was overheard and she blushed, covering his lips with her fingertips.

"Good thing you don't know what you're talking about and you have it wrong," he said.

A bit chagrined, Smitty mumbled, "I'm sorry. I mean…"

As her words trailed off without completing her thought, Rigby asked, "Why did you say Mount Rushmore?"

"Oh, some project Congress is doing. I suppose I'm not supposed to talk much about it, either. I just thought maybe that's what you were doing because of Roosevelt. Did you know Franklin Roosevelt was the president who dedicated the monument in 1941? Well, never mind."

"You're working with Congress on this project."

"We're the Smithsonian. Congress comes to us for information from time to time."

Interesting, Rigby thought. Certainly, a conflict of interest for his young friend, yet she would be in position to know some things that might show him a connection between Mallory's investigation, the Speaker's Mount Rushmore project and President Roosevelt's fishing expeditions near the treasure island. But for the life of him, he could see absolutely no connection.

Chapter 8

Rigby and the woman finished their drinks, paid the bill, and headed for the door. He wanted to follow Rigby but he had invested $300 with the waitress and he also needed to know what she had learned.

As Rigby and the woman passed him, he pulled his Washington Nationals baseball cap lower so the bill would cover his face, and he waved a handful of dollar bills at the waitress as if he were a customer anxious to settle up and move on. The waitress hurried toward him.

He decided to tell her that he would come back for what information she learned. He would offer more money to be sure she would keep the appointment. He would then follow Rigby. Maybe he would come back to speak to her. Maybe he would not return if he were able to get what he wanted immediately retribution for stopping his attack on the Lincoln Memorial.

The waitress stood next to him and he was about to explain his intentions of returning later when he noticed that Rigby and his companion were standing on the sidewalk in front of the bar, continuing their conversation. If they stood there, he would not leave. He kept an eye on Rigby and took the opportunity to say to the waitress, "Tell me all."

"Hard to hear all. I was working. Got snatches here and there. They seemed comfortable with each other all right. No lovey-dovey talk, but pretty friendly. Maybe you're right, mister. Maybe the guy is cheating on your sister with that woman, like you said. I think they might be planning to go off together to some romantic hideaway. Some island they kept talking about. She said it was romantic."

"What's the name of the island?" the man asked.

"Not sure. Cocoa, Cocus? Maybe Coconut. Didn't

hear clearly."

The man watched as Rigby hugged the woman on the street, a clear sign they were about to depart in different directions. He didn't know what he expected to learn from the conversation between Rigby and the woman. He had to focus on pursuing Rigby.

As he was about to thank the waitress and follow as the FBI man walked away, the waitress said, "They might also be planning to visit Mount Rushmore."

Mount Rushmore. America's grandest monument. Why would Rigby be going to Mount Rushmore? Did the FBI think Mount Rushmore was *his* next target? The idea hit him like a thunderbolt. Should Mount Rushmore *be* his next target?

Through the large plate glass window of the bar he saw Rigby moving out of his line of sight. He wanted to follow, but he needed to know more.

"What did he say about Mount Rushmore?" he asked her.

"Actually, it was the woman who brought it up."

He was surprised. Had he guessed wrong about this woman? Was she more than Rigby's lover? He knew Rigby saw her on occasion. Had he guessed wrong about their relationship? Did she work for Rigby, work for the FBI?

Women had important roles in this land, to his great sorrow. He looked for her in the street but she was already gone.

The waitress continued talking. "…hear much. But they mentioned Mount Rushmore a couple of times. I heard the word *project*. They also mentioned President Roosevelt. Isn't he one of the presidents on the side of the mountain?"

He shrugged. What difference did it make to him? He looked outside McGillicutty's Bar & Grill again. Rigby was lost in the street traffic and the gathering dark of the night.

No matter, he thought. He was formulating a plan for even greater revenge. He would damage this biggest of all

American monuments. In the process, he would ruin Rigby's *project*, whatever that was. Destroying Rigby's project would also ruin the man. Rigby would pay for his interference at the Lincoln Memorial. He would pay with terrible damage to Mount Rushmore and to his reputation, if not his life.

What was the American expression? Killing two birds by throwing a single stone. That sounded right.

Chapter 9

"There, señor," the pilot said, pointing to his left. "Parque Nacional Isla de Coco." In his heavily accented English the pilot added, "Cocos Island National Park. The whole island is a park."

In the passenger seat of the De Havilland Beaver, Rigby leaned toward the pilot's side of the plane and looked out the window. Below the whirling propeller, he spotted their destination. No one could miss the island. Not that it was big as islands go, maybe three miles wide by five miles long. But placed against the vast Pacific Ocean, Cocos Island looked like a lone black period on a sheet of white printing paper.

As the plane gently banked and made for the island, the black dot reformed itself into a plush green tropical bed of flora and fauna.

The plane dipped and Rigby could see the churning waves below. The choppy water would make for an uncomfortable boat crossing from the Osa Peninsula in Costa Rica, about 330 miles and maybe thirty hours away. He was offered an opportunity to travel that route, but Rigby appreciated that the Bureau had sprung for the plane ride. He had gone through all the proper channels, first contacting the legation office at the U.S. Embassy in Panama. They did all the diplomatic protocol procedures to get Rigby through customs in Costa Rica and made the arrangements for the seaplane to travel to his island destination.

The pilot's plane was associated with the national police, the Fuerza Publica. Rigby was to be delivered to the island where park rangers who lived there would greet him. He actually dreaded that meeting because he had no answer for the first question the park rangers would ask him: How can we help you?

He had picked up some background information on President Roosevelt's trips to the island from FBI sources, and begged a few more tidbits from Smitty by offering her a future weekend of dinner and the theater. None of the information offered a clue as to why Paul Mallory thought FDR had created some mischief that would discourage his appearance on Mount Rushmore, or that the president himself had stumbled on buried treasure.

As the pilot descended toward the island, Rigby spotted a dark spot below the surface of the water. The spot was moving. Rigby brought it to the attention of the pilot, who laughed.

"Fishes going to school, I think is the way you say it. One-eyed Jacks, probably."

The size of the spot indicated a swarm of fish in the hundreds, Rigby guessed.

"The waters around the island are filled with all sorts of sea life. That is why it is so popular with the divers, señor. See, some dive ships below."

Rigby could see the large seagoing vessels that probably could carry fifty or so passengers and crew. He also saw some smaller sail craft anchored in the bay.

"You'll find hundreds kinds of fishes here, señor. Yellowfin tuna, giant mantas, sailfish, and all sorts of sharks like the hammerhead and the biggest of all, the whale shark. So don't fall in, huh? Unless you're looking for mermaids, yes." He laughed and Rigby gave him a good-natured smile.

The pilot steered the craft into a wide loop over the island so his passenger could view the mountainous jungle landscape. Rigby spotted a number of waterfalls tumbling over cliffs and looked down on a dense forest that would be hard to penetrate. It really didn't matter, he thought. If he didn't know what he was looking for, what difference did it make where he decided to look?

The pilot completed his loop and nudged the plane

down steadily as he approached one of the island's inlets. The pontoons touched the water and bounced slightly then came down and up and down once more on the rough surface, finally gliding to a stop.

As the pilot turned off the engine a steady rain began to fall, big drops of water plopping on to the windshield.

"Get use to this, señor," said the pilot with a snort. "Rainy season. It is why everything is so green. I hoped to get you ashore before the clouds started to cry but alas..." He swept his hand across the horizon. "I see your ride to shore is here."

Rigby spotted a man in a poncho with a hood rowing a small boat between anchored sailing ships and making for the seaplane. He gathered his backpack and patted the pilot on the back, thanking him for the ride. The pilot informed him that he would depart as soon as Rigby cleared the plane in hopes of getting off before the rainfall intensified.

Rigby opened the plane's door and backed onto the pontoon. The rubber soled hiking boots held the wet surface well enough. He shuffled to his left, grabbed his pack, and closed the door. Slipping the backpack on, he grabbed the strut attached to the wing and turned around to face the arriving dinghy.

"Hop in," called the rower from beneath the hood in clear English. "Let's get to shore before the downpour. There's a poncho under your bench."

Rigby slipped into the boat and with two hands on the pontoon, shoved it away from the plane. The man with the oars proceeded to row toward shore using a practiced and powerful stroke. The rain intensified, pelting the water's surface with a repeating rat-a-tat-like machine gun fire. Rigby removed his backpack and quickly covered himself with the poncho.

Once they had moved a few yards away, the pilot turned on the plane's engine and started taxiing toward the open sea.

With the noise of the engine and the rhythmic splat of falling rain, Rigby chose not to try conversation with the rower. He watched as the plane cleared the inlet on the surface of the water; the engine revved, and the plane scooted along the water until it jumped into the air, water trailing off its pontoons like foxtails.

He wondered how quickly he would call the plane to return and pick him up. He expected to be on the island no more than twenty-four hours. Long enough that he could tell the Judge and the Speaker of the House that he had investigated FDR's far-off fishing island and found nothing.

The dinghy reached the edge of the shore, scraping the sandy beach. The rower retracted his oars, scampered out of the boat and pulled it a few more feet onto the beach before tying a line from the bow through an iron rod cemented into a boulder. Rigby gathered his bag and leaped onto shore.

Following the oarsman, Rigby ran through the rain and into the jungle. Pushing aside large ferns that encroached on the trail, the men soon came upon a tin-roofed one-story building, the roof clanging under the heavy rain. The roof extended a couple of feet out and over large glass windows. A pile of rocks stood in front of dark green wooden planks with yellow-painted letters carved into the wood:

Bienvenido
Base Chatham
Parque Nacional Isla de Coco

The park ranger station at Chatham Bay. Rigby was told there was a second ranger station at Wafer Bay, both on the northwest side of the island separated by the Presidio Peninsula, probably no more than a mile apart.

Rigby followed the other man under the overhanging roof and shook himself free of rainwater as best he could. He then followed the man inside.

45

The ranger station was what he expected. Bureaucratic papers posted on the wall, a desk and a counter with information about the island. At the desk a man in a ranger uniform stood and extended his hand.

"Fernando Oliveira at your service, señor. We were told of your coming but the reason was rather fuzzy."

"Fuzzy orders for me, too," Rigby said, taking the man's hand.

"You met my partner here at the post," Oliveira said with a nod at the oarsman.

"Many years ago," the man said, flipping the hood back off his head.

Rigby got a full view of the smaller man's face. Specks of white in Brillo-like hair, large brown eyes, small ears and a deep scar that crossed the fleshy point of his nose. Rigby still remembered when the knife carved Pedro Campos's nose.

"You are surprised to see me alive, no?" Campos said. His expression was stern. He did not extend a hand toward Rigby.

"I knew you survived so I'm not surprised to see you. I am surprised to see you here."

"I'm the one who is surprised, Rigby. Federal Bureau of Investigation? You were a bum when I knew you. You're still a bum, only one with a badge."

Campos starred hard at Rigby, who returned the look. Oliveira interrupted the stare-down with a question.

"Okay, I get that you're old acquaintances. Did you have to arrest this old-timer?" Oliveira said, pointing at Campos and hoping to lighten the moment.

"You remember my story how I got this scar," Campos said to the younger man as he traced his finger along the scar line across his nose.

Oliveira told Rigby, "This place can get pretty lonely. I've heard all his stories. The scar story I've heard a hundred times."

46

"Rigby was with me when it happened," Campos said, clearly gearing up for another re-telling of the tale.

"I thought you were guarding some cargo in the Philippines."

"Rigby was there."

"I traveled the world after college," Rigby explained.

"Only he wasn't there when I needed him," Campos said. "We were both hired to stop the gangs from raiding the warehouse. The warehouse owner was cheap. He figured to put a couple of young guys in the warehouse and the gang would go somewhere else to steal. We were a couple of drifters coming from different places, didn't know each other, but we worked for little."

"Next to nothing," Rigby said with a smile.

Campos wiped his arm across his mouth as if squelching a response. Then he said, "The gangs came anyway. Wanted what was in the warehouse. Tape decks or something like that."

"Last century technology," Rigby said.

"So they bust in carrying clubs and knives. One fool holds me while another cuts me across the nose. Where's Rigby? He slipped out to get a cup of coffee without telling me. I have to kick the knife man away before he cuts off my nose."

"I came as soon as I heard the commotion," Rigby said, defensively. "I got you out of that fix with the metal pipe to the cutter's head."

"A little late, no?"

"So you're that guy," Oliveira said, as if he just met a mythical figure he had heard about all his life.

"It was a brawl, but we won," Rigby said.

Campos ground a fist into the palm of his hand. Rigby wondered if he were reliving the battle or had some present day use for the fist.

"Last time I saw you they were carting you off to the hospital," Rigby said.

"You never came to visit," Campos said.

"I had a ticket for the next day. I was shipping out to Australia. You knew that. I did everything I could for you. Once you were headed to the hospital there was nothing more I could do. I'm only sorry I couldn't stop the cutter."

"Great for storytelling. And women find it manly," Campos said with no humor as he traced the scar across his nose again. "Don't worry, amigo, the warehouse owner was generous enough. He paid for the doctoring, gave me a ticket home and pocket money. Who would've thought he'd be the one that had my back."

Rigby decided it was time to change the direction of the conversation and get on with his assignment. "That action in the warehouse must have made you think of quieter places." Rigby pointed outside at the island. "Never figured you for a nature boy, though."

"Job's a job when you need one. Same as in the Philippines."

The younger ranger also seemed tired of the tension simmering in the cabin and asked Rigby if he wanted a cup of coffee. "Then you can tell us what we can do for the FBI way out here."

Rigby accepted the coffee and joined the two rangers at a table in the back of the station. As the rain drummed away on the tin roof, Rigby told them as much as he could about his mission. He was assigned to find a connection to President Franklin Roosevelt and the supposed hidden treasures on Cocos Island. He repeated the research he'd reviewed, which said that while Roosevelt visited the island many times and even talked with treasure hunters, there was no indication that the president himself went on a treasure hunt or that anyone associated with him found any treasure, although a few crewmen from the USS *Houston* may have given it a shot.

Rigby concluded his review with a question: "Did Roosevelt or his party leave anything behind that you know about?"

"Nothing," Campos said.

"There's a plant species common to the island named after President Roosevelt because of his visits. That's all that I know," Oliveira added.

Maybe it's a poison plant, Rigby thought, trying to make sense of his mission to the island. He said, "What about the treasure hunting?"

"That's all illegal now," Oliveira told him, "unless you got permission and that's rarely given. This place has been picked over for more than a century and hardly anything's been found. Probably all stories."

"But there are caves and volcanic tunnels. If I was going to hide a treasure this would not be a bad place," Campos said. "Maybe a treasure is still here, no?"

Oliveira shrugged. "Stories."

"This President Roosevelt, he used crutches and a wheelchair, no?" Campos asked.

"That's right," Rigby replied.

"Well, he would go no further than the beach if he came ashore. Too mountainous."

Oliveira asked, "Have you contacted the sailors on his ship? Are any still alive?"

Rigby shook his head. He didn't expect to have any luck going in that direction but he figured that to be thorough he should see if any sailors from the USS *Houston* still survived.

"So what do you want to do?" Campos asked. "Sit out the rain for a day and call the plane back?"

"I suppose I should see the island some while I'm here. I came in at Chatham."

"Bahia Chatham," Oliveira corrected.

"Chatham Bay to you, Yankee," Campos said.

Rigby nodded. "Then Wafer Bay, or Bahia Wafer..."

Oliveira smiled at the appropriate pronunciation.

" ...is over the ridge. Wafer Bay was one of

49

Roosevelt's stops on the beach. I should probably go there."

"I will guide you," Campos said in a voice that gave pause to both Rigby and Oliveira. "Once the rain lets up. But, your search will turn up the same as all those treasure hunters who came to this island before you. Nada."

Chapter 10

Pedro Campos led the way over a narrow trail, trekking uphill, the ground soaked with rain squishing under their feet. Rigby had considered Campos's harsh tone and sharp stare in the cabin and wondered if Campos intended to do him harm for not being quicker to help him so many years ago. It wouldn't take much in this jungle-like environment to find a slippery rock over a rushing waterfall.

Rigby dismissed the idea. Campos still blamed him for the disfigured nose, but he wasn't a man to seek revenge. At least, that wasn't the Campos he knew before the knife fight.

Campos might be spared the need to punish Rigby. The treacherous terrain and wet conditions might cause an accident. Rigby had already slipped a number of times trying to crest the hill.

Rain began to fall again. Rigby freed his poncho from his backpack and slipped it on. As he continued up the hill he lost his footing and started to fall. Frantically, he reached out to the nearby moss-draped tree but couldn't hold on. He fell hard against a large rock partially covered by tangled vines.

Campos heard Rigby's cry as he hit the rock and turned around. "Injured?" he asked. Rigby shook his head and Campos muttered, "Too bad."

"Think I found something, though."

Campos joined Rigby and looked down at the rock that Rigby clung to, his knees soaking in the wet ground.

The rock was covered with carvings, some more easily legible than others. Sitting in the center in broad letters was the name of a ship: *Sweet Martha, Newport, RI*. Below that were a name and a date: *O. Potter 1839*.

"Ancient graffiti," Campos said, putting a hand under Rigby's arm and pulling him to his feet. "No treasure map. Come on."

Rigby followed Campos. The wetness from kneeling on the ground and from the rain was soaking through the lower part of his trousers. He looked at the ground as he walked, as much to seek out trouble spots before the trouble occurred as well as to find a sturdy broken branch he could use as a walking stick.

They reached the summit of the hill and stopped to catch their breath. "Used to be easier," Rigby gasped, trying to start up a conversation.

"Used to breathe better." Campos pointed at his scarred nose.

Rigby moved on toward the sound of rushing water. They soon came upon a river, which cascaded over a nearby cliff.

"Stay clear," Campos said. "The power of the current can pull you over the fall."

Rigby figured that the ranger in Campos was speaking automatically. His long-held anger was not slackening.

"Does this river empty into Wafer Bay?" Rigby asked.

He heard no response from Campos. The river and the nearby waterfall were loud. So was the rain. He turned to Campos to shout louder.

Campos was not paying attention to him. He stared off into the backcountry away from the bay. Rigby followed his gaze and looked at the palm- and fern-covered canyon, a waterfall tumbling over a distant cliff. Birds swooped through the canyon as the palm fronds swayed in the breeze. Then Rigby spotted what had warranted Campos's attention.

Standing out against the green backdrop, Rigby could see a royal blue—something. The blue was moving. Rigby shielded his eyes from the rain and stared, finally making out the shape of a person hiking a trail that ran along a cliff. The blue he recognized as the hiker's shirt. The hiker had on brown pants and a wide-brimmed hat.

"Not supposed to be here," Campos said. "No one signed to be up in that part of the island today."

Campos swung his backpack off one shoulder and opened it to pull out a pair of binoculars. He trained them on the distant figure. Rigby wondered if he could get any kind of clear view with the rain falling harder.

"Not supposed to be here," Campos repeated. "Dangerous."

The hiker was using vines growing down the side of a cliff as a handhold to move along a ledge.

"I've got to go after that fool," Campos said. "It's rough going. You should go back to the station."

"And leave you again. Not on this trip."

Campos shrugged and marched off quickly. Rigby strained to keep up. He didn't want Campos to think him incapable of handling himself in these difficult conditions.

Campos followed the trail, making decisive movements when the trail forked.

Following closely, Rigby shouted ahead to Campos asking if they could get close enough to call to the hiker.

"I don't want to scare him, I want to arrest him."

"Why?"

"Unless I miss my guess, he's a treasure hunter."

"I thought they weren't allowed on the island?"

"They're not." Campos quickened his pace.

They soon arrived at the spot where they'd first seen the blue shirt. The trail narrowed and clung to the edge of a steep drop into the canyon. Campos began edging along the trail. A waterfall was ahead, water cascading from a higher point right past the trail and down into the canyon. The trail headed directly toward the fall.

A loud squeal erupted to their left and a creature bolted from the underbrush. It barreled against Campos's right leg, causing him to lose his balance and teeter at the edge of the cliff. Rigby reached out and grabbed Campos's arm, holding him steady as the ranger rotated his other arm like a helicopter to regain his balance.

The animal—Rigby could see it was a pig—panicked and reversed course, darting around the men's legs in search of safety. It turned the wrong way and slipped on the wet surface, propelling itself into the air with a loud squeal as it plunged to the canyon floor. They followed the fall of the pig as it crashed into the rocks below and remained motionless.

"Feral pig," Campos said. "Sailors left them long ago and their descendents make a home on the island."

Campos looked down at Rigby's hand still gripping his arm then glanced at the remains of the pig below. Whatever went through his mind, Campos said nothing but gave a slight nod toward Rigby and removed his arm from Rigby's grasp.

Campos looked down the path to the waterfall. He did not see the hiker. "This path ends," he said. "Where did he go?"

Chapter 11

Campos followed the ever-narrowing trail along the top of the ledge, making his way toward the water dropping on to the trail and into the canyon below. Rigby stayed behind the ranger, being sure to plant his foot firmly with every step. As they reached the waterfall the sound of the rushing water became louder. Water splashed onto them, harmlessly mixing with the steady rain.

The trail ended at the waterfall with no hiker in sight.

"Did he fall off the ledge?" Rigby asked Campos over the roar of the water.

The ranger shook his head. To be sure he edged toward the cliff and looked into the canyon. Water from the fall landed in a pool directly below. Perhaps a man could have plummeted into the pool and sank to the bottom. But Rigby was sure either he or Campos would have seen the body fall.

The ranger motioned for Rigby to move back along the ledge trail. As they took step after careful step both men held the vines on the cliff wall, at the same time pushing a hand through to see if an opening existed in the wall. They hit rock each time.

Rigby had crossed the ledge about halfway to where the trail widened. Again he pushed through the vines, and again he hit hard rock. Then, he saw the end of the vines move.

The movement was slight. Rigby stopped and watched the longest vines on this section of the rock wall move slowly away from the wall a couple of inches then collapse back toward the wall. This happened over and over. Rigby looked at the ends of the vines to both sides of him, but they were not behaving like the ones that had caught his attention.

Rigby pushed his fist through the vines at waist level and again hit the rock wall. Down at his feet the vines continued to do their slow dance.

"Keep a hand on my shoulder," Rigby told Campos, trusting that the ranger's anger toward him had abated after Rigby saved him from hurtling into the canyon when attacked by the pig.

Slowly, Rigby dropped to one knee on the narrow ledge, keeping a firm grip on the vines. When he felt steady and secure as possible kneeling on the ledge he freed one hand from the vines and reached toward the ends of the ones swaying just above the trail. He could feel a soft breeze on the wrist above his glove. He pushed his gloved hand into the vines and toward the wall. This time his hand met nothing solid but moved through the vines into open space.

"Something here," he reported to Campos. "Hold on."

He felt Campos's hand tighten on his shoulder as he lowered himself more and reached around the open space, feeling for where the rock wall ended maybe two feet above the trail. Examining the width of the opening he guessed it was no more than two-and-a-half feet wide.

"Someone could get through here," he said.

"Move out of the way, I'm going after him."

"I'll go with you, and since I'm down here I may as well go first. Hand me that light attached to the side of my pack."

Campos did as he was asked and slapped Rigby on the shoulder as a sign to tell him to go. Rigby lowered himself even farther, becoming a human snake on the wet surface, and slithered through the vines.

The narrow opening went only a few feet into the mountainside when it started to widen. The expansion of the tunnel continued dramatically until, barely six feet into the tunnel, Rigby could stand up to his full height. He sent the beam of his flashlight around the walls, revealing a cave-like tunnel, its ceiling a couple of feet above his head.

Campos joined Rigby and whispered, "A lava tube. The island is the top of an old volcano. Lava created the tube when it cooled but left behind these channels. The lava flow must have ended at this point and tapered to the small opening."

"He must be up ahead." Rigby shone his light on footprints in the dirt.

Campos said, "Turn off your light. I'll keep mine on and point it straight down on the ground. We'll see where we're going but not give away that we're coming after him."

They took off their wet ponchos and dropped them on the ground. Rigby clicked off his flashlight and walked with Campos deeper into the cave.

The lava tube took a slight turn to the right ahead. Rigby tapped Campos's hand and pointed to a splash of light on the ground coming from around the bend. Campos immediately clicked off his flashlight.

They crept into the tunnel as it elbowed to the right. They moved silently, for any sound would carry in the deathly stillness of the cave. At the edge of the turn, each man put his back against the cold stone. Campos was closer to the edge and ever so slowly inched around the bend so that he could see into the next part of the cave.

He suddenly pulled back. Putting his lips next to Rigby's ear, he said that the treasure hunter was kneeling on the ground, his back to them, lamp at his side, looking at something on the ground.

"Sneak up and grab him. I'll come around with the flashlight ready to take him out if need be."

Rigby nodded and circled around Campos, ready to strike. He realized they had no evidence that the man was doing anything wrong, other than treasure hunting without a license. However, Rigby saw another opportunity to bury the old feud with Campos by helping him do his job.

Rigby charged around the bend. He saw the back panel of the royal blue shirt, the wide-brimmed western hat as the treasure hunter knelt on the ground next to a flashlight.

Rigby wrapped his arms around the treasure hunter's arm and chest—and let go immediately, his sudden clutch and release causing the person to fall to the ground backward. He'd realized instantly in putting the bear hug around the treasure hunter's chest that he…was a she.

The woman toppled to the dirt. The cowboy hat flew from her head, releasing her strawberry blonde hair. The woman was about forty, a tanned, pretty face peppered with a few freckles. She looked up with fear in her eyes at Rigby and Campos, who now stood next to him.

"Who the hell are you?" Campos demanded.

The woman said nothing. Her eyes darted around the dark cave, doubtless looking for a weapon to defend herself with, or a way to escape. Rigby understood the fear instantly. He had seen it when his one-time fiancé had been confronted by men in a lonely spot intending to do her harm. Something he could not prevent as they accosted her and left him with both everlasting guilt and a purpose to defend the defenseless. He also understood that if this woman were a treasure hunter, as Campos suspected, she might think that they were there to take the treasure from her and leave no witnesses.

"We're not going to hurt you," Rigby said. "Do you speak English? Espanol?"

He saw that she understood what he was saying. Jerking his thumb in the direction of Campos, Rigby continued: "This is a park ranger. I'm an FBI agent from the United States."

The woman's eyes narrowed as if she was trying to decide whether to believe him. An FBI agent on Cocos Island seemed rather incomprehensible.

Campos stooped down toward her and the woman reacted defensively, scooting away from him. He picked up the item she had been looking at on the ground and shone his light on it.

"Of course: a treasure hunter, and she has a map. Where did you get this phony map? You got a permit to look for treasure here?"

With the men making no further advance on her, the woman seemed to relax a bit. She boosted herself to a sitting position and said in a firm voice, "I got the map from my husband."

The woman had a slight British accent and that made Rigby again think painfully of his former fiancé and their lost relationship. She had survived the attack, but his inability to prevent it had finished them.

"Where's your husband?" Campos asked.

"Dead."

"Where's the body?"

The woman stared at Campos defiantly. "In a country churchyard outside Nottingham."

"A bit out of your jurisdiction," Rigby said to Campos with a smile.

"How long ago did he die?"

"Over a year ago."

The park ranger did not let up on his prisoner. "Are you alone on your treasure hunt? Where did you come from? You can't exactly sneak onto this island."

The woman stood up and dusted off her clothes. The men kept their lights on her. Rigby noticed that she was short, maybe five-three, but decided she was quite attractive.

"Are you arresting me? If so, no more answers until I talk to my solicitor."

Campos contemplated her question for a moment. He then softened his tone when he spoke. "What's your name and where are you from?"

"My name is Danielle Warren. Danni. I live in the United Kingdom."

"You know it's illegal to dig for treasure on the

island without a permit. Too many people dig holes in this place, harming the environment. I could put you under arrest."

"Do what you're going to do, just let's get out of this burial chamber."

Campos was not through with his interrogation. "Where did your husband get this map?"

She shrugged.

"It's phony you know. They're all phony, no? These maps that bring treasure hunters on a fool's errand. It leads to nothing."

The woman said, "Not this map."

"Not this map?" Campos scoffed. "What—not this map?"

"This map did not lead to nothing, as you would say. This map led to something."

Rigby looked at Campos. Had the woman found the treasure? A treasure connected to Franklin Roosevelt?

"Not to be believed," Campos said.

"What did you find?" Rigby asked.

Danni Warren picked up her lamp from the ground and signaled for the men to follow her.

"No tricks," Campos cautioned.

They continued along the lava-created tunnel for maybe twenty yards. While the tunnel continued on, there was an opening to the left. She held her light up and stepped back for the men to see into it.

Rigby and Campos stepped forward. They shone their lights into the opening, a small alcove off the main tunnel that must have been created by lava testing a new route.

The lights worked down toward the ground and froze. On the floor of the alcove they saw two skeletons. The skeletons were laid out as if they were in a coffin, arms folded across the chest. Both were dressed in pants and shirts that had mostly disintegrated.

Cut into the back wall of the alcove were the words: *Bloody Sword.*

Chapter 12

"The pirate," Rigby said. "Benito of the Bloody Sword."

Campos nodded and turned to Warren. "Where's the loot?"

"I don't know."

"You said you found something with the map."

"I did. These gentlemen, whoever they were. I followed the notes on the map. It led me to the tunnel and then to the alcove and the skeletons."

"Maybe the treasure is buried beneath the skeletons," Rigby said.

"I don't think so," Warren said. "I think the map was made to find the bodies."

"Why?" Rigby asked. He wondered if the bodies were the evidence Paul Mallory was after to discredit Roosevelt. "What did your husband tell you about the map?"

"Nothing. I found it after he passed. After much research, I realized it was a map of Cocos Island. I learned about the treasures buried on the island."

Campos let out an exclamation of disgust.

"I knew it could be fake," the woman said. "I read that all the treasure maps to the island were considered fakes. A way to prey on the gullible."

"So what made you go to the island if you learned the maps were fake?" Rigby asked.

"I...I was desperate. I wanted it to be real."

"I think you're holding something back. You're not saying all," Campos said.

"You're very clever, Mr. Ranger. I *am* holding something back. See the inscription on the upper left? Read it."

Campos held the map up to Rigby's light. Rigby could see that the inscriptions on the map were in English, written in an elegant longhand. The map contained longitude and latitude numbers, the names of the bays written out, and directions to the cave opening. On the lower right was the word, *COLOR*. The item Danni Warren referred to read: *The bones of those who tried.*

"Maybe I've seen too many movies," she said. "I thought that was a curse. You know. Some people tried to get the treasure but they failed. Cut down by some murderous traps protecting the treasure like in those Indiana Jones movies. It was a warning not to come after the treasure. Now that I'm here, I'm thinking different. The map was straightforward: *here lie bones.*"

"Of the men who tried. Tried what?" Rigby asked.

"Bones," Campos muttered. "Why would anyone make a map to bones?"

Rigby thought: could be a memorial of some kind. Or the memorial could be covering treasure.

He said, "We've got to dig. That's the only way we'll know. The carving says it's Benito of the Bloody Sword. He's tied to one of the treasures here. When did the Bloody Sword do his pirating?"

Campos told him, "Benito Bonito was a pirate around 1820. Some of the legends mix him up with the Treasure of Lima. Others say he buried his treasure in Australia, not Cocos Island."

"This carving of the words *bloody sword* is here, not Australia," Danni Warren said.

Rigby turned his light on the skeletons. The scraps of clothes that clung to the bones gave little indication of the period in which they were worn. Rigby thought there was enough left to question whether the clothes were from the early 1800s.

He knelt between the two skeletons and could see that they had been laid carefully in their final resting place.

He ran his light over the first skeleton. The poor fellow must have been five-eight, maybe five-nine. He turned his light on the other set of bones. This one was shorter by an inch or two and also displayed something the first one did not: a missing chip of bone in the rib cage and another carved chip out of the humerus bone from the left arm.

Rigby didn't think he would be too far wrong if he guessed the missing bone chips had been made by bullets.

One more thing about the smaller pirate caught Rigby's eye. There was something clutched in the skeletal hand. Rigby said a little prayer to himself to respect the dead and then reached for the object in the skeleton's hand.

He held it up for the others to see. It was a small folded scrap of cloth with faded colors of red and blue. He was pretty sure what the cloth stood for and Danni Warren confirmed his thinking when she said aloud, "Why, that's a piece of the Union Jack."

The pirate held the corner of a small version of the British flag.

"Did the British do in Benito?" Rigby asked.

"There are a number of legends how he met his end," Campos replied. "But they might have finished some of his men."

"If they were sneering at them by having them hold the flag of their executioners, why would they lay them out so carefully? I don't know if that makes sense."

"I don't know that any of this makes sense," Campos said. "I will tell you what we're going to do. We're going back to the ranger station where we'll question Mrs. Warren further. I will contact the Ministry about the map and ask them to bring some archeologists with shovels. We'll see if the bones are hiding something beneath, no?"

"I've told you all I know," Warren said. "You can't force me to go with you."

"Yes, I can," Campos said. "You are treasure hunting on the island, which is prohibited. You're under arrest. I will turn you over to the Fuerza Publica if you resist."

With that Campos pointed his flashlight down the tunnel that led to the narrow entrance.

The small party walked to the cave entrance, the men deciding to leave their ponchos behind for now. Campos insisted on Rigby crawling through the opening first so he would be there when Mrs. Warren came out.

Once all three were outside the cave and back in a light rainfall, Rigby made his way along the ledge, holding onto vines as he went. Eventually they reached the wider trail and spread out as they started down the trail, Danni Warren leading the way.

A loud report echoed through the canyon, lifting a flock of squawking birds from tree branches all around them.

Campos grunted. He grabbed at his neck as he fell to his knees. Rigby reached out for him and saw blood gushing from the man's throat. Campos fell from Rigby's grasp, toppled over and hit the ground...dead.

Chapter 13

R igby grabbed Danni Warren and pulled her to the ground.

The woman cried out, "Oh, my God!"

Rigby looked around but saw nobody. He reasoned the shot came from a rifle some distance away. The shooter could be hiding anywhere in the jungle. Rigby wished he hadn't had to surrender his handgun when he entered the country. He knew they had to get away from open ground. There was no knowing if the bullet was meant for Campos and the shooter was gone, or if the shooter was after the woman. Maybe he was after all of them just for target practice.

"See those boulders to the left?"

She nodded.

"That's your safe spot. I'm getting up first. I'll zigzag to that clump of trees over there." He pointed. "As soon as I go you head for the boulders. I'll get into the jungle with you and we'll make our way to the ranger station at Wafer Bay. The gunman will have a difficult time following our trail."

"It won't be eating cake for us, either," she said.

Her words were different somehow, the accent had mutated. Fear, he figured. He could see the fear in her eyes, but there was a determination there also.

He nodded at her. "Ready?"

She briefly grabbed his hand and gave it a squeeze. Then they split up. Pushing off the ground, he moved like a running back maneuvering from side to side around orange cones in a practice drill.

A shot rang out, kicking up dirt by his foot. He changed direction. Another shot. He could feel it buzz by his ear like some angry bee.

A third shot. This one sounded different. He went to ground and looked around. Warren was on the move. The last bullet had been meant for her. The bullet chipped the boulder a moment after she dove behind the large rock.

Rigby scrambled to his feet and sprinted into the line of trees. He took a moment to catch his breath. He also took the opportunity to scan the landscape from his hiding place. He saw no one.

The birds continued to screech their protest for this noisy disruption of their paradise but there was no sign of the shooter.

Rigby plunged deeper into the jungle. He called her name softly. She replied, and he could tell from the direction of her voice that she was no longer behind the boulders but moving along the palm trees and brush.

He caught up to her in an open spot among the trees with a crater in the ground like a large foxhole that had filled in over time. A dig for treasure, he figured.

They dove into the foxhole and stayed low.

Warren pulled a cell phone from her pocket but Rigby shook his head.

"No reception."

She checked anyway and discovered that he was right.

"We can only make slow progress through the jungle," Rigby said. "If we want to get to the bay faster we'll have to use the trails. That means the shooter can move faster, too."

"He'll have a clearer view to shoot at us," she said.

"Yes. We'll have to be careful. Let's stay in the trees for a bit longer and angle northwest. Where did you come from? Did you take the trails up from Wafer Bay?"

She shook her head. "I'm off a sailboat that's anchored north of the island."

"Help on the boat, then?" he asked.

"If we can get there. There's a four-man crew and

other passengers."

"Ready to go?"

Warren nodded.

As they rose, Rigby said, "You have enemies?"

"Many," she said as she ran toward the next protective stand of trees.

They remained well shielded for a couple of hundred yards then came to a decision point. A trail cut in front of them. They could make quicker time on it but they would be exposed. Rigby looked at Warren and knew she was making the same calculation.

"Let's go for it," she said.

He admired her spunk and hoped she had good judgment. Together they hopped over a downed tree and ran to the trail. They came to a stream and Warren stopped.

"Can't stop," Rigby said. "Get your feet wet."

He took her hand and they waded into the stream together, testing the depth of the water and the texture of the stream's bed. Though muddy, the water was only ankle deep.

They were tiring now and Rigby knew it. He could hear Danni Warren's labored breathing. He also breathed hard. His long-ago marathon training was no preparation for these jungle sprints. He knew they had to keep going but he also knew they could not outrun the bullets. Maybe the only way to escape the gunman was to trick him. Make him think they went one way when they really went another. Circle back and take the shooter down by surprise. Very risky...the shooter had the gun.

On they ran, but slower now. If only the gunman got discouraged with the chase and stopped.

The rain intensified. Rigby could see fog creeping toward them. He guessed they were close to Wafer Bay. But he did not know where the ranger station was there. He did not know where trails existed that might take them down the cliff to the beach. From photos he saw of the inlet before he left on his journey he knew there were cliffs standing behind the beach.

Danni Warren stopped running. She crouched down, putting a hand on each knee and gasping. Rigby looked around but did not see the gunman.

"Just a little farther," he said. "Listen. You can hear the fast-rushing water from the river, where it goes over the waterfall."

She listened carefully and her lips turned up into a small, encouraging smile. Then they heard another rifle shot.

Rigby grabbed her arm and dragged her toward the river. They were on the run, but with no place to go. The river loomed before them. Rigby had no idea where the trails were. He didn't know if any help was out there for them, someone who heard the shots and was coming. The one thing he did know was that the gunman was not giving up his pursuit. He figured the guy was in good shape because he was maintaining the chase while carrying the rifle and who knows what else.

Another report from the rifle, louder this time.

Rigby felt the bullet rip through his shirt at the shoulder and scrape his upper arm.

Without stopping to examine his wound, Rigby whirled, grabbed Danni's hand and pulled her toward the rushing water. He did not hesitate as he leaped into the river clutching Danni's hand and pulling her along with him.

They splashed hard, sank a few feet then bobbed to the surface, moving along with the current. Through water dripping across his forehead and blurring his vision, he could see that the current was carrying them swiftly toward the waterfall.

"Hold on," he yelled at Warren, "we're going over the fall!" He wrapped her in a bear hug as the water picked up speed.

They both screamed as the river threw them into the air but managed to cling to each other as they fell. Time seemed to stand still for a moment. No sound, no sight, a dream-like lightness.

Rigby tried to relax, anticipating the impact. They hit a pool of water with a loud splash and sank to the bottom, hitting it hard then popping back up.

"You okay?" Rigby gasped.

Warren nodded and buried her head into his shoulder.

He sprang back and she saw his wounded shoulder for the first time.

"What about you?" she said.

No accent at all. No time to question.

"A scratch. Let's get out of here. He won't give up."

They climbed out of the pool, water sheeting off of them. A quick glance as they were going over the side gave Rigby a view of the bay. They still had some jungle to traverse. Exhausted, they followed the water streaming toward the beach.

The killer couldn't follow them now, Rigby thought. Still, they ran through the brush like the characters trying to escape raptors in *Jurassic Park*. He remembered Smitty telling him that Cocos Island was supposed to be the model for the dinosaur island in *Jurassic Park*. He wondered why that thought flashed through his mind when he was trying to escape his own terror. Then another thought about Smitty: seeing a scowl on her face as she demanded, "Who was that woman?" running with him. Despite the situation he couldn't resist a smile. Maybe his inner conscience realized they were out of danger and he could relax.

After another few minutes of dodging boulders and maneuvering around trees, their skin scratched by bushes and branches, they emerged onto the beach. A heavy fog hung offshore no more than twenty yards.

They stopped to gulp air. Rigby was soaked from everything they'd endured. He looked cautiously up and down the beach and then spotted a rowboat sitting on the sand at the edge of the surf.

If the shooter was coming down a trail he might trap

them on the beach. Rigby still did not know where to find the ranger station. It was not visible from the beach. Pushing out to sea would be a certain way to escape. He shared his plan with Warren and, as exhausted as she was, she agreed.

They ran to the boat. Danni jumped in and began freeing the single oar from below the seats. Rigby pushed the eight-foot craft off the beach, took a couple of steps into the surf and pulled himself into it. They jostled around each other as Rigby sat on the stern thwart preparing to row. Warren held up the oar.

"Only one," she said.

He nodded and took it. He would have to use it as a paddle working both sides of the boat. He pulled hard on the left a few strokes, then the right. The tide was going out, easing Rigby's task, helping to pull the boat out to sea and into the encroaching fog.

"Do you think the shooter is on the beach?" Danni asked as she abruptly stood to look back to the shore.

She lost her footing and stumbled. Rigby grabbed for her and rocked the boat. He lost his grip on the oar. It fell overboard and quickly floated away on the crest of some surging whitecaps.

The boat drifted seaward deeper into the fog. Rigby had no idea of their position or in which direction they were drifting. He listened for the beat of waves on a shoreline, hearing nothing but the rhythmic rise and fall of the wooden boat on the ocean.

Looking around he saw there was nothing in the rowboat to assist him—no lights, no food. There was nothing to direct the boat.

Exhausted from the chase he lay back down in the belly of the boat next to Danni and waited to clear his mind and make his next move.

Chapter 14

Rigby had not intended to fall asleep but he did. Checking his watch, he realized that he and Danni Warren had slept for thirty minutes. The boat drifted along in a wide sea. Fog still wafted around the vessel, and though it was lessening, he could not see land.

He shook Danni, who had collapsed with exhaustion. "We're adrift."

She came awake with a start. "Where…where are we?"

"I wish I knew. We can't be too far from the island. See?" He pointed to a bird circling above.

"Can we follow the bird to land?"

"We can't keep up."

"We can use our hands," Danni said hopefully. She stretched over the stern, put her hand in the water and stroked. Suddenly she pulled it out.

"Oh my God!"

"What?"

"Hammerhead."

Rigby peered into the ocean. He could see the shark with its strange flattened head in the shape of a hammer, eyes—as someone once described to him—like lights at the tips of an airplane's wings.

"The motion of your strokes attracted his attention. Sit tight and he'll go."

"Then what can we do?" Warren asked. He heard the concern flaring in her voice.

"We have to sit and wait for the fog to lift. Then we'll be spotted." He hoped that he believed what he was telling her.

When the fog finally lifted they saw nothing but

water and sky in every direction.

Rigby continued to encourage Danni with hope that they would soon be picked up by a passing freighter or dive ship out of Costa Rica headed to Cocos Island.

Time passed; night filled the open sky. Rigby knew they would not be spotted at night without any lights. He told her they would be found in the morning. The rain had stopped and the sun painted the sky red before it dropped from sight.

"Red sky at night, sailor's delight." Rigby echoed the old ditty. "It will be clear tomorrow. They'll see us." He tried to keep them occupied with conversation and not think of the danger they were in.

"We haven't formally met," Warren said, holding out her hand. "Danielle Warren of London and Bournemouth."

Her accent was thicker again.

"Ah, Mrs. Warren," he said with a slight bow of his head. "Zane Rigby, Washington, D.C. I'm afraid I've only one location I call home, and a relatively small apartment at that."

"I'm sure it's a very nice flat." The accent even stronger.

"You're not who you pretend to be, are you?" Rigby said.

"Whatever makes you say that?"

The accent thinner that time.

Rigby said. "Your accent comes and goes. When you're under stress you sound a lot like me."

She studied Rigby for moment then a bemused smile captured her lips.

"Acting. I sound like you because I hail from the same place as you. The country, I mean. You know what they say. When in Rome ... or in my case: *When in London.* I work the accent to fit it. Less of an outsider and *all that rot.*"

The thick British accent at the end of her little speech

came with a laugh.

"You're an FBI agent, you said. What on earth are you doing here?"

"Working a cold case."

"Until that shooter heated it up. Was he after you or that poor ranger that you were with?"

"Could he have been after you?" Rigby asked. He noticed her reaction and was surprised. She seriously considered his query but did not answer.

Rigby had very few pieces in the evidence pouch he kept in the back of his head to make him believe the gunman was after him. Paul Mallory had been murdered and he was on the island because of that murder. More likely the shooter was after Campos and wanted to eliminate any witnesses.

"So you think someone is mad enough with you to shoot you down," he said.

She surprised him again when she held up two fingers with each hand to make quotation marks and said, "My stepchildren."

"That gunman was no fifteen year old."

"My stepchildren are older than I am, Mr. Rigby," she said. "Looking for treasure is not the only kind of gold digging I do."

Not only did she make her confession to him matter-of-factly, she showed no guilt.

"I see I've made you speechless," she said when he did not respond. "Alvin was seventy-two when I married him, I was twenty-seven. Mirror opposites we used to call each other. Yes, he was rich. It may not have been a romantic love but I was a good companion to him for ten years until his death. Now his children are contesting the will. He left everything to me. The solicitors tell me it will be a tussle. There are six children from his previous marriage. When I found the map…"

She didn't finish her thought. Rigby said, "You thought a treasure would be insurance. You wouldn't lose any of your lifestyle in case the court wasn't kind."

"Something like that. Plus, I needed a vacation. A tropical isle seemed just peachy." She smiled at him.

"So the shooter could have been one of Alvin's children or hired by one of his children."

"There are six of them," she said again.

They settled down for the night and both slept restlessly. Dawn broke clear. No rain in sight. Nothing else in sight either in any direction all the way to the horizon.

The reality of their situation started to sink in. Danni said they might not be rescued. Rigby discouraged her from the thought but it sat on his shoulder like an ominous blackbird of death.

The tropical sun started to cook. There was little shade. They took turns lying in the hull using a bench as cover for their faces as the other watched for a ship or a plane.

Both were hungry and thirsty. Rigby had read of survivors at sea forced to drink urine to subsist. He wondered when his body would demand such a move.

They challenged the monotony of the day with small talk. Wisely, they stayed away from the subject of food.

"My face is burning up," Danni said sitting on the seat across from him, after both were silent for a while as they scanned the horizon. "I don't want to lie under this bench again".

"We could take off our shirts for a while to cover up but then our bodies would feel the sun." His voice, like hers, had become raspy from the lack of water.

"Why, Mr. Rigby. How bold and on our first date."

"I promise to stare only when you're not looking."

She didn't hesitate to follow his suggestion, unbuttoning her blue shirt and removing it, covering her head with the shirt like a shawl. She wore a matching royal blue, lacy bra.

"From Harrods," she explained and turned to look at

the horizon.

The sun continued to cook. It wasn't long before Warren felt she needed to protect her torso from the sun. She slipped the shirt back on and slid into the hull, using the bench to cover her face while she took a nap.

Rigby tried to keep watch but the sun wore him down. His eyes fluttered and as much as he battled against it, he realized sleep would overtake him. If he fell asleep, he wondered, would he ever wake up again.

Then, sleep overwhelmed him.

Chapter 15

Rigby sensed a change around him. He heard the beating of great wings. A shadow fell across his face, mercifully blocking out the savage sun. The blackbird of death was now flying above them, coming to get them.

He blinked. The shadow was thicker than any cloud could make. The beating wings came at a rhythmic, engine-like consistency.

He opened his eyes. The bird was a mechanical one, a helicopter. What was a helicopter doing out here? There were none on the island, as far as he knew.

Rigby sat up and looked to the open sea on his left. He turned to his right and was astonished at the sight. He reached down and shook Danni Warren by the shoulder. She snapped awake.

"What?" she said in her voice made nearly inaudible by her dry tongue and throat.

"The cavalry's here," he said.

Warren looked in the direction he indicated and her mouth opened in amazement. Off in the distance steaming toward them was a strike group of two cruisers, two destroyers, and a supply ship surrounding a massive aircraft carrier, all flying the flag of the United States of America.

A line dropped from the helicopter and a sailor in dive gear slid down and jumped into the sea. He paddled over to the rowboat.

The diver asked in Spanish if everyone was all right. Rigby answered in English. "We're okay. We're Americans. I'm an FBI agent."

"Hang tight, partner," the sailor said with a Texas twang. "We'll get a basket down here and lift you aboard the chopper then haul your bones over to Abe and get you checked out."

"Abe's a doctor?" Warren asked.

"No, ma'am. Abe is the USS *Abraham Lincoln*, finest Nimitz class aircraft super carrier in the whole United States Navy."

After his last case, Rigby thought he'd had enough of Honest Abe but suddenly he had a new appreciation for the man and his namesake.

One at a time, the diver guided them into the basket lowered from the chopper, which hoisted them up, giving each an exhilarating ride to the helicopter—although Rigby kept his eyes shut for most of it. They were transported onto the deck of the *Abraham Lincoln*, the length of more than three football fields with a half-a-dozen F/A-18 Super Hornet strike jets sitting quietly on deck, ready to sting.

Taken below decks, Rigby and Warren were separately checked out by medical personnel, and an intelligence officer questioned each of them about their experience. Rigby couldn't help notice the sailors standing at the back of the room wearing 9mm Berettas. He told the officer of the shooting on the island and of their harrowing escape.

Rigby and Warren were reunited after the examinations and offered clothing from the ship's store, each selecting a hooded sweat shirt with the *Abraham Lincoln* logo, the ship's motto: *Shall Not Perish* above a profile of President Lincoln, which was placed above the deck of the aircraft carrier with the ship's hull number 72 clearly visible. Once dressed, they were brought to the Ward Room for a meal. They ate slowly following medical orders, but they ate plenty.

"Admiral on deck," whispered the sailor picking up their dishes with a nod toward the officer entering the room, accompanied by the two sailors Rigby saw earlier sporting the Berettas. "Don't piss him off. He's transferring to the Pentagon in a couple of days. He wants everything to run smooth."

The admiral crossed the room and took a seat at the table.

"Agent Rigby, Mrs. Warren, I'm Admiral Anderson Rosshowe, Chief of Staff for the strike group."

"Admiral, thank you for the rescue and the hospitality you've shown us," Rigby said. "You can bet I'll be wearing this sweatshirt proudly around DC every chance I get."

"You saved our lives, Admiral," Danni Warren said, "I'm so grateful. I want you to know if your chef ever gets out of the Navy, he could open a bakery. The key lime pie was delicious."

The admiral did not smile. He placed his hands on the table and leaned forward.

"Agent Rigby, I have to detain you."

Rigby laughed. "As if I can go anywhere."

The admiral's face held the same hard expression.

Rigby lost the smile. "What gives?"

"You're wanted by Costa Rican authorities for the murder of park ranger Pedro Campos."

Chapter 16

Rigby was stunned. Why would anyone think he killed Pedro? They must have found the body and discovered he was missing. Okay, he could see how they might misunderstand the situation.

"We can straighten this out, Admiral. Pedro was an old friend. I told your intelligence officer what happened. There was a shooter who gunned him down then chased Mrs. Warren and me off the island. He tried to kill us, too. When they couldn't find me they must have put two and two together and came up with five."

"Apparently, they have a witness," the Admiral said, maintaining his somber air.

Witness? Who else was in the jungle and why were they lying?

"I have a witness, too." He touched Danni Warren on the arm.

"That's right," she said. "Agent Rigby didn't have a weapon. Someone was shooting at *us*. The three of us had just come out of a cave when the ranger was shot."

"Cave?" the Admiral echoed.

Rigby and Warren exchanged a glance. Neither appeared eager to tell the Admiral about the search for treasure or the skeletons placed in the cave by the Bloody Sword.

"Yes, cave," Rigby said, "there are many on the island."

The Admiral shook his head. "Looking for one of the treasures."

Rigby and Warren again exchanged a glance, this time one of surprise.

"Legends like that are not secrets to men of the sea,"

80

the Admiral said. "Look, agent, we're on the same team. Landing on this ship is like stepping foot in the good old USA. This is sovereign United States territory. No one from the Costa Rica police is going to set foot on Abe and arrest you. We get our orders through the chain of command. The State Department is already involved. That's how we knew you were on a wanted poster. We can put you and the lady on a COD and send you to San Diego and you can deal with State from the comfort of your own home."

The information came at him fast and Rigby tried to process what the Admiral was telling him while at the same time asking himself about the witness who implicated him in Pedro's murder. Was the so-called witness also the shooter? That would be a neat way to get rid of him. The shooter would claim he saw Rigby gun down Campos and *poof*, no more Rigby. He could not identify the shooter and wouldn't know if the shooter and the witness were the same person.

He decided if that was the shooter's plan, it would go awry because of Danni Warren. She saw the whole thing and would be a credible witness.

"What's a COD?" Danni asked the Admiral.

"Carrier Onboard Delivery. A C-2A *Greyhound* twin-engine cargo transport plane we keep around for missions like this. We can take you where you need to go."

"I'd rather catch a ride on one of those fighter jets," she said with a smile and perhaps a hint of guile, hoping the request would be fulfilled. She quickly realized her response was insensitive to Rigby's position being accused of murder and put a reassuring hand on his. Rigby found the touch warm, even sensual.

To Admiral Rosshowe he said, "I didn't kill Pedro Campos and I can prove it. I'll go back to Costa Rica if necessary."

"I don't send you anywhere until I hear from chain of command. I imagine we're talking to State as we speak."

"You don't get to be an admiral without making

some quick decisions on your own," Rigby chided him.

"That may be true, Agent Rigby, but I don't need to make a hasty decision just now. No life at stake."

"I need to talk to the Bureau."

"I'll make it happen. For now, enjoy our world class hospitality." The Chief of Staff snapped his fingers.

Rigby and Warren were escorted by one of the gun-toting sailors that had been following them around since they came aboard. While one sailor pointed out a couple of locations as they went and explained that the nuclear powered ship carried a complement of over 5000 personnel, ninety aircraft and its own zip code, he would have made a terrible tour guide at Universal Studios or anywhere else. Whether following orders or looking for an excuse not to talk too much, he used the word "classified" a half-dozen times to put off questions from the pair.

Rigby sensed they were not wandering aimlessly and he soon ended up with Warren in adjoining rooms in the Flag Quarters, which the sailor explained was set aside for VIPs visiting the ship. However, he also set limits to their VIP status when he said that he and his gun would be just outside.

"Well, I think we've established one thing," Rigby said as he settled down in a chair next to a small table. "The shooter wasn't one of your stepchildren. This charge of murder against me says that the killer was after me."

"Or the ranger. He's the one who's dead, after all," Warren said. "And if you knew my stepchildren you wouldn't rule them out, either."

"How much are you worth anyway? Must be a pretty penny if you think these folks would take drastic action to see you never return to merry old England."

"A pretty pound actually. Maybe as many as fifty million of them."

"Hmm. Would you like to go to dinner?"

He smiled at her but Danni's response was a look of curiosity and contemplation. What was she thinking? He thought there was a spark between them as they stared hard into each other's eyes. The heat began to build inside Rigby.

Danni broke the spell, saying, "Most of it is frozen in the banks until the court decides about the will. I'm left with a meager amount to live on in the meantime. Still want to go to dinner?"

"Sure," Rigby said. "Make it McDonalds till the frozen money starts to melt."

A tap sounded on the door, followed by a junior officer entering the quarters. He informed Rigby that the Director of the FBI was on the phone for him. He pointed to a telephone in the corner.

"This should be interesting," Rigby muttered.

Danni Warren said she would leave but Rigby discouraged her. "Stay for moral support."

The officer left and closed the door. Rigby picked up the telephone receiver.

"Rigby."

"Who'd you kill?" the Judge snapped over the phone line as if she were in the next room.

"I didn't kill anybody," Rigby said. "Someone took shots at us when we came out of a cave on the island. The park ranger with me was killed."

"Did you find the treasure in the cave?"

How about a word of sympathy for the dead man, he thought. More than he should expect.

"No."

"Anything on Roosevelt? Know what Mallory was after?"

"Not a clue."

"The Speaker isn't going to be happy," she muttered and Rigby realized he was not supposed to hear her inner thoughts. "Well, I need you back here. We've heard from the Monument Bomber again."

The Bomber! Despite Rigby's desire to get back on the Monument Bomber Task Force and his obsession with bringing the Bomber down after the son-of-a-bitch eluded him twice, Rigby had not thought about the Bomber while on the island. He was pre-occupied with his odd assignment to figure out what Paul Mallory knew about FDR.

If the Judge was calling him in specifically to deal with the Bomber, he felt things must be getting hot and his chance at redemption was near.

As earnestly as he could, Rigby said, "How can I help you with the Bomber?"

"He sent another letter. He mentions you by name."

Rigby wondered what network the Bomber was working in and how much information he had about his personal life. When Rigby thwarted the Bomber's effort to destroy the Lincoln Memorial there was no press release issued praising his effort. Like many individuals who served this country, no one followed them around with a bullhorn touting their achievements.

If Rigby was surprised by the Judge's information being named in the Bomber's letter, he was completely floored when the Judge said, "He mentioned you in connection with what our code breakers believe is Mount Rushmore."

"Mount Rushmore..." Rigby didn't finish.

"Exactly," the Judge said. "How did he know about Mount Rushmore? Is someone inside talking to him?"

Important questions that needed answers, Rigby thought, including the one she did not voice but stood out among all the questions—did Rigby somehow tip the Bomber?

"How did you make the connection?" Rigby asked.

"The letter said he will destroy four monuments at once along with Rigby, and his *project*. He underlined the word project. You're working with the Speaker to help with his Mount Rushmore project. The sculptures of four presidents. It wasn't too difficult a puzzle to solve."

"Makes sense."

"I'm going to have to talk to the Speaker about this," she said. "I'm not so much worried about the politics as I am about the objective. We have to assume that Rushmore is his next target."

The Monument Bomber is going after the largest monument of all, Rigby thought. There was logic to it. But there was no sense in the Bomber spilling the beans. In Boston, he had used subterfuge to hide his real target when he hit Old Ironsides. Rigby thought he might be doing that again. How could he get close to the monument to do any damage without hurting himself? His criminal history indicated he wasn't that type.

"So you want me back on the Task Force," Rigby said.

"Not exactly. I want you to continue to do what you're doing. Don't be shy about taking your investigation to Mount Rushmore."

"The Speaker won't be happy if I go public with this."

"Don't talk about the Speaker's project. Just don't be shy about saying whatever case you're working on will take you to Mount Rushmore, and go there. I'll take care of the Speaker. If we're right about the Bomber's next target, the Speaker will want us to stop him or he won't have a project."

"You're using me as bait," Rigby said.

"Mount Rushmore's the target now. *Mount Rushmore*! We have to stop him."

"You think he'll make himself known because of me."

"He's obsessed with you for stopping his last attack. His letter indicates that."

When Rigby said nothing right away, the Judge added, "This is the Task Force. You always wanted back on."

"And FDR?"

"Two for one, the way I see it. You'll be dealing with

the Bomber *and* Mount Rushmore, which is central to the Case of Historical Significance your office is investigating."

"Whatever that case is, since nobody seems to know," he said.

"Whatever it is," the Judge agreed.

Rigby had to smile. He found common ground with the Judge over the seemingly unsolvable FDR investigation.

"I've got to get rid of this accusation hanging over me, that I shot Pedro—the, ah, ranger."

"Being taken care of," the Judge said. "State's on it. Talking to Costa Rican authorities and getting word to the military to get you off the carrier. I understand you might have to go through a hearing in Costa Rica, but it's perfunctory. It'll keep goodwill relations between our countries. Then head up to South Dakota. We'll send in a team and be ready for the Bomber. Go relax and have a day of R & R in San Jose."

Double R. Just like the code name for the *project*.

Rigby hung up and said to Danni, "Looks like I'm going to Mount Rushmore."

Chapter 17

Danni Warren squealed like a schoolgirl as the Navy plane lifted off the deck of the aircraft carrier. She threw an arm around Rigby in excitement. He liked her being that close. The plane flew them low across the Pacific, over the jungle and mountain peaks of Cocos Island and on to Juan Santamaria Airport in Costa Rica's capital city of San Jose. At the airport they were met by a thin man wearing a gray suit and gray tie who identified himself as Robert Hamilton from the Consular Section of the American Embassy.

No federal officer was there to arrest Rigby.

Hamilton explained that a hearing to discuss the incident on the island was set for the next morning with a magistrate. Hamilton said he would accompany the couple to the hearing but that he could not represent Rigby as an attorney.

"Do I need a lawyer?" Rigby asked. "I thought this was pro forma. I've got to get back to the States."

"Costa Rica officials are sensitive to this sort of thing, as you might expect. The killing of a government official and an American agent involved."

"I didn't kill anyone," Rigby said.

"Of course. I was just expressing their point of view. Their sensitivity." Sweeping an arm across the terminal and airport in front of him, Hamilton continued: "Do you know about the man this airport was named after, Juan Santamaria?"

Rigby shook his head.

"He's a Costa Rican national hero. He was a young man killed in battle with the forces of William Walker, an American who conquered Nicaragua and set out to establish

87

a slave empire in Central America in the 1850s. There's a nationalist strain that must be appeased when dealing with provocative actions of Americans in this land. You should know your history when you come to a foreign land, Agent Rigby."

Diplomat and bureaucrat all rolled into one, Rigby thought. This gray guy would be no fun to hang around with all evening. He hoped he didn't have to. Looking at Danni, he wondered if she were interested in stepping out for the evening and leaving Mr. Hamilton behind.

"So what's the program? Where are the cops?" Rigby asked as they entered a waiting Embassy car.

"Your agency director made a special request for our assistance. We're doing our best to cooperate. As I said, I'll accompany you to the hearing in the morning. For tonight, we've secured a pair of rooms at the Marriott for you and your witness, Ms. Warren. While you're here, even though you have a serious charge levied against you, because of your status, willingness to appear and return to the country on your own, insistence from our staff based on your assurance that there is simply an error, and the influence of your government, you are free to have this evening for yourself. There will be no detention. You can come and go as you please. I'll pick you up in the morning and go over the procedure then, unless of course you'd like to spend some time now."

Rigby had no intention of spending any more time with Robert Hamilton but he did have one important question for him. "Who's the witness against me?"

Hamilton shook his head. "Not my department."

"Thank you for your support," Rigby said, "I think we'll just talk in the morning."

"Very well." Hamilton looked relieved that his duty with the couple was temporarily done. "Is there anything else you need before we part ways?"

"I'd like to go to the Gold Museum," Danni Warren

said.

"What's that?" Rigby asked.

"What's it sound like?" Danni said.

"The Pre-Columbian Gold Museum," Hamilton volunteered. "Located underneath the Plaza de la Cultura. It has a considerable collection of over 1600 artifacts of Pre-Columbian gold dating back to 500 A.D."

"I told you I'm into gold." Danni smiled.

"You may be late," Hamilton said. "It closes for the evening about this time. But the plaza is not difficult to find. The museum is under a McDonald's restaurant."

Rigby shrugged. "The stars are aligned. The place for our dinner date."

Hamilton's driver took them to the Plaza of Culture but Hamilton was correct: the museum was closed. Danni expressed disappointment but Rigby promised to take her there the next day after the hearing. The offer did little to lift her spirits. He told Hamilton that they would forgo their McDonald's date and suffer through a four-star restaurant experience.

Hamilton made it clear it was time for him to leave so he ordered his driver to take the couple to the hotel and said he would pick them up in the morning. He directed them to a nearby shopping area when both Rigby and Warren complained that they had no outfits. Except for shirts and sweatshirts picked up on the aircraft carrier they were still in the clothes they wore when they escaped the island.

The shopping excursion was sponsored by Rigby's American Express card. Danni had no wallet with her. Rigby hoped he might get a reimbursement from the Bureau because of the action he saw that required the purchase of new clothes and the bags in which to carry them. As far as a reimbursement from Danni, he simply hoped the court considering her husband's inheritance would rule in her favor because she sure knew how to shop.

"You already have two outfits," he said with the

impatience of an old married man waiting for his wife as she tried on more clothes.

"Don't you like this one?" she said emerging from a dressing room wearing designer jeans and a blue blazer over a white blouse, her hands held behind her back.

"You sure like the color blue."

"Are you referring to the shirt I had on in the cave or what I was wearing on the rowboat?" Her eyes twinkled to add emphasis to her smile. He had no trouble remembering the blue, lacy bra.

"Both," he said. "Can we leave now? I'm getting hungry."

"Wait, I wanted to show you one more thing."

From behind her back she produced a sheer, sleeveless, see-through yellow top. "How do you think this would work with my boat look?"

"I believe you'd be arrested everywhere but the Riviera."

She laughed softly then said that at least she would purchase the jeans from the clerk who was already running the tab on Rigby's credit card. Soon she had changed into one of her new outfits and was carrying the rest of her purchases in a bag.

Rigby and Warren made their way to the hotel, inquired about a top restaurant and spent the evening enjoying each other's company, reliving their recent adventure.

"You said you found the map going through your husband's things after his death. He never said a word about it?"

"Nothing."

"Was it hidden in a safe?" Rigby asked. A treasure map had to be hidden away securely, he reasoned.

"No safe. In a drawer in a wall unit in his study. I recall there were a couple of things in the drawer mostly to do with his childhood. He grew up in Cornwall in the southwestern part of England. I'm trying to remember. There was a schoolbook he owned as a child, a toy train, I recall, and a picture of his much older brother who died before the war. I think there was fifteen or sixteen years between them. Different mother."

"Anything with the map?"

"To me it appeared that things were put in the drawer by happenstance. Some of the papers were clipped together. The map. His brother's picture. There was also a calling card, too. It was from a U.S. Marine general. I don't remember anything on the card—except that the general's name was Orville. Nothing else in the drawer that I recall."

"You still think the map only led to the bones?" Rigby asked.

"Do you?"

The conversation ventured off into different territory as dessert was served.

Soon Rigby hailed a cab and they returned to the hotel. Rigby walked her to the door of her room.

"Thanks for showing a girl a good time," she said, touching his upper arm.

He nodded. "It was a nice dinner."

"Dinner, my word! I was talking about crawling though a cave, dodging bullets, hurtling down a river waterfall, being adrift at sea, getting hauled onto an aircraft carrier by helicopter, then flown to the mainland. I can hardy wait to see what you have in store for our next date."

She kissed him on the cheek, opened the door, entered her room, and after a moment of hesitation closed the door, leaving him alone in the hallway.

He found himself very much wanting a second date with Danni Warren.

Rigby walked to the next room and let himself in. He was tired. He stripped to his underwear and prepared for bed. Once under the covers, though, he didn't feel like sleeping. He wondered what the next day had in store. The hearing was supposed to be perfunctory, but if someone claimed he murdered Pedro Campos, it had to get complicated. He tried to review the incident at the cave, both inside and outside, but his thoughts would wander to the smiling, freckled face of Danni Warren. She would not leave his mind.

A soft rapping snapped him out of his trance. There it was again. He pushed off the covers and got out of bed to investigate.

The knock came from the connecting door to Danni's room.

Without thinking about his state of undress, concerned she may be in trouble; he hurried to the door, unlocked it and pulled it open.

Danni stood at the door wearing her designer jeans that she bought that day and the sheer see-through yellow top that she had shown him. She wore nothing underneath it.

"You never told me what you thought of this top," she said hoarsely.

"Hate it, get rid of it," he replied as he helped her pull it off over her head.

Chapter 18

Rigby awakened alone. He reached over to Danni's side of the bed but she was gone. He rubbed his eyes and checked the clock next to the bed. 8 a.m. He'd overslept. They only had a half hour to get ready and meet the embassy man, Hamilton, in the lobby.

He threw back the covers and went looking for Danni. Not in the bathroom. He went to the adjoining room door and knocked. No answer. He tried the handle. The door opened and he went in. He figured she was way ahead of him, getting ready for the hearing.

"Danni, I just got up. You want me to run down and get us coffee? Danni?"

No response.

He went to her bathroom: empty. Maybe she was having breakfast at the hotel restaurant.

Then he noticed the area around the sink contained no personal items. No toothbrush or any other overnight things they had picked up the day before. He went back into the bedroom and looked in the dresser drawers and the closet. Nothing. Not even the sleeveless see-through yellow top. She'd bought more than one outfit, so she had packed up and taken everything with her.

He refused to believe that she had left him. Not after last night. She was an early riser, he decided. She was having breakfast and her bag was checked with the hotel bellman.

He hurried back to his room, took a quick shower, put himself together, wearing his off-the-rack blue suit and red tie and hurried down to the lobby.

Robert Hamilton was waiting. "Are you and Ms. Warren ready?" he asked as he rose from a broad leather chair.

93

"She's having breakfast," Rigby said curtly as he walked past Hamilton toward the restaurant. But he didn't believe it. She was not going to be in the restaurant.

He scanned the restaurant from the entrance. She was not there.

"We have to hurry," Hamilton said. "We must not be late for the hearing. Where is Ms. Warren?"

"She's not going," Rigby said with resignation. More overpowering was his sense of betrayal. She was his key witness. She knew he did not kill Pedro Campos and her testimony would be enough to let him walk. But she did a disappearing act at his moment of need.

After the closeness and sincere attention they paid each other throughout the last thirty-six hours—especially the last eight—he never expected this.

"Not going?" Hamilton said. "I thought she was the witness to help exonerate you."

"I don't need a witness; I can speak for myself." He wondered why he was covering for her after she had deserted him.

"The government has a witness of its own." Hamilton dug into a pocket and pulled out a folded paper. "I was sent a document this morning. See here. Besides you, the magistrate will hear from Park Ranger Fernando Oliveira."

The young park ranger. He didn't see anything, Rigby knew. He probably suspected Rigby because of the sharp words between Campos and Rigby renewing their twenty-five-year-old feud. Oliveira was guessing that the old animosities led to gunfire. Pretty hard to do since neither Campos nor he carried a gun.

Even if he could convince the magistrate that Oliveira was guessing, Rigby would still be in a fix. He'd have to wait to have his story verified. They would have to uncover the rifle shells scattered on the island that would match the bullet that killed Campos. That would take time.

Or perhaps Oliveira had another reason for telling his

story. He and Campos didn't seem to be the friendliest compatriots. Could he have found a way to terminate their association and pin the blame on someone else?

Whatever the reason for the accusation, it would take time to clear up without Danni. All the while the Monument Bomber would be planning his attack on Mount Rushmore.

Hamilton jerked Rigby's sleeve and said, "Come, let's go. This will be hard on you but you have to face the law."

They walked to the front of the hotel and Hamilton pointed him toward the Embassy car. As Hamilton entered the car from the right, Rigby circled around the rear of the vehicle to its left side. When he got there, instead of opening the door he held up his hand to a taxi that had just dropped off a fare.

The taxi screeched to a halt in front of him and Rigby jumped in. He could hear Hamilton yelling, "Hey! What're you doing? Where the hell are you going?"

Rigby ignored him. To the driver he said, "Speak English?"

"Si, señor."

"Juan Santamaria airport. If this car follows, lose it."

Rigby tossed a number of bills in the front seat. The driver smiled, displaying a missing tooth, then jammed down the accelerator.

Rigby settled back. He knew he was headed for a mountain of trouble. He would be a fugitive from Costa Rican justice. The State Department would not be on his side, although he noticed the Embassy car was not chasing him. He imagined Hamilton was glad to be rid of him. He had no idea what the Judge would say to him. His job was on the line and he knew it. He decided he was doing his job the best way he knew how by getting back to the states to protect Mount Rushmore.

All this flashed through his mind, though the nagging thought that would not go away was why Danni Warren had run out on him.

Chapter 19

Rigby directed the taxi driver to the terminal where the Navy C-2A *Greyhound* had dropped him the day before. He was taking a gamble, but remembered the pilot's commander telling him to report back the following day.

Cutting through the terminal, he could see the Navy plane sitting outside a nearby hangar. Men were servicing the plane, preparing it for flight. The pilot must be nearby. Rigby moved through the private terminal seeking out the pilot.

What he saw instead were a couple of police cars rolling up to the terminal. Four officers got out. Rigby was sure they were looking for someone and he had a pretty good idea who.

Hamilton must have scurried over to the court to say that the man he promised would appear had run away. He didn't want the scar on his record. Blame it on the crazy FBI agent.

Rigby had no time to lose. He started asking the same question to everyone in the terminal: Where was the pilot of that U.S. Navy plane?

He found his man in a small rest area set aside for visiting pilots. Amid the constantly running television, chairs, and a sofa suitable for catnaps and piles of magazines, the Navy pilot was working an old coffee-making machine.

"Pilot," Rigby said, a bit out of breath from his frantic search.

The Navy man turned around and recognized his passenger from the day before.

"Naval aviator, sir," he responded.

Rigby acknowledged the correction with a nod and

looked at the leather patch on the man's flight suit containing the winged shield over a fouled anchor and the aviator's name and rank.

"Lieutenant Connors, I need your services again."

"My orders were to fly you and the lady here, spend the night and return this morning to Abe. I'm airborne in just a few."

"I've had a change of plans and I need a lift," Rigby said.

"I can't change plans without orders."

Rigby looked through the pane of glass next to the rest area door expecting the federal police to come barreling through at any moment. "Can you raise the Chief of Staff for me?"

The pilot shrugged. Rigby could almost see in the expression an exasperated declaration: "Civilian!" but he put down his coffee cup and waved Rigby to follow him.

The aviator led Rigby out a door onto the airfield and straight for his plane. After exchanging a few words with the maintenance men and the Marine guard who had accompanied the flight from the USS *Abraham Lincoln*, Lt. Connors entered the plane, followed by Rigby. Connors headed for the cockpit and powered up his radio. Rigby took a seat beside him.

"Foxtrot whiskey five this is lima delta four, over."

Lt. Connors flipped a switch and a squawk box chirped to life.

"Lima delta four this is foxtrot whisky five, over."

"Request authorization to return with half of delivery package."

"Lima delta four this is foxtrot whiskey five. Do not launch, stand by for further instructions, repeat do not launch."

"We need to speak to Admiral Rosshowe," Rigby interrupted without knowing if the radioman on the carrier could hear.

There was silence for a moment, then the response, "Stand by."

Rigby felt it took hours to find the Chief of Staff even though only a few minutes had passed. He scanned the grounds in front of the plane looking for his pursuers.

"Lima delta four this is foxtrot whiskey five. The Chief is present."

"Admiral, I need to get out of here. Pronto."

"Now?"

"Yesterday. But I'll settle for now."

"I had a report you were turned over to the Consular corps."

"Didn't work out. He wasn't my type. Stickler for the rules."

"We stick to the rules here, too, Agent Rigby."

"Unless we're at war with a terrorist."

The Chief of Staff was silent.

Farther down the field, a police car had entered that section of the runway and was making its way toward them.

"Admiral?" the pilot said.

Out of the squawk box, Rosshowe's voice was loud. "You're really trying to scuttle my Pentagon appointment, Rigby. Is that what you're telling me? You're on a mission to stop a terrorist?"

"We think the Monument Bomber will strike again. Soon."

There was no hesitation from the Admiral. "Our original orders from the Pentagon were to take Agent Rigby where he wants to go. Those orders still stand, Lieutenant."

"Aye aye, sir."

The aviator turned over the engine. The firing of the engine caught the attention of the police in the vehicle. They started driving toward the plane.

"Good luck, Agent," Rosshowe said. "We're all on the same team. Over and out."

Connors hollered over his shoulder, asking if the

crew were all on board. When he was answered in the affirmative, Connors called to the tower that he was ready to taxi into position.

The police car stopped about twenty yards away and two officers emerged from the car. Rigby scrunched low in the co-pilot's seat.

"These fellas are suspicious," the pilot said, "but I don't think they know you're on board."

The plane slowly taxied toward the runway. One of the police started questioning the maintenance men who had serviced the Navy plane. As the plane went past the police car, the pilot saw the conversation between the officer and the service operator become more animated. The maintenance man pointed to the plane.

"Bingo," Connors said. "Time to fly."

He maneuvered the plane onto the runway as the police scrambled to the vehicle to chase them down and call the tower.

The runway was clear and Connors was given an okay to take off. He didn't hesitate in immediately pushing the plane toward takeoff speed.

"Fasten your seatbelt, sir. We're getting out of Dodge just ahead of the law."

Chapter 20

He used a technique called lock bumping: slipping a specially cut key into the door lock and banging or bumping it all the way into the lock allowed the key in that split second to get under the lock's pins. Turn the key and the lock is open. It was that simple. He went into the Asian woman's apartment and closed the door behind him. He knew she would not be there. He had watched her leave and followed her to the subway entrance.

His patience had been running thin. For days he heard nothing about Rigby, his mission, and what he was doing. Was he at the mysterious island that the waitress in the bar had informed him about, or more importantly, had he already gone to Mount Rushmore?

He wanted to make his attack on the monument when Rigby was there. He had already begun preparations. This would be the most daring action of his war on America. It would make the most noise. Be the most spectacular. Be heard around the world.

It would also be the most expensive and require the most preparation. His supporters were forthcoming with the resources he needed. They were excited about his plan and the news it would make. He was gathering material.

But he needed to know Rigby's plans.

Listening to the Asian woman's phone calls with an electronic eavesdropping device had not been too difficult. He learned that her name was Veronica Wong. He learned she was a researcher at the Smithsonian. He learned she liked movies and talked about them with friends and that she had a mother living in San Francisco. He learned nothing about Rigby.

Until yesterday.

Veronica Wong was talking to a fellow Smithsonian researcher about some project she was working on and was late in finishing.

She told her colleague on the phone that she knew she was late but she had received an emergency call from her friend Zane Rigby. He was on a ship somewhere and made a quick request for a few items. Rigby needed them before he headed to South Dakota.

He hoped he would find more information about Rigby in her apartment.

He closed the door behind him and looked around. The apartment was of medium size. It had an uncomplicated layout. He crossed the simply furnished living area and went through the bedroom door. It was a good-sized room, easily accommodating a bed and bureaus along with a large desk containing a computer and telephone, a fax machine and lots of papers scattered on the desktop.

He crossed to the telephone and looked around the papers without touching anything. He noticed a notepad by the phone partially covered by a loose sheet of copy paper. He moved the loose sheet and instantly realized he'd found what he had come for.

On the top of the sheet was a large letter Z. Below that was scribbled: Z on ship/ Mt. Rush / three days / Genl Orville, Marines, WW 2 / Danielle Warren, Eng. / 4 Presidents Inn.

The Z must be for Zane. Along with the reference to Mt. Rush, he was sure these were notes Veronica Wong took when talking to Zane Rigby. He had no idea what all these notes meant, nor did he care. The information he needed was that Rigby was headed for Mount Rushmore and would be there in three days staying at the Four Presidents Inn. He suspected that was close to Mount Rushmore.

Three days began yesterday, he reasoned. So Rigby expected to be at Mount Rushmore tomorrow. It would take some doing, but he believed he could be there to meet Rigby and finish his business with him.

Chapter 21

"The FBI doesn't *create* international incidents, Mr. Rigby, we're supposed to *fix* them."

He had arrived in San Diego the night before courtesy of the U.S. Navy but decided he needed a good night's sleep before reporting to the FBI. Despite expecting a severe reaction, he decided he might as well go straight to the top. As the first rays of the morning sun poked through his uncovered hotel room window, he phoned headquarters and asked for the Director. She took the call immediately, sharp tongue unsheathed.

"An FBI agent to be questioned about a murder *runs away*! Now, doesn't that make for a juicy headline? You're a fugitive, Mr. Rigby, or didn't you know that? Costa Rican police put out a bulletin for your arrest."

He let her continue her tirade without interruption knowing it would be futile to break in anyway.

"Where the hell have you been? Where the hell are you now?" She paused a moment, then continued, urgently. "No. No. Don't tell me. When the State Department asks me, I can honestly say I don't know. They have asked me every damn hour. What were you thinking, Agent Rigby?"

Finally, he spoke up. "I was thinking about protecting Mount Rushmore."

The Judge was silent. Rigby looked out of the hotel room window at San Diego's Mission Bay. What a peaceful scene; the water lapping the sand. No stress. He was shocked when the thought of retirement flashed through his mind. It didn't last. He thought of another beach he recently visited—with bullets flying all around.

"I'm okay now, thanks for asking. Been a rough few days being shot at, chased into the sea, adrift on a small boat."

"Yes, yes. Then you were supposed to be in a Costa Rica courtroom to tell that story but you didn't show up," the Judge said.

"Circumstances changed. I asked myself, *What would the Director do in this situation?*"

"Don't screw with me, mister."

"Think about this," he began, the attitude in his voice sharpening to match her tone. "Someone said I murdered a government official because I previously had cross words with him. I had a witness that could tell the court I had nothing to do with the killing. The morning of the hearing my witness disappeared. I had no defense. The court would probably delay my leaving the country until I could prove my innocence. I knew that the Monument Bomber was active and I was *told* I had a special role in stopping him. So, Director, I'm asking you if you were in my shoes, what would you have done?"

She answered his question to his satisfaction by ignoring it. "Are you headed to Mount Rushmore?"

"The plane leaves later today."

"The Task Force is already on the ground there. Agent Miller is in charge. Backup is provided by the Denver field office."

Miller. No picnic there, he thought. Then again, he wasn't on the Task Force. As he understood it, he was bait, acting as a free agent in more than one sense of that word.

"How do I fit into the plan?" he asked.

"It's become much more complicated. You're a wanted man. Some cop on the beat could arrest you. The FBI can't be working with you in any visible way."

"Buy me some time. Tell the Costa Rican government that I had to be pulled to counter an immediate terrorist threat. Tell them you believe my story and that I'm innocent." He paused. "You do believe me, don't you?"

"Of course. You're innocent until proven guilty."

The Judge's answer gave him no confidence. He plunged ahead. "While you're telling them all this, send some agents to find Danielle Warren, my alibi."

"What about that? She said she'd testify and then disappeared? Could she have been kidnapped?"

Rigby thought about this and considered the fear she had of her stepchildren. He knew better. She had run out on him.

"What was this woman to you?" the Judge asked.

A good question. Whatever Rigby thought might be developing between them, apparently for Danni Warren they were just ships passing in the night.

"We both found ourselves in the wrong place at the wrong time."

His cell phone buzzed. He pulled the phone from his ear and checked to see who was calling. Smitty.

"Got to go," he said to the Judge. "I'll contact you from South Dakota."

He hit a button on the screen that ended the call with the Judge and connected to Smitty.

"Hello, Smitty. Were you able to find anything for me?"

She didn't rebuke him for calling her Smitty. She didn't charge across the phone line full of bluster. She spoke softly as if she were puzzled and a little afraid.

"Z, I think someone's been in my apartment."

He could tell she was not playing a prank.

"Get out quickly," he said.

"No. There's no one here now. I came back from shopping and have been all over the place. Put my jacket away in the hall closet. Used the bathroom, hung up my new clothes in the bedroom closet. Had a glass of water from the kitchen. There's no one here."

"What made you suspicious?"

"My desk. I can swear that papers have been moved around on my desk. I looked closer and saw a pad of paper was not where I left it. It was right next to the sheet of paper I used to scribble notes when you called me. The General with the name Orville and Danielle Warren. The last call you made. I looked on that pad and I could make out the indentation from someone writing on the sheet they removed. Looks like it said, Four Presidents Inn."

Rigby was immediately struck by the possibility that the Monument Bomber had hooked into Smitty. How did that happen? The relief he felt was that there was no leak in the FBI. It was quickly overwhelmed by his concern for Smitty. He reasoned the Bomber—if it were the Bomber—would not do anything to his information source. Still, Rigby did not know how the Bomber was getting his information. Had he put a tap on Smitty's phone?

"We've got to talk, Smitty, but I want you on another line. Go to a friend's apartment and send me an email with the phone number. I'll call you from a landline."

"Now?"

"Right now. And, Smitty. Make sure you're not followed."

Chapter 22

A little over an hour later Rigby and Smitty were talking again. In an age of almost universal ownership of cell phones it was hard to find a pay phone, but Rigby had, down in a dank basement corridor of a downtown San Diego government office building. Smitty was at a friend's house.

"Borrowed my neighbor's car and visited a friend who has a farmhouse in the country," Smitty said with an air of satisfaction that she pulled off her assignment well. "Lots of open space here. I could tell if I was being followed and I wasn't."

"Good," Rigby said, "be sure you keep using your head. Stay with your friend for a few days and don't go to your place alone."

"What's going on, Z?"

"I'm on the trail of a terrorist. I don't know how, but I think he latched onto you to learn more about me. I can get you protection."

He wondered if that were true. Would the FBI support him, a fugitive from justice? Rigby told himself Smitty was out of danger because the Bomber needed her to track him. However, he was not naïve enough to realize that one way for the Bomber to learn where he was hiding was to make life very uncomfortable for Smitty.

"Did you have enough time to get some information for me?" he asked.

"You never give me enough time, Z. But I got some preliminary stuff."

"Let's have it."

"What's your connection to Danielle Warren, anyway?"

Same question the Judge asked him about Danni.

"We were supposed to testify in a court room together but she disappeared. I want to know a little more about her."

"You should read *People* magazine," Smitty said. "I found an article there. It was titled, *The Gangster's Niece and the Billionaire*. She used to be an actress, never made it big, moved to England, and was seen around town with high rollers. Ended up marrying one. Big-time industrialist. Alvin Warren. She was twenty-seven at the time; he was in his seventies. When he died ten years later, she became a very rich woman—for a week—until the old man's kids contested the will. British courts are dealing with it now. And the British tabloids. You can *imagine* what that's like. In fact, there was a new court filing this week. The old man's children claimed she disobeyed court orders by taking a piece of the old man's property out of the country. She's not supposed to take anything out of the estate until the court decides the rightful owner."

"What did she take?" Rigby asked.

"Get this. A map. Funny, huh? The old man's kids got all hot and bothered about a map."

Funny, Rigby mused. These kinds of maps get people killed.

"Go back," he said. "Gangster's niece? What's that mean?"

"Oh yeah. Get this. Apparently your lady friend is a great-niece to Marvin Rothman of Murder Inc. and the Jewish mafia. A contemporary and friend of Meyer Lansky and Mickey Cohen and that bunch."

Smitty paused. As if she were listening to the words she spoke for the first time she asked, "Say, is she your lady friend?"

Rigby ignored the question. "You mean *Dimes* Rothman?"

"Uncle Dimes. Couple of times he'd overcome his adversaries by poking them in the eye, gunning them down when they were blinded, and placing dimes on their closed, dead eyelids. Earned him his nickname."

Rigby let out a low whistle. "What about the general?"

"There's no record of a General Orville in the United States Marine Corps either in the decade before or during World War II."

Was Danni lying to him about the calling card? Was the guy an imposter? If so, what did he have to do with presenting the map to Alvin Warren?

"I did play a hunch though," Smitty continued. "Orville might be a first name. Everyone's heard of Orville Wright. So I got help and searched the records of a first name Orville Marine Corps general. Let me tell you, that wasn't easy."

"And?" Rigby asked impatiently.

"I found one. Lt. General Orville Randolph. Born 1904, that's the year after the Wright Brothers flew the plane in Kitty Hawk, so maybe his mother or father was amazed by human flight. General Randolph died in 1982. He served in Washington for the most part during the war. Got his promotion to Brigadier General in June 1944 and Lt. General in January 1955."

"Is there any record of him having dealings with Danni Warren's husband?"

"I didn't find anything."

"Okay. Thanks, Smitty. Keep looking."

"I did find something else though."

"What's that?"

"Remember you had me look up stuff about Franklin Roosevelt's visits to Cocos Island?"

Remember? Rigby almost chuckled to himself.

Smitty continued: "Well, in the 1930s Orville Randolph was a Marine Colonel. He was in charge of a detachment of Marines that sailed on the USS *Houston* with President Roosevelt to Cocos Island."

Chapter 23

The bar at the Four Presidents Inn in Keystone, South Dakota was all Old West, from its swinging half-doors at the entrance to the pudgy Rubenesque nude above the bar, to the wood paneling and framed prints of cowboys, Indians and western vistas. The one-time mining settlement of Keystone was now a town of hotels, catering to Mount Rushmore visitors. Rigby stood at the bar nursing a beer in a bottle, contemplating his next move. He was trying to capture a bomber with no idea where the man was and how to run him into the ground.

He wondered if keeping his job with the FBI depended on him stopping the Bomber. He had failed to come up with anything on Cocos Island to understand why Paul Mallory was murdered. The Speaker of the House would not be happy. His old acquaintance, Pedro Campos, was dead and he was a fugitive from Costa Rican justice. The Director of the FBI was not happy. The State Department was making inquiries about him. If the Bomber succeeded in damaging Mount Rushmore, everyone in the government from the president on down—hell, everyone in the country—would not be happy. He expected somehow he'd be the fall guy.

He just hoped nothing else would go wrong.

A handcuff was slipped over his wrist and clicked shut.

He jerked away from the bar and looked at the woman holding the other end of the handcuff. She was black, tall, athletic-looking, sporting a couple of gray hairs. She carried an air of authority.

"You're under arrest," she said.

He nodded at her. "Special Agent Miller. Can I buy

you a beer?"

"How about we go someplace where we won't be seen together and not tip off the bad guy," she said, looking around at the few patrons in the bar.

"My place or yours?"

"Why Agent Rigby, I didn't know you cared. Since we're here, your place is closer."

"Don't you think you ought to undo the cuffs or are you planning on using them when we get to my place."

"You've got an overwrought imagination." She undid the cuff from his wrist.

Rigby gave Agent Kendra Miller his room number and headed to the elevator. She followed a couple of minutes later and soon joined him in his room. Miller stood by the window looking out at the traffic flowing on Keystone's main street. Rigby had flopped onto the bed adjusting the pillows as a backrest.

"This road has a number of names and a route number attached to it," Miller began without any greeting or a reassurance that the handcuffs trick in the bar was not a gag. "One of the names is *Holy Terror Trail*. I'm not sure why it's called that but it will be apt if we don't stop the Bomber."

"I'm here to help anyway I can," Rigby said.

She looked at him suspiciously. "You know, Agent Rigby, I used to look up to you. You were a model for younger agents like me. Wanting to be a success, trying to do things the right way. Then…"

Her voice trailed off. She watched more traffic go by.

Rigby said, "I've had a few unlucky breaks but I get the job done. That's the bottom line."

She turned to stare at him. "Get the job done. Arresting the young California congresswoman for playing footsy with her boyfriend? Letting the Bomber get away not once but twice? Running from the Costa Rican authorities? You know this Bureau is button-down collar with a single color tie. You're a tie-dyed t-shirt in comparison."

Rigby thought her analogy was over the top but he understood what she was trying to say. He offered a response in a measured tone, not wanting to rile her.

"Sometimes you have to go it alone without your blockers, Kendra, to score the touchdown."

She stared at him and raised her voice a notch. "Not on my team. You're working for me now and you do as I say. I know I was your junior but this is my deal. I get to play the cards as I see fit."

"I'm your ace in the hole."

"Unfortunately, for you, Rigby, you're the card that's turned over for all to see."

Rigby laughed. Within three exchanges with Agent Miller he had been a tie-dyed t-shirt, a football player and a playing card. It all added up to one thing in her mind and she was telling him: the independent Mr. Rigby was playing by her rules.

"What's the plan?" he asked.

"I have agents around the monument. We're cooperating with uniformed park rangers. Nothing will appear out of the ordinary. The agents will look like tourists. The only exception is you. You will look like an FBI agent. The button-down kind. I might even have you wear the windbreaker with the big, yellow FBI letters on the back panel. You'll walk around, talk to the rangers, maybe to the tourists. Be visible. You'll be watched. Different members of the team will pick you up. We'll be looking for anyone who is following you or acts suspiciously. At the same time, we will closely monitor the visitors to the memorial. The Bomber will have a hard time sneaking a bomb onto the grounds."

"If he's after me all he needs is a gun."

"You're a secondary target. He's the *Monument* Bomber, after all."

"Always second best," Rigby said.

"Just remember, Agent Rigby, I'm in charge here. You follow my orders. We'll catch this guy before he gets to you. There's no way he can get through our net unless he can fly."

Chapter 24

He didn't know how to fly but he didn't need to. They would have defenses against flying a bomb into the monument. He had studied the precautions. He knew there was a no-fly zone posted around the monument on certain holidays like Independence Day, July 4. That would not be the only defense to protect the monument from an air attack.

He had a surprise for them. He also had a surprise for Elmer Stanton, the Cessna pilot who approached him across the end of the runway at the airport in Spearfish, South Dakota, about sixty miles north of Mount Rushmore.

"Mr. Micah J. Nabb?"

"Yes, that is correct. You are Elmer Stanton?"

Stanton stuck out his hand and the two men shook.

"Thank you for agreeing to help me on such short notice," he said in pretty fair English although he could not hide his accent. He would use that vulnerability as a positive in his scheme.

"I've just recently decided that now is the time," he continued. "I must do this. I understand your customs somewhat. I have been in the country some years now. I want to do something she will remember."

"Oh, she'll remember this, Mr. Nabb. She'll be talking about it for the rest of her life."

"It is a good thing to do?" the man going by the name Micah Nabb asked innocently.

"Pretty unique, I'd say," Stanton replied. "Not that it's unheard of, but it ain't common. She'll be impressed."

"Is this the plane?" Nabb nodded toward the Cessna.

"No, that one will pull the banner. The clincher, I like to call it."

"Ah, the clincher," Nabb repeated. "Good." He didn't

know why these Americans so often had to make pet names for things, or shorten every phrase to a word or a set of initials.

Nabb looked around and said, "Where is the plane that makes the smoke?"

"This baby right here." Stanton pointed at another small aircraft across the runway.

"That little plane," he said doubtfully. "All that smoke?"

"Nothing to it," Stanton said. "Just a pressurized container with low viscosity oil. Inject the oil into the hot exhaust manifold and it vaporizes into dense white smoke."

"How long do the letters last in the sky?"

Only a few minutes with the wind and all. We're up maybe 10,000 feet, but we're making letters the size of the Empire State Building. It'll get her attention."

"But the letters will be gone so quickly," Nabb said.

"That's why you're smart to come in with the clincher," Stanton responded with a wink.

Still trying to sell him, Nabb thought. Trying to reassure this naïve, lovesick person he presented to the pilot that he was not overspending by sending up more than one plane with messages. The man who called himself Nabb didn't need convincing. The cost was immaterial to him. The dual distraction was the important thing.

"I'm putting the banner together over in that storage building yonder. Want to take a look?"

"Of course," Nabb replied.

They walked across the airfield to a corrugated metal building standing by the far end of the runway.

"Now exactly where will your lady be?"

"She works in the gift shop at Mount Rushmore. I've arranged for a friend to bring her outside when the skywriting begins."

"Rushmore, huh?" Stanton whistled. "Don't think the authorities want us buzzin' around there."

"But you will be so high in the sky."

"That's true with the smoke. But we have to come in much lower with the banner."

"The clincher," Nabb said.

"Yeah." Stanton smiled. "They'll understand, I guess, when they see the smoke. Everyone's a romantic."

That is what Nabb was counting on. Americans and their romantic streak.

Stanton opened the door to the metal building. A wave of heat pushed out at them. Lights were on and the men walked into a jumble of airplane parts, tools, spools of cloth, sewing machines and an array of items that allowed for construction of banners that were dragged along behind an airplane.

"Here's yours," Stanton said, pointing to a banner on a worktable. "The boys are out to lunch but they'll finish it up soon."

Nabb could make out little of what the final product would look like but he saw a sketch of the banner taped above the worktable. The words read: *Say Yes, Gwyn. Love MJ.* He had chosen the name of the little girl who lived on the first floor of his apartment building when he first came to America. She always smiled at him when he entered the building. He chose the initials he often heard associated with a player of basketball that his neighbors revered.

"Yes. Yes, very good," he said. "How could she say no?"

"No way," Stanton replied.

"You will be ready on time?"

"We can go up tomorrow morning. That's your schedule, right?"

Indeed it was. Enough time to prepare the other planes and give Agent Rigby a ringside seat for the show of destruction.

Chapter 25

The lady was almost as wide as she was tall and came waddling right toward Rigby. He waited patiently for her arrival. She was panting a little as she stopped in front of him. They were on the viewing deck across from the Mount Rushmore memorial. Sweeping an arm toward the sculpture the woman said, "Just gorgeous. Gorgeous."

Rigby nodded.

"So I want to know, who was the president who dedicated the memorial and was he unhappy that he wasn't up there with the others?"

Rigby was not surprised that he had been asked a question. As the only person walking around the visitors' center wearing a suit and tie the tourists thought he was a member of the memorial's staff. He had been peppered with questions all day, just the way Agent Miller wanted it.

He actually knew there were different answers to this question. Because of World War II, the dedication of the completed monument didn't happen until President George H. W. Bush finally did it. As Smitty told him, Franklin Roosevelt dedicated the Jefferson head on the monument, and Calvin Coolidge held a ceremony here before the monument took shape. Considering the mission he was on, he thought the second part of the woman's question ironic about the dedicating president not being a face on the monument. Yet, he played dumb. Miller also had scripted his answers to all inquiries.

"Sorry I can't help you, ma'am. I'm an FBI agent. I'm not attached to the monument."

"FBI? My. Why are you here?"

"Keeping an eye out. Can't be too careful these days. Tell your friends that everything is fine."

"Oh, I will, Mr. FBI agent. As soon as I get the answers to my questions about the president from someone who knows." She brushed past him and opened the door to the visitor's center.

Spreading the word about the FBI agent was part of the plan, Rigby knew. Make sure that the Bomber knows he's here. Make sure the FBI agents watching Rigby pick up the Bomber. Simple. Rigby doubted it would work. The Bomber wasn't going to show himself. If the Bomber's intent was to kill Rigby, that would not be hard to do.

He was in the open and word had spread about the FBI agent. The Bomber would know who he was. The Bomber's chief mission was to damage the memorial. Rigby knew how he worked and what was most important to him. Rigby also knew that as bait to attract the Bomber into the FBI net, he had to play his role.

Rigby looked across the Grandview Terrace at the muscular agent dressed like a hiker. He knew the stock boy in the gift shop who followed him around in the store as if he were a shoplifter was one of the younger agents. The interracial couple holding hands by the entrance to the pathway that meandered under the great sculpture also were agents. This was the new FBI, not Mr. Hoover's FBI.

He appreciated the backup but felt certain it was a waste of resources.

Rigby spent the entire day at the memorial. Between giving out directions to the gift shop, cafeteria and every bathroom in the whole complex and talking to tourists, he also spent some time looking up at the great faces on the side of the mountain.

The sculpture was truly awe-inspiring. He took a moment in the visitor center to read about the sculptor, Gutzon Borglum. He remembered the name. Borglum was responsible for the Lincoln head bronze in front of Lincoln's Tomb. Rigby had rubbed the nose for luck when he was in Springfield. He was assigned to Springfield to be *away* from

119

the Monument Bomber. The reverse was true at Mount Rushmore.

Borglum had received an invitation to carve the mountain at the request of the state historian, who was trying to bring more visitors to the state, Rigby had read. The guy knew what he was doing, Rigby figured.

Borglum had been carving Robert E. Lee into Stone Mountain in Georgia when he got the invitation, the information at the park headquarters said. That was in 1924. FDR made his speech in 1936, a dozen years later, and that was the dedication of the Jefferson head. Washington had been finished a couple of years before but Lincoln and TR were yet to come.

In the end 400 workers sculpted the huge sixty-foot-high carvings in granite from October 1927 to October 1941.

He looked at the stoic faces that represented American Democracy over its first 150 years. He wondered how proud the men represented on the mountainside would be of the current state of America. Would they be ashamed of the constant political bickering today, or would they understand? It was the intransient nature of today's politics highlighted by the fight between the president and the senate majority leader that conjured up the scheme to expand Rushmore. The presidents on the mountain all had their own political problems, he knew, although he wouldn't do well if someone required him to write an essay about what those problems were.

He imagined the pile of granite rubble visible at the base of the mountain, the result of years of dynamiting and cutting to shape the rock, were the presidents' symbolic tears for the condition of the country.

The thought made him sad for a moment. Quickly he realized he was working for the best damn country on Earth, one that could work toward solving its differences. That, too, is what the men on the mountain stood for. He was determined to protect that heritage.

He wondered what the mountain would look like with FDR and Reagan up on the mountainside. He had seen the drawing in the Speaker's office but knew the real thing would be different. He tried to be an architect planning the addition of the two presidents.

A voice next to him broke his concentration. "Why is it called Mount Rushmore?"

Another tourist. He knew his job. Direct the tourist to a park ranger or the visitor center. He turned to the man who asked the question and paused.

Rigby studied the man standing next to him. He was shorter than Rigby. Darker complexion. He sprouted a scruffy beard. His eyes were brown and cold. Rigby tried to remember the face of the man who carried the instrument case at the Lincoln Memorial intending to attack the monument had Rigby not intervened. The Monument Bomber who had eluded Rigby's grasp in DC.

The man noticed Rigby's inquisitive look. Rigby wanted to keep the man with him. Give him more time to decide if the Bomber was within his grasp. Instead of relying on the script of Agent Miller, Rigby answered the man's question.

"He was a New York lawyer who came to South Dakota for clients who were interested in a tin mine. He admired the granite peak. When asked its name he was told it had none so his friends named the mountain after him."

"That so," the man said. Rigby noticed a trace of accent.

Just then the heavyset woman who had asked Rigby about the president who dedicated the monument walked by on the viewing terrace with some friends. Waving to Rigby she said in a loud voice, "That's the FBI agent I told you about."

The man next to Rigby reacted to the revelation. He moved a step away from Rigby, stuffed a small pair of binoculars he was carrying into a jacket pocket, and hurried

121

toward the platform exit leading to the Presidential Trail that ran beneath the monument.

Rigby didn't hesitate. He moved immediately to follow the man, signaling the undercover agents to join him.

"Stop. FBI," Rigby called after the bearded man.

The man broke into a run.

Rigby and the other agents raced after him.

Off the Grandview Terrace, the bearded man charged onto the trail. He was in an all-out sprint now. Rigby was on his tail, but a couple of the younger agents were faster and better dressed for the run. The Asian woman and African-American man who acted as hand-holding lovers were catching Rigby as they climbed a short set of stairs and followed the paved trail, wooden railings on each side of the paved path.

The bearded man picked up his pace and Rigby felt he was falling behind the man. The other agents were almost beside him now. Rigby was blowing hard, sweat cooling his back and beading his forehead.

The bearded man vaulted over a railing, leaving the trail. A blanket of granite stones covered the base of the mountain and rose up along the lower mountain like some sort of crumbled pyramid that had kept its outline as it fell in upon itself.

The man ran onto the rocky landscape. The stones blown off the face of the mountain had settled into an interlocking jigsaw puzzle of sorts, barely walked on for three-quarters of a century. Yet, as the bearded man made his way across the sea of stones they moved beneath his feet. He threw out his arms to keep his balance.

Rocks that had been loosened by his footfalls came rolling down the hill at the man's pursuers. Rigby dodged a bouncing stone. The woman agent fell and cried out as she hit a sharp stone and split open her jeans at the knee, exposing a bleeding cut.

The bearded man scrambled higher. His effort sent

stones and rock chips flying back at Rigby. He was forced to throw an arm across his face to protect his face and eyes.

The man was making progress. The FBI agents were falling back.

Where could the guy go? Rigby wondered. Eventually he would have to climb the faces on the mountain and no one could do that, not without equipment, anyway.

Suddenly, a second figure appeared in Rigby's peripheral vision. He looked to his right and saw the muscular agent dressed like a hiker scampering across the rock pile as if he were a mountain goat. The hiker made great strides across the stones as the bearded man struggled to keep his footing. The suspect probably didn't see the guy coming.

It was over quickly. The hiker blindsided the bearded man and flattened him onto the stone. They rolled over a couple of times, moving back down the hill toward Rigby and the other agents before coming to a stop with the FBI agent sitting on the man's chest.

The bearded man's resistance was gone. He breathed hard as the other gasping agents encircled him.

Rigby was breathing harder than anyone but he was also sure his adrenalin pumped faster than any of his fellow agents.

He'd finally caught the Monument Bomber.

Chapter 26

Ignoring the cuts and scrapes on the man's face resulting from the wrestling on the rock pile, Rigby started questioning him as soon as the man's hands were secured in handcuffs.

"Where are the bombs?"

The man stared at him as if he were trying to interpret a phrase in a foreign language.

"There are children here. Don't put their lives in danger. Tell me where the bombs are and when they're set to go off."

"What you talking about, man? Bombs? What bombs?"

Rigby blew out a breath. He did not have the patience. He reached out and grabbed the man by the shoulders. "You're going to talk to me, now! No one is going to die here today, unless…"

He let his voice trail off menacingly.

The female agent touched his wrist and a shake of her head told him this was not the way the FBI did things. He knew the standing policy on interrogations. But, he sure as hell wasn't going to let this guy succeed with his last mission. The guy was not going to blow off George Washington's nose.

Let her be the good cop. As long as she got him to talk quickly.

"Let's take him inside," the female agent said. "The park rangers have a place we can interrogate him."

"What interrogate? I ain't got no bombs."

The agent playing the woman's boyfriend fished a wallet from the rear pants pocket of the man and pulled a small two-way radio from his own pocket. He called in information to Agent Miller as the others carefully worked their way down the unstable slope.

**

Forty minutes later Rigby sat staring into a cup of coffee in the visitor center cafeteria. He did not hear Kendra Miller approach.

"No need to be so glum," Agent Miller said as she pulled out a chair next to Rigby.

He took a sip and placed his cup back on the table. "Easy for you to say. I've been chasing the Bomber for months."

"We'll still get him. No need to be down. It was still a good collar."

"You don't suppose…" Rigby looked up at her with a hopeful expression. "He could be both a bank robber and the Bomber?"

"Not unless he's Superman and can fly across the country with the speed of a bullet." Miller smiled. "The moment you were chasing the Bomber away from the Lincoln Memorial, our friend, Mr. Raul Mesta, was holding up a bank in Honolulu. He also has a string of bank robberies on his résumé here in the west from Oregon to New Mexico. He panicked when he heard the tourist identify you as an FBI agent. Thought you were looking for him. Looks like he's responsible for the bank job in Cheyenne that happened two days ago. The FBI was hot on his trail, or so he thought. No need to tell him any different. It's good for the Bureau's rep."

Rigby nodded at all this but still had a hollow feeling inside. The Monument Bomber was still out there. Still a threat to America. Still a threat to its historical past and monuments. Still a threat to him. Was the bomber even in South Dakota? Was all his prancing around at Mount Rushmore a waste of time and resources?

Rigby sighed.

Miller noticed and said, "You need something stronger than coffee. Come on. The workday's over. I'll join you and your escort for the ride back to the hotel and we can have a drink."

"I thought we weren't supposed to be seen in public together," he said, reminding her of their meeting in the Four Presidents Inn hotel bar.

"I didn't say the drink would be in public," she shot back, more in the tone that Rigby was used to from Agent Miller.

Still, Miller's sympathetic air made him realize he was letting his emotions show too much. Yes, he was disappointed and frustrated that the mysterious bomber might be lurking and they had no idea where he was. Rigby knew he shouldn't wear his emotions so openly that even hard-as-nails Kendra Miller had sympathy for him.

Rigby pushed the coffee cup away, stood and followed Miller through the cafeteria to the parking lot.

An agent had been assigned to him for protection as he made his way to the memorial and his hotel. The agent drove them back to the hotel, where Rigby joined Miller in the promised libation, not in the hotel bar but in a meeting room set aside for use by the FBI. When they were finished, Miller bade Rigby goodnight and the escort agent walked Rigby to his room, saying that he would pick him up in the morning.

Rigby spent the evening watching a movie about an FBI agent catching bank robbers who wore presidential masks in their heists. Where do these writers think up this stuff about how the FBI operates? he wondered. Well, if it's a good story...

He drifted off to sleep, not looking forward to another day of watching the four presidents on the mountain and telling tourists where they could find the bathroom.

The knock on the door came a bit early as Rigby was

slipping on his suit jacket. "Coming," he said as he adjusted his tie before opening the door.

In the doorway stood a swarthy man about five-seven with scars on his face wearing a collarless button-down shirt, a Washington Nationals baseball cap and holding a Glock 17 pointed at Rigby's chest.

"You will come with me, Special Agent Rigby."

The voice carried an unmistakable accent. Rigby squinted as if trying to focus on the man's features but he knew that was not necessary. He was certain this time. He was staring at the Monument Bomber.

"Come, come. No foolishness," the man said as he removed Rigby's gun and tossed it into the room.

Rigby left the room and walked down the hotel corridor in the direction indicated by the Bomber, the Glock firmly against Rigby's spine. They proceeded through the fire door at the end of the corridor. Rigby's room was on the fourth floor. They had gone down one flight of stairs when Rigby heard a door open in the stairwell one floor below.

The Bomber faced Rigby, gave him a threatening look and reached into his inside jacket pocket, pulling out his FBI badge and identification.

Ordering Rigby down the stairs, they met a woman from the housekeeping staff carrying towels. The Bomber did not hide the gun. Instead he held up the case with the FBI badge and flashed it at the woman, who only had eyes for the big weapon.

"FBI," the Bomber said. "I'm taking my prisoner to jail."

The frightened housekeeper gave a slight nod. Her lower lip quivered and she never took her eyes off the gun.

The Bomber shoved Rigby in the back and they continued down the stairs, exiting the building into the rear parking lot. There was little activity in the morning hours. The Bomber directed Rigby to a sedan and ordered him into the rear seat. Rigby complied as he studied the man's face.

Was the man nervous? Hesitant? Would the gunman take his eyes off him, give him an opportunity to take the guy down?

"Put your hands out in front of you," the Bomber demanded as he leveled the thunder end of the pistol at Rigby's forehead. There was menace in his voice.

Rigby stuck out his hands and almost immediately the wrists were trapped inside his own handcuffs, which the Bomber has taken from Rigby's belt.

The Bomber released tension from his tight facial expression. He looked around to see that they were still alone in the parking lot and scanned the hotel windows for signs of life. Satisfied he was carrying out his mission in secrecy, the Bomber took a roll of duct tape from the floor of the rear seat and cut two pieces off the roll with a pocketknife. He slapped both pieces over Rigby's mouth and pressed down hard. Rigby's protests came out as muffled gags.

The FBI agent knew his chances of escaping whatever fate the Bomber had in mind would diminish if he drove him out of the parking lot. He wasn't going to let that happen without a fight. Rigby dropped his shoulder and tried to push against the Bomber with sudden force, knock him off balance.

The man staggered, kept his footing and rewarded Rigby with a blow to the forehead with the butt of his gun.

Rigby dropped back into the rear seat and the Bomber wrapped a yard of duct tape around his legs. The Bomber searched Rigby's pockets, removing his cell phone and dropping it into the front seat. He found the key to the handcuffs and threw them next to the cell phone.

The Bomber closed the doors, started the car and eased it out of the parking lot, clearly intending not to draw attention with a screeching of tires.

Rigby looked out across the parking lot and the row of windows at the rear of the hotel, hoping that somebody had seen his abduction and would call the police.

He saw nobody.

Chapter 27

The Bomber drove the car into the Black Hills. He did not speak. Rigby could not speak. The radio was off, the drive made in silence. Rigby wondered if anyone coming down the opposite side of the road would see him gagged in the back seat and call the police. He doubted it. The opportunity never arose. The Black Hills in the morning was a lovely, but lonely place.

The Bomber followed the curving road as it steadily climbed into the hills. Ponderosa pines dominated the landscape. The packed forest pines with their dark green needles looked black from a distance, giving the hills their name. Fern-like plants covered the ground beneath the pines. A deer broke from the forest up ahead, scampered across the road and disappeared on the other side.

Up into the hills the Bomber drove until he came to a tunnel carved into the hillside. It was square and short, just a way through the rock for the road to continue.

The Bomber went through the tunnel and stopped the car in the middle of the road. He turned and looked at Rigby, his eyes alive with excitement. He said, "Look behind you."

Trussed up like a Thanksgiving turkey, Rigby had difficulty moving. He squirmed and pushed and turned his head. He saw the tunnel behind him, and framed by the tunnel walls in the distance was the Mount Rushmore Memorial.

"Like a painting on the wall, yes?" The Bomber said. "They did this with other tunnels, also. To show off the mountain."

A car came up the road behind them and the Bomber drove his car off to the side of the road and parked. The car slowly went by and disappeared around the next curve.

When the car was out of sight, the Bomber exited the vehicle and pulled out his gun. He opened the rear door and took out his knife.

Rigby believed his end was near. He struggled against his restraints. He could hardly move. His position seemed hopeless. Fear overtook him. It was not a fear of death, but rather failure. A fear that the Bomber would succeed in blowing up the monument and continue to attack America and Americans. In this moment when he was about to die, Rigby felt only shame for failing to stop the Bomber.

The Bomber brought his knife down toward the floor of the car and Rigby's bound legs. He cut through the duct tape, freeing Rigby's legs.

The Bomber stepped back and, motioning with his gun, he ordered Rigby to follow.

With a sense of relief, Rigby obeyed. He was still alive. He still had a fighting chance. He guessed the Bomber was intending to finish him with a bullet deep in the woods. He would attack before that could happen.

The Bomber directed Rigby into the forest, ordering him to climb the hill that the tunnel ran through. There was no path. Rigby maneuvered around pine trees and snapped off broken branches in his way, his abductor close behind him.

Rigby began his calculations. Could he outrun the man? Could he grab a branch in his bound hands and turn on his captor before the Bomber got a shot off?

Crack!

Rigby felt a blow from the handgun to his neck and back of the head. He stumbled and fell, momentarily stunned. He felt his legs being twisted around and focused on the scar-faced man, who was once again taping his legs together.

Rigby kicked out with his legs. The man pulled back. Too late. The legs were bound.

The Bomber dragged Rigby along the ground to a

nearby tree and produced a rope that he must have left there earlier. Soon, Rigby was tied securely, seated on the ground against the tree and facing the Mount Rushmore monument in the distance.

To Rigby it meant one thing: he was not going to die, at least not right away. The man would not go to all this trouble and then kill him. The Bomber wore a sick grin. He reached over and yanked the tape from Rigby's mouth, searing his skin.

"FBI Agent Rigby," the man said and spat in contempt. "Tied like a lamb for slaughter."

"Don't set off the bombs," Rigby said in a scratchy voice. "You'll kill innocent people."

"You Americans kill innocent people all the time in your wars," he said, then added in a burst of anger, "In my country!"

The Bomber caught himself, took a breath. He was gaining control, presenting an image of calm and reason.

"Few will die," the Bomber began. "There is always a price to pay. Maybe some; that cannot be helped. It is the American heart that I am after. Destroy the way you self-glorify. Remove your legends and your myths by destroying your memorials to yourselves. I want you to see this happen. The tunnels are built to look upon the monument. From above the tunnel here you will have that same view."

The Bomber pointed toward Mount Rushmore in the distance and Rigby understood that they were in the woods directly above the entrance to the tunnel on the side closest to the monument. He could see the four presidents in the distance, as if looking at a small soapstone replica of the famous memorial.

"You will see it all. They will not stop me. They will be distracted. They think they will stop me but they will not understand. They will be in Bunker Hill again."

The Bomber had tricked Rigby at the Bunker Hill monument. He used deception and was proudly proclaiming that he would do so again to achieve the same success.

"They will think rescue has come but it will not be rescue, it will not be U.S. military, it will be me. It will be destruction."

The sound of an airplane engine caught the Bomber's attention. He looked up in the sky and smiled.

"Ah, yes. It begins. You, Special Agent Rigby, have a seat by the ringside."

Before Rigby could speak, the Bomber leaned over and reapplied the tape over Rigby's mouth, making sure that it was secure.

"I must put the last phase of the mission into place. I will come back when it is over and you can tell me how magnificent it was. I would free your hands and leave you with a camera to record history, but somehow I don't trust you to be here when I return."

The man laughed with delight. He was enjoying the moment and expected that nothing could stop his mission of destroying Mount Rushmore. Rigby feared he was right.

Chapter 28

The Monument Bomber reached the lonely airstrip just as the skywriter began spelling out a message in white, smoky letters on the blue-sky canvas. The airstrip was at the base of the hills surrounded by forest. It was rarely used. There were no facilities, just a landing area cut out in a meadow at the edge of the forest. The drones had been delivered the day before and camouflaged just inside the tree line.

The Bomber marveled at the resources his contacts in America could bring to bear for his mission. He never met them but imagined they were wealthy men who felt a strong loyalty to their native country and disgust at the war their adoptive country brought to their homeland.

He knew he had little time with much work to do in such a short period. He hurried around the crafts, loosening the camouflage tent cords from the pegs in the ground. Once all the cords had been freed, he dragged the tent off the three replica aircraft.

They looked like Navy F-4 Phantoms, NAVY printed on the fuselage with the single star on the wings. The drones were 80" long and 65" from wingtip to wingtip. The interior of each plane was packed with C-4 plastic explosives, enough, he hoped, to turn Mount Rushmore into a faceless mountain again. They would be controlled by a GPS system and remote control.

Looking to the east, he could see the smoky message in the sky taking shape. *Will You*....

The sequence of events would happen fast. The skywriter would distract the Americans. They would be defensive about the plane with a banner. The drones would surprise them. By then, it would be too late.

Chapter 29

Special Agent Kendra Miller looked up into the morning sky at the letters taking shape over the Black Hills.

Will You Marry M...

The park superintendent, a woman of fifty who did not bother to cover the gray in her hair, joined her.

"Isn't that romantic," the superintendent said with a broad smile.

"Maybe," Miller responded. "But I don't like it. We better get our defenses ready."

"Defenses?" the superintendant said. "You mean...?"

The superintendent did not even want to say the word. Her smile was gone and a nervous twitch worked her eyelid.

"The missile," Agent Miller said.

"You really think...we need it?"

"Maybe."

The FBI agent's cell phone rang. She answered and listened. The agent assigned to escort Rigby spoke to her. "Rigby wasn't in his hotel room. I looked everywhere. No one's seen him."

Miller clicked off the phone.

"Get the Stinger ready now!"

The superintendent nodded, took a two-way radio off her belt and barked orders to the park ranger on the other end.

Chapter 30

Rigby watched the airplane dip and curl and sweep the sky, trailed by white smoke. The pilot was leaving a message in the sky above the monument. To Rigby's surprise the message did not denounce America. It was a marriage proposal.

Will you Marry Me, G...

Rigby sensed he was witnessing the first step in the Bomber's plan. The Bomber said there would be a distraction. Could this be it? He thought it was.

Mount Rushmore was in imminent danger and he could do nothing. He pulled the rope holding him against the tree. There was little give. In frustration, he tried to pull his hands apart, as if he had the strength to snap the handcuffs. The cuffs dug into his wrists.

Rigby leaned back against the tree. He was a sad mix of adrenalin to do his job, fear that the Bomber would succeed, and the empty feeling he hated when he experienced it before: failure.

The Monument Bomber had beaten him in Boston. Rigby outsmarted the Bomber in D.C., but this game wasn't a record of wins and losses. One major defeat and it was all over. Unlike a sports team that suffered a loss but looked forward to redemption the next year, there would be no next year for him or for the monument. The monument would be destroyed and so would he. Watching it all from the seat provided by the Bomber. Then the son-of-a-bitch would return and finish him.

A tree branch on the ground snapped behind him. His ears tuned into the sound. He heard another crunch of a step on the needles and leaves. He wondered if the Bomber had already returned.

Too soon, he thought.

What kind of animals called the Black Hills home? Would a bear be so bold to approach a human for sport? Did a mountain lion smell a meal? Rigby knew he had no defense to chase away a determined animal beyond thrashing around or mumbling through the tape covering his mouth.

Another crunch of branches.

He tensed for the first strike.

Suddenly a hand appeared from behind him and reached toward his face. The hand grasped the end of the tape covering his mouth and yanked it off.

He yelped in pain and turned to see the person who now moved into his line of vision.

Danni Warren?!

Chapter 31

He moved the drones shaped like Navy planes into position at the end of the airstrip. He set the GPS system, turned on the engines and adjusted the dials, ready for takeoff. But the planes would not take off until he released them. He pulled remote control devices from a backpack and tested each one. The engines on the planes revved. Everything was working as it should.

He looked at stacked cubes of explosives filling the first plane. This would make a loud bang, he thought, and set off a fire and a light show that would be seen for miles.

He thought of Rigby sitting on the hill above the tunnel with a perfect view of the coming explosions, and he smiled.

Stepping away from the planes, remotes in hand, he was eager for his surprise to take off and fly to the monument. This would be his most spectacular triumph yet. The world would know he would not rest until America was punished for her crimes. America would come to know that her monuments and myths fooled nobody. America was not the land of freedom and equality that it claimed. He would literally blow the mask off America's lies.

He looked up into the sky, waiting for the plane pulling the banner. He hoped the little adjustment he made to that plane's radio when Elmer Stanton had left him alone for a moment worked as expected. Soon after the plane passed by he would launch his messengers of truth and destruction.

Chapter 32

R igby was stunned. Danni Warren smiled weakly at him as she held the tape that had covered his mouth.

"Where did-did ..." he stammered.

"I followed you," she said.

He didn't understand and his shoulders rose in a gesture to let her know he was confused.

"You told me you were coming here to Mount Rushmore. I needed to explain to you what happened in Costa Rica. I came to see you this morning. I was in the car in the parking lot working up my courage about what to say to you when I saw you come out with the man. It looked like he was bullying you so I followed."

Questions, rebukes, condemnations, concerns all rolled around inside Rigby's head. For a moment he wondered which expression would jump first off his tongue.

"When your car pulled off the road I drove past and around the corner. When I saw he left without you I came to look for you. Let me free you," she said as she started to move around the tree.

"Never mind that," he said. The danger from the Monument Bomber focused his mind. The man was operating as he had before: subterfuge and decoys. Rigby said, "Do you have a cell phone?"

She nodded and produced one from her pants pocket.

"No time to explain. Dial the number I tell you and put the phone to my ear."

Chapter 33

The drones' engines were grinding smoothly in their idle position and did not drown out the noise from the small plane approaching from the north. He looked up and saw the plane pulling the banner.

Say Yes, Gwyn. Love MJ

He stared into the distance in the direction of the memorial. The sky was filled with fading, smoky letters, drifting and thinning. Soon the message would be obscure, just a patch of thin clouds.

He made the final preparations for his own planes full of explosives to lift off and follow soon after the banner plane came closer.

**

Rigby heard the plane and turned toward it, pointing in the sky with both his hands. Danni Warren had freed him from the tape around his legs and from the rope that held him to the tree but she could do nothing about the handcuffs.

"What is it?" she asked, then saw the banner and read it aloud. "*Say yes, Gwyn, Love MJ*. Persistent chap. He's pushing her to say yes. Following the proposal he wrote in the sky."

"No!" Rigby exclaimed. "It could be a bomb." Or could it be another decoy, he thought. Had he made the phone call in time?

**

Special Agent Kendra Miller stood next to the ranger holding the five-foot-long Stinger missile launcher on his shoulder.

140

The ranger told Miller he hoped this day would never come. He had been trained in the use of the Stinger rocket launcher as a precaution. Since 9/11, attacks using airplanes as weapons against all kinds of structures had to be considered a real possibility. To protect the memorial, a MANPAD, Man Portable Air Defense System, had been reassigned from the military to different locations around the country. Personnel were trained in handling the missile launchers to confront direct threats.

Miller turned to an agent manning a radio nearby. They were on the flat top of a rock outcropping about halfway up the mountainside.

"Did you raise the pilot?"

"Still trying, ma'am."

The agent spoke into his hand-held microphone.

"To the Cessna flying near the Mount Rushmore monument. Do you read me? You are in restricted airspace. You must turn back. Do you read me? This is the FBI. Over."

There was no response from the aircraft.

"Keep trying," Miller said. To the ranger she asked, "Are you ready to fire?"

"Are you sure about this, ma'am? He's just hauling a banner. Just a civilian."

Miller showed no emotion. Her duty dictated her hard stand. "Be ready to take that plane down if he doesn't respond."

The ranger swallowed visibly but said nothing.

**

Elmer Stanton brought his plane into a downward glide heading toward the four massive heads on the mountain. The banner he was pulling caused the plane to shimmy from the swirling wind, requiring him to maintain pressure on the yoke to keep the craft steady.

It was beautiful day. The lucky lady Gwyn would be dazzled by Mr. Nabb's double-dip proposal of skywriting and a banner. He wondered if she was already in tears. And, he hadn't reached the destination yet.

The radio sputtered out static. He wished he had time to fix the darn thing. Probably a loose wire. He discovered the problem as he was about to take off. What could he do? He needed to cement the proposal to the lucky lady, Gwyn. He would fix the radio when he got back.

**

"That plane is heading straight for the mountain," Agent Miller said, her voice spiking with tension. To the agent holding the radio she yelled, "Again. Try again!"

The agent repeated his warning but received no response.

Oh my God, she thought, her mouth going dry. She had to make the call. What if the ranger was right? What if some pilot doing his job was just planning to circle the monument with a marriage proposal? A pilot with a family?

She could hear the agent repeat his warning.

What if the pilot were a suicide bomber set on destroying this cherished monument with no regard for the lives he would take with him?

The plane continued its descent toward the monument. She could not wait until it got over the visitor's center.

**

Elmer Stanton saw a flash down below. It looked like a small spark. From the spot of the flash he saw a dot in the sky. The dot was coming toward him. Coming very fast.

**

142

Zane Rigby and Danni Warren watched the plane with the banner jerk up and then dissolve into many pieces. The explosion ripped the little aircraft apart, the banner freed from its mooring, fluttering in the tides of wind in the atmosphere, falling more slowly to the earth than the pieces of the plane.

"It exploded," Warren said. "The bomb?"

"A bomb would have made a bigger explosion," Rigby said. "It was a decoy."

**

The Monument Bomber heard the explosion and smiled. He thought, *I suppose I don't get a refund because the banner didn't stay up as long as promised.*

He turned his attention to the remote controls. His drones shaped like fighter planes with their special delivery were already off the ground and on their way to destiny with the heads on the mountain.

**

"Look," Rigby said.

He pointed to three planes, each with U.S. military markings. Yet they seemed small.

"Will they shoot those down, too?" Warren asked.

"No," he said softly.

**

"More planes approaching, Agent Miller," the agent on the radio said. "Hard to see from here but they look like American fighters."

"Load up," she ordered the ranger. "To be safe."

"There are three of them. Reserve missiles are back

in storage. We never expected an invasion. I don't have more ammo to re-load."

**

"Why don't they shoot?" Danni Warren cried out as the new planes darted across the air headed straight for the presidential heads.

Rigby said, "They can't re-load in time. That's what he was counting on."

The three planes still appeared small to Rigby. It wasn't the distance that made them look small. They were drones of some kind.

The drone planes glided effortlessly through the sky, heading toward their destination. Only a few thousand yards now from the mountain.

"Nothing to stop them," Rigby said, more to himself than to Danni.

One thousand yards. Rigby watched in mesmerizing horror.

Five hundred yards.

Despite all their efforts, they had been unable to stop the Bomber.

He had failed.

Again.

Three hundred yards.

A whooshing sound caught his ear and quickly rose in volume. Rigby suddenly saw speeding objects above.

Three missiles streaking across the sky.

The lead drone was hit mid-section and exploded in a huge fireball. In rapid succession two more missiles caught the small drone planes, setting off more explosions. Rigby and Warren stepped back from the echoing of the blast roaring through the mountains, fireballs painting the sky.

They watched the spectacular event in awestruck silence. Smoke from the exploded drones drifted across the sky. Debris from the explosions fell toward earth at the base of Mount Rushmore.

An instant later two needle-nosed F-16 Fighting Falcons screeched across the sky in a blur, traveling at Mach 2.

As the F-16s passed the four presidents the pilot closest to the monument tipped his wing in salute, then the two planes turned skyward and zipped into the wild blue yonder.

Warren's cell phone rang.

"Yes."

She listened for a moment then held it out to Rigby. He started to reach with his cuffed hands but she again placed the phone to his ear.

"Rigby," he said

The voice on the other end said, "This is NORAD command. Hold for Admiral Rosshowe at the Pentagon."

Rigby heard a click on the line.

"Rigby?"

"Yes."

"Got 'em."

"I saw. Saw it all. Thanks."

"Thanks for your phone call, Special Agent. Like I told you on ship, -- same team."

Chapter 34

"Why the hell did you run out on me?"

They were in Danni Warren's rental car working their way back down the mountain to the village of Keystone.

Rigby had called in reinforcements but the Monument Bomber never returned to claim his prize. Given the explosions of the bombs before they hit their target, Rigby wasn't surprised. Now headed back to town, he concentrated on the mysterious Ms. Warren.

"I didn't run out on you. Not really."

"I was being questioned about murder. You were my witness."

"I know. I know," she said with a mix of exasperation and remorse evident in her deep sigh. "I got a phone call."

Rigby, seated in the passenger seat, was looking straight ahead. Now he turned to her.

"I didn't hear a phone. I certainly remember we were together that night and *real* close."

"Yes, it was nice." She smiled. "I was awake. I heard the buzzing of the cell phone in the next room. The door was open, remember?"

He remembered. He remembered it all.

"It was from my solicitor. My stepchildren…they found out I had the map to the Bloody Sword treasure. They claimed it was part of the estate. That under the court's ruling I was not to take anything from my husband's estate until a final disposition of the will occurred. They were going to send the authorities after me."

Rigby weighed her story. Smitty had told him about the map and the stepchildren's lawsuit so he knew that was true. He considered if this was a worthy excuse. It didn't add up.

"Don't tell me you ran off to express the map back to England. You didn't need to pack your bags to do that."

She laughed. "No, silly. I had no intention of sending the map back to England. I decided to go back to the island as soon as possible. I know I said on the island that the map just led to the graves. But, I thought, why would anyone do that? I decided I had to dig to be sure before I was forced to give up the map."

Rigby was stunned. "You went back to the island?"

"Yes."

"And left me in the lurch?"

"Whatever that is. I don't think I did it."

"You were my witness that I didn't shoot Campos." Rigby knew he did not have to explain but made the statement sternly.

"Didn't they get my letter? I expressed it over."

Rigby made a gesture, hunching his shoulders. He didn't understand.

"I wrote out what happened on the island. I didn't mention the treasure map and the Bloody Sword site. Just that I met you and Mr. Campos hiking on the island. We were returning to the ranger station when someone opened fire, shot poor Mr. Campos, and chased us off the island, firing at us all the time. I paid a messenger to take it the Costa Rica court."

Rigby studied her. Could she be telling the truth? It sounded like a feeble lie. Yet, he'd been in enough strange situations in which he knew a seemingly feeble lie was actually true. Did she really think that a letter from her would exonerate him if she wasn't there to answer questions?

Danni Warren was sophisticated in many ways, more sophisticated than he was, although he never gave himself high points in that category. It wasn't a matter of knowing that her presence in the courtroom was more important than her letter. The woman that he thought he had been so close to was more interested in how things worked out for *her*. There was no affection in their tryst, just a one-night stand. Any feelings he developed that night were foolish.

After a moment of silence, he asked, "You went back to the site?"

"I wanted to know."

Her tone had changed. No longer was she the helpless woman asking for forgiveness. As soon as they began talking about the treasure site, Danni Warren was the adventuress.

"When Campos and I found you in the cave you said the map just led to old bones. That was to get rid of us. So you could go back and get the treasure for yourself."

Danni Warren said nothing.

Rigby put aside any sense of betrayal he harbored over her disappearance in Costa Rica. There was the matter that brought him to the island in the first place.

"You dug in the cave? Where the skeletons lay?"

"I intended to."

"What did you find?"

"Nothing. I didn't dig. There were police all over the place because of the shooting. I couldn't get close."

He looked at her again. He tried to see her eyes, to look deep inside her in search of the truth. She kept her eyes on the road.

Danni must have sensed his stare. Without taking her eyes off the road she said, "Please believe me. I very much wanted to find that treasure, make no mistake. But I did not abandon you. I'd never do that. There's probably nothing there, anyway. What the map led to was a gravesite, not a hidden treasure. The bones belonged to a couple of pirates who sailed with the buccaneer known as The Bloody Sword."

Rigby told himself he shouldn't believe her. Yet, it

was possible. If she had found the treasure, would she have come looking for him? Had she found the treasure, and had she come looking for him, what did *that* mean? That the night in Costa Rica was more meaningful than he previously thought?

He looked over at the attractive lady driving the car and decided he preferred his most recent thoughts about what she thought of him to his original conclusion.

"I wouldn't have been a helpful witness for you anyway. They would have doubted me because of my family. I suppose you know about that."

"You're related to Dimes Rothman."

"Distant. Still, there it is. Always comes up. I never told you, but you knew. I tried to be an actress in Hollywood and was making some good strides until they learned about my family. Great-niece of a gangster! I wasn't getting the job offers I wanted. They wanted to typecast me as a bad girl. Some San Fernando Valley porn producer wanted me to star in something called, *The Gun Moll and Her Rod*. No thanks.

"I didn't want my family hurt by the publicity, telling America that we were related to Dimes Rothman. I decided to start over in England. Many English actors come to America. I thought I'd reverse the trend. Get a fresh start. I met Alvin in England. He was wonderful to me; pursued me. My family found out and encouraged me to get close to him."

"Why?"

"They said my uncle wasn't all bad. They said he did good things and that Alvin might be able to prove it. Improve the family's reputation."

"What good things did Dimes Rothman do?"

Danni smiled. "It doesn't matter. My family said I would find something to prove Dimes was a mensch. You know what that means? A good guy. Alvin knew nothing about Dimes. But he was so kind and so *generous* to me. So much validation for who I was. When he asked, I agreed to marry him. Some reporter found out about me. *Gangster grandniece to marry industrialist.* That kind of magazine cover helps some careers but it didn't help mine. I can't escape the family history."

Rigby took it all in and didn't respond. They remained silent the rest of the drive.

When they arrived back in Keystone, Rigby was ordered back to Washington immediately.

Special Agent Kendra Miller told him, "The Director has a lot of questions that only you can answer," in a way that meant she would be happy to be 2000 miles away when Rigby faced the music.

Danni volunteered to accompany him to Washington and speak up on his behalf.

She had come back to him when she didn't have to. Now she was willing to go to DC with him when she didn't have to.

When they landed at Reagan Airport, Rigby had a message on his cell phone to come directly to the Director's office. He was told to bring Danielle Warren with him. It made sense. Agent Miller had reported what happened in South Dakota. Danni had helped Rigby thwart the Monument Bomber's attack on Mount Rushmore. She probably was in line for a citation.

Instead of an awards ceremony, Rigby and Danni were ushered into a small conference room near the Judge's office. The FBI Director was there and she was not alone.

"Agent Rigby, I believe you know Detective Rory Denver."

Rigby nodded.

"You are Danielle Warren?"

Rigby answered for her. "Yes. She's the woman who helped stop the Monument Bomber."

The Judge nodded.

Rigby knew something wasn't right. He looked at Denver and said, "How's the murder investigation?"

"Just got a big break," Denver said, leaning back in his chair and studying Rigby and Warren closely. "We finally confirmed some interesting fingerprints we found at the murder scene."

"What makes them so interesting?"

"We found the fingerprints in Paul Mallory's bedroom. They belong to Danielle Warren."

Chapter 35

All eyes were on Danni Warren. She showed as much surprise as the others in the room. After a long moment she said, "Mr. Mallory's dead?"

"You admit being in Mallory's place?" Denver said.

"In his bedroom," Rigby blurted out. His eyes widened, his face a mask of complete surprise.

Danni searched the faces of the law enforcement people in the room. "Of course, I admit it because I was there. But, he was very much in the pink when I left him."

"What were you doing there?" Rigby said. It came out as a demand, as if he had every right to know. That brought a suspicious look from the Judge, which Rigby ignored. He didn't care what the Judge thought.

"Is it anybody's business?" Danni said to everybody in the room but delivering the message directly at Rigby.

"It's *my* business," Denver said. "Mallory was murdered. Do you own a gun?"

"They wouldn't let me take it on the airplane," she said mockingly. She was not backing down.

"Your Uncle Dimes give you one?" Denver chided.

"Every time..." she muttered, shaking her head in disgust.

Turning to Rigby, the cop said, "You didn't know she was with Mallory?"

Rigby didn't have to shake his head to answer the question. His body language provided the answer. Rigby now understood why the Washington cop and the FBI Director were conducting this interrogation together. Since they learned that Rigby knew Danni Warren, they expected he knew Warren had some connection to Mallory. He hadn't revealed that connection. This little conference was as much about Rigby withholding information from the Judge as it was to question Danni Warren about Paul Mallory.

Danni said, "I don't understand what this is all about. I visited Mr. Mallory when I stopped over in Washington on my way to Costa Rica. I was with him for maybe forty minutes. He was very much alive."

Very much alive in the bedroom, Rigby thought.

"How did you know him?" Denver asked.

"He phoned me in England."

"Phoned you?"

"Well, not me really. He wanted to talk to my husband, Alvin Warren. My husband had passed on. I ended up on the telephone with him."

"What did he want?"

"I couldn't help him. He wanted to talk to my husband about his older brother. I never met the man. He died many years ago."

"What did he want to talk to your husband's brother about?"

Rigby looked across the table at the Judge. He didn't know how much she had told the detective about the Speaker's dramatic proposal to fix the partisan bickering and Mallory's attempt to disrupt that. Rigby figured there was no way to keep the information secret from the cop. Otherwise, how to explain his own visit to Mallory? He had left that to the Judge as he headed off to Costa Rica.

The Judge made no effort to stop Danni from answering Denver's question.

"He wanted to know about a meeting Robert Warren had with President Roosevelt on an island off Costa Rica in the 1930s. Mr. Mallory was writing about it for a magazine or something."

Denver seemed puzzled by Danni's answer. Rigby guessed the detective saw no motive for murder in a 1930s conversation.

The Judge said to Denver, "I explained why one of

153

my agents was visiting Mr. Mallory, why he was at his townhouse and discovered the body."

"Yeah," the cop said.

Rigby understood that the cop knew about Project Double R but the Judge was not sure that Danni knew and if she did not, the Judge wasn't about to reveal anything.

Denver said, "If you had nothing to tell Mallory over the phone, why visit him in DC?"

Danni looked at Rigby.

Rigby said, "Tell him."

She sighed. Paused a moment, then looked at the detective. "Mr. Mallory told me that Robert Warren was on the trail of buried treasure. After he told me that, I searched Alvin's things and found a map attached to a photograph of his brother. I discovered it was a map of Cocos Island; the one Mr. Mallory talked about. I decided to go there and look for treasure. I thought I could find out more information from Mallory that would help my search. I stopped in DC on the way to Central America."

"So you showed him the map?"

"I'd be a poor fool if I did something like that now, wouldn't I? Give away the whole store? I think not. I stopped to get more information. He left me his phone number when we spoke by phone. I told him I was in the states and thought I'd drop by and see if he had any luck with his research. Get him to talk about what I was interested in—in a roundabout way."

"And what did he tell you?"

"I want to understand something." Danni's voice was strong but Rigby sensed fear. "Are you asking me these questions because you think I had something to do with Mr. Mallory's murder?"

She turned to Rigby as perhaps the only friendly face in the room. "Should I be answering these questions without a criminal defense lawyer present?"

Rigby didn't know how to respond. He wanted to

hear the answers she would provide as much or more than the Judge and the detective. He also felt a responsibility to protect her.

Finally he figured out an answer to satisfy both mandates. "Telling the truth, Danni, will help the detective and reassure him you did nothing wrong. Get you on your way quickly."

She sighed again. She was tiring from the interrogation. Rigby wondered if she was deciding to follow his advice. Tell the truth or try to wiggle her way out of any difficult circumstances.

"I didn't show him a map, he showed me one."

"A treasure map?" the Judge asked.

"A map of Cocos Island, one that showed with red circles where many of the diggings occurred on the island. He kept it in his bedroom," Danni said firmly, staring straight at Rigby. "I followed him upstairs—we were in conversation—to get the map then we retreated to his study where he pinned it to a wall."

Could be true, Rigby thought. He had seen the island map on the wall. Of course, it could have always been on the wall of the study. Danni could have seen it there and made up the part about following Mallory to the bedroom to retrieve it.

The cop asked, "Did Mallory seem nervous to you? Did he mention any visitors coming? Was he complaining about anybody or anything?"

Danni shook her head to each of his questions.

"He gave me a few minutes, talked about the island and the treasure hunt. He seemed upset that I couldn't provide him with any documents about Robert Warren's trip to Cocos Island or how he died. I could tell he didn't really want me around. Once I saw the map he had and realized he wasn't interested in talking about treasure on the island, I left. The next day I was off to Central America. I didn't know he was dead.

"Now, I've answered all your questions. If you are not through with me, I'm certainly finished with you."

Chapter 36

Rigby followed Danni Warren out of the conference room but no words were exchanged between them until they exited the building.

"Are you sure it's all right to be seen with me, a murder suspect?" A drink could have been chilled with her words.

"You're not a murder suspect," Rigby said. He didn't sound convincing.

"You didn't stick up for me in there."

"I told you to tell the truth. I told you that's the best way to end the suspicion. And it was."

"Not completely," she said. "There's still at least one person suspicious. You."

Rigby admitted to himself that he was still contemplating Danni's answers about her visit to Mallory. Her visit to Mallory's bedroom, in particular. Could she be a killer? Did Murder Inc. still run through her veins?

Suddenly, her expression changed. Her lips curled into a pleasant smile. "I like that," she said. "You're jealous."

He *was* jealous. His concern was not that Danni might be a killer; it was that Danni might have been more interested in another man. Twenty years of FBI training undone by a pretty face. He wanted to be surprised by his reaction, but he wasn't. He explored his feelings honestly. What about her feelings toward him? Either she thought he could help her find the Cocos Island treasure or she cared for him more than a one-night stand. The latter idea seemed unreal but he had no other explanation.

Looking at the attractive woman who obviously relished a sense of adventure, he found the thought pleasing.

157

A small smile moved his lips.

"What?" she said.

"What what?" he responded.

"The smile. What were you thinking?"

"Nothing."

"About me?"

"Why would you think that?"

"Because," she said, "you just came from an interrogation about my possible involvement in a terrible crime. Yet, you choose to be here with me and you're smiling."

His smile grew a little wider. "You're a detective, are you?"

"So I'm correct?"

"Of course not. It was a nervous smile because I just realized the next step for me to untangle this mess is to have a word with Smitty and I don't know how to explain *you* to *her*."

He explained Smitty to Danni as best he could as they took a taxi to McGillicutty's Irish Bar and Grill in the Cleveland Park section of town. Smitty wasn't easy to describe. He avoided the obvious psychological arguments having to do with father figures and puppy love and emphasized a woman with brains that carried around a pack full of jealousy on her back. He realized there was nothing he could say to Smitty about Danni. Danni was a good looking woman and she was with him. That would be enough for Smitty.

**

"And you are?" Smitty asked Rigby's companion as she took a seat at the table Rigby and Danni had laid claim to at McGillicutty's.

"Danielle Warren."

Smitty brightened. "Yes. Yes you are. I recognize

you from the magazine photos."

Rigby disdained the celebrity culture that seemed to put a spell on the country. He remembered Smitty telling him that Danni had made an appearance in *People* magazine because of her May-December marriage to the rich Alvin Warren. The Gangster Girl and the Billionaire Boy. Hardly a boy. In Smitty's eyes Danni had reached some level of celebrity status. That would make the meeting with Smitty more comfortable than he had imagined.

"Where did you meet Zane?"

"We ran into each other on the island and had a few adventures together."

"What kind of *adventures*?"

Rigby said, "The kind where bullets are flying. The kind that demands that we solve this puzzle and you are the only person I know that can help us do it. What did you find out?"

Smitty took a moment to study the sculptured features of Danni Warren before turning her attention to Rigby.

"There is absolutely nothing more on FDR and these treasures. We know he went to Cocos Island four times on fishing trips and that he talked to some British treasure hunters one time at least. Had lunch with them. That was in the ship's log. Otherwise, no mention of treasure."

"That general you traced down for me, Orville Randolph. You said he served on the ship FDR used most often."

"The USS *Houston*."

"Yeah, that's the one. Maybe there's a connection."

"Randolph was a Colonel in charge of a Marine detachment on the *Houston*. I don't see a connection," Smitty said.

Rigby turned to Danni. "Are you carrying the map?"

She was taken aback by the question. He understood. The treasure map was a valuable commodity. Not something to be displayed in public. But who in the bar would know what they were looking at?

"I'm sure you have it," he said. "You wouldn't leave it anywhere out of your sight."

Danni looked at Smitty, letting Rigby know that she was concerned about revealing the map in front of her. He dismissed the concern with a wave of a hand. "Smitty's gonna help us get to the bottom of this."

Danni nodded, a bit reluctantly, he thought, and reached into her bag. She pulled out an envelope and took the map from its protective covering.

"A real treasure map?" Smitty said in a low voice that did not conceal her excitement.

"I'm not sure what it is," Rigby said. "A map of Cocos Island that shows the resting place of some old bones."

He unfolded the map and placed it in the center of the table. He pointed to the lower right corner of the map with the inscription: *The bones of those who tried.*

Below the inscription was the one word: *COLOR*.

"I see it but I don't understand it," Warren said. "The bones were the pirates' remains we found. What *COLOR* means, I don't know."

"I think our friend Smitty here told us," Rigby said.

"I did?"

"*COLOR,*" Rigby said, "could stand for…" He pulled a pen from his pocket and wrote on a paper napkin the same letters but added some periods: Col. O.R.

"Colonel Orville Randolph," he said.

The women looked at the name in surprise.

"Then it's not a treasure map made by pirates," Smitty said.

"No treasure?" Danni said with obvious disappointment.

"I don't think so," Rigby said. "More 1930s than eighteenth century."

"Could the answer to what's buried on the island be on President Roosevelt's ship?" Danni asked.

Smitty shook her head. "If that's the case then I'm afraid the answer's lost. The USS *Houston* was sunk by the Japanese in the Battle of Sunda Strait in 1942."

"Randolph was killed?" Danni asked.

"No. I already told Z that Randolph made general and sat out the war in Washington. He died in the 1980s."

Rigby aimed a thumb at his chest to answer the question on Danni Warren's face that the reference to Z was Smitty's pet name for him.

"The *Houston* was sunk along with an Australian ship, the *H.M.S. Perth*. Not all hands on the *Houston* perished. As I recall when I looked up this information for you when searching about Roosevelt, about a third of the thousand-plus member crew survived. Many ended up in prison camps and suffered a lot building a railroad between Thailand and Burma, the one made famous in that movie about the bridge over the River Kwai. William Holden's character in the movie told fellow prisoners-of-war he was on board the *Houston* when it sank."

Rigby considered the possibility that someone from the old ship might know what Roosevelt was up to on Cocos Island that captured Mallory's attention. But that ship went down seventy years ago. Another dead end.

Smitty continued: "The survivors started an association to commemorate the ship. *The Galloping Ghost of the Java Coast* the ship was called. Apparently, survivors and descendants keep the memory alive. From what I read about what those brave souls went through, it's a memory worth keeping alive."

"Maybe there's some records about Roosevelt on the ship?" Rigby asked with a spark of hope that the trail had not gone cold after all.

Smitty shrugged. "Maybe."

Chapter 37

He was not surprised to find them at McGillicutty's. He peered in through the plate glass window from under his Washington Nationals baseball cap. Rigby was there with the Asian woman. Another woman shared their table. He hoped neither of the women would leave with Rigby. It would be their ill fortune if they did.

Rigby would not live to see the sunrise.

He considered his desire to end the life of the man who foiled his plans—twice. He wanted to stay alive and continue his mission of destroying America's soul by destroying its self-made myths. But, his failures had been costly.

He failed to destroy Lincoln's Memorial. He requested expensive drones to blow up Mount Rushmore and had done no damage. Lincoln's Memorial and Mount Rushmore still stood. Unscathed.

Because of Zane Rigby.

His backers had abandoned him. He was on his own and that meant his resources would be limited. That also meant his targets would be limited.

One target, however, he knew he could reach—*had* to reach to avenge his failings. He would kill Rigby.

The task was made harder because Rigby now knew what he looked like. The baseball cap would protect him for only so long. He would have to strike quickly.

Why set a trap? he thought. Do it now. Do it here. He felt for the bulge in his jacket pocket. Loaded and ready.

He would follow Rigby when he left the bar and shoot him at the first good opportunity. He was not concerned with the many people walking the street. The shots would create chaos and he would use that chaos to escape.

He settled on a bus bench and waited for Rigby to exit the bar.

Chapter 38

Rigby left McGillicutty's Bar & Grill ahead of the women, pausing a moment at the doorway to scan the street in both directions. When he waved the women forward he made sure that he stood on the street side with the women between him and the buildings as they slowly ambled down the street toward the Metro station.

Rigby would twist and stretch every few moments as if he were trying to work out some kinks.

Smitty noticed the unusual behavior and asked, "What's got into you?"

He stopped in front of an abandoned storefront with a *For Lease* sign in the window. With no light coming from inside the shop, the glass acted like a mirror. Rigby nodded toward the glass.

"Look into this storefront. See the reflection of that fellow with the baseball cap a few paces behind us?"

"Yes," both women said.

"I recognize him from my...ah, adventure in the Black Hills."

"The man that kidnapped you?" Danni whispered.

Rigby put a restraining hand on her elbow so that she would not turn around to look at the man and give away the fact that he was recognized.

"The Monument Bomber."

"Are you sure?" Smitty said, excitement mixed with fear in her voice.

"I'm sure. The same guy who was in your apartment."

"Let's get him," Smitty snarled and Rigby had to admit she looked mean.

"Down, tiger," he said. "We have to make sure no

one gets hurt. Especially you two. He's after me."

"He's dangerous," Danni said, touching Rigby's arm.

"He won't be so foolish to attack me with so many people around. Let's walk so he doesn't get suspicious."

They headed up the street. He lost sight of the Monument Bomber but felt sure the man was behind him.

"What are we going to do?" Danni asked.

"Call a cop," Smitty said.

"We keep heading to the Metro station where I say goodbye to the both of you. You go into the station and I'll go past it. There's a bar just beyond, the Station Bar, it's called. I'll take a seat inside the bar. He'll wait for me to come out. As soon as you're out of sight you call the FBI and tell them what's happening. While the Bomber is waiting for me, they'll swoop down and grab him. Nobody gets hurt."

Smitty protested. "What if he's suspicious? I mean, he knows where I live. He's been in my apartment. Why would I be taking the Metro? I live right here."

"He doesn't know if you and Danni are going to a party or the movies. He won't be concerned about our separating. In fact, he'll welcome it. Easier for him to come after me."

Rigby recited a phone number that would get them directly to the operations center inside the Bureau. The FBI would respond immediately.

At the Metro Station entrance, Rigby waved goodbye to the women and watched them go into the station. He then went past it and came to the bar. He paused, looked at the bar for a moment as if making up his mind, looked back to the station, as if he was checking to make sure the women were not following him, then walked in and took a seat at the bar.

Chapter 39

He watched as the women accompanying Rigby entered the Metro station. Rigby waved goodbye to them. He would be alone now. This would make the job easier. If Rigby walked to his residence, he would follow. If he walked to a car, he would attack before the FBI man could drive away. The victim of a carjacking, they would say. No matter, Rigby would pay the price for interfering with his mission.

Rigby did not go far. Just past the station entrance, the FBI man stopped in front of a bar, paused a moment, then entered.

The man sighed. This was something he had not expected since Rigby had just left another bar. He contemplated whether excessive drinking would weaken the man's reactions when surprised by an attack. Yes, that would be a benefit, but it also meant he would have to wait.

Not that he had anywhere to go. He had already been told that his failures meant he had no more allies he could rely on; no more suppliers for the weapons and bombs he would need. All the time preparing…all the time attempting to prove to his brothers fighting the Americans in the battlefields of their homeland that he was worthy…all lost.

A bomber without bombs was a worthless figure. Failure was not his fault. The FBI agent had been lucky. He could redeem himself in the eyes of his benefactors and receive a warm embrace from his brothers in his homeland if he were successful in his next missions—starting with the repayment of all he owed Special Agent Rigby.

The FBI agent had been lucky. Up until now.

**

Rigby sat at the bar and ordered a beer. He could see the peak of the Washington Nationals baseball cap through the plate glass window. The Bomber was waiting for him. He would not have long to wait. Rigby imagined agents were already racing toward the location. The Monument Bomber's freedom could be measured in minutes.

**

He fidgeted. He rubbed his thumb against the index finger on his right hand as if warming up the trigger finger to do its work.

How long would Rigby sit there? How long would he need to wait to have his revenge?

Why should Rigby make him wait? He should command this situation, not his prey. He thought again about the FBI man going from one bar to another. It made little sense to him.

Rigby was up to something.

He had not survived this long, an agent in a foreign land, without reacting well to his instincts. The throbbing in his forehead told him something was wrong. He had the urge to run, to get away from this street and seek refuge.

He would do that. *After* he finished his mission. He would have his revenge even in a crowded bar. He had no fear.

He reached into his pocket and fingered his pistol.

**

Rigby saw the baseball cap as the man walked through the door. He had his glass to his lips and immediately let the beer drop from his hand, the glass shattering on the bar top, the brown liquid splashing on his shirt and running over the edge of the bar streaming to the floor.

167

He reached under his jacket, unsnapped the guard on his holster.

The Bomber already had a revolver out. It was leveled at Rigby.

Rigby pulled out his handgun knowing that it was too late.

The Bomber stopped a couple of yards away. His mouth opened as he took an awkward step forward. Blood gathered at his lips. He jerked forward. The gun dropped from his hand. He crumpled slowly to one knee. Blood foamed from his mouth, staining his teeth red and flowing across his chin.

The Monument Bomber looked up at Rigby. The FBI agent could see the man's eyes—sorrowful yet defiant.

The Bomber collapsed onto his face. Inside the bar a woman screamed. Lying face down on the floor, the man's back was exposed. A bright red spot where the bullet entered had blood staining his shirt at the entry hole.

Rigby looked up to see FBI agents rush into the bar—but there was nobody.

No agents. No Danni. No Smitty. No cop. No soldier. Nobody.

The entrance to the bar was open and light foot traffic walked in both directions. None of the passers-by bothered to look into the bar. They were not aware a man had been shot.

Rigby jumped off his bar stool and pulled his credentials from his pocket, holding them high to inform the bar patrons that the FBI was on the case. A quick examination of the man on the floor confirmed what Rigby knew: the Monument Bomber was dead.

But shot by whom?

Chapter 40

Screeching tires and slammed car doors pulled Rigby's attention away from the dead man as a cadre of FBI agents swarmed into the little bar, led by the Director herself.

"Is that him?" the Judge said, studying the body.

"That's him." Rigby rose slowly to his feet.

The Judge smiled. "A great victory for the Bureau."

Agents were already at work securing the area, talking to the bar patrons.

The Judge stepped closer to the agent inspecting the body and her smile faded. Rigby could see she picked up the significance of the bullet wound in the Bomber's back.

"Who shot him?"

Rigby shook his head.

"No police? Not one of ours?"

"The shot came from outside. Right through the open door. Didn't seem to rile the neighbors. I'd say a silencer or something a long way off from the buildings across the street."

The Judge considered this for a moment before ordering a search of the area. Once her orders were being carried out she returned to Rigby. "The FBI knew that the Monument Bomber was not working alone. He was getting his equipment and financial support from a clandestine network of supporters. One supporter felt the Bomber was becoming reckless, might reveal his contacts. Or just maybe he was cashiered in one of the oldest ways known to mankind."

Interesting way of putting it, Rigby thought. All the Judge's explanations seemed reasonable, yet Rigby couldn't help but feel there was more.

The Judge said, "We've got to get our press people

169

on this immediately. The Monument Bomber is dead. Raise his scalp to the world and say the FBI got its man."

"The FBI didn't get the Bomber," Rigby said. "Somebody else brought him down. There's another assassin out there."

The Judge stared at Rigby and then did something that surprised him. She put a hand on his shoulder and steered him into a corner away from the other agents and bar patrons.

Once there, she sighed and looked into Rigby's eyes. "It's important that we spin the story in a positive way. This country is teetering on the edge. The president is not speaking to the Senate leader. The Senate leader doesn't take calls from the White House staff. The budget is in lockdown and the government is shutting down. The people can use a bit of good news now."

She looked around to see if anyone was listening before continuing.

"Speaking of which, Speaker Gaines is demanding to hear from you about his special project. What do you have for him?"

"I've been a bit occupied with this guy," Rigby said, jerking his thumb at the figure on the floor.

The Judge nodded. "We get that. The Speaker and I are pleased about what you did at Mount Rushmore. Now it's time to move on. I'm laying off so-called non-essential workers because of the fiscal crisis. In my mind the Bureau is not the same without them. They're all essential. Our operations will suffer. America's security will suffer. The Speaker wants to announce his idea to the world and maybe break the ice. Put things on track. But he can't do it until he knows the truth. Getting America moving again is up to you."

**

Speaker Gaines' aide, Richard Nolan, greeted Rigby in the reception area of the Speaker's office and walked Rigby back to see his boss.

"You know we're going to shut down the government in a matter of days if the president and congress don't patch up their differences. You know what that means." Nolan paused a beat before continuing: "You and I won't get paid."

Nolan said it with a crooked smile but somehow Rigby thought he heard a bit of panic in the man's voice.

"My poker partners will be unhappy to hear it," Rigby replied with a smile of his own.

They entered the Speaker's office and found Marshall Gaines, suit jacket off, putter in hand and a number of balls scattered around a makeshift hole consisting of a Styrofoam cup on top of an artificial grass mat. The Speaker immediately put down the golf club and walked across the room to greet Rigby.

"I fool myself that putting a few balls will ease the tension and help me think through a solution to the problems facing the country. I hope you can help me find that solution, Special Agent Rigby."

"I'm at your beck and call, Mr. Speaker. But I've been dodging bullets on Cocos Island and dealing with the Bomber in the states."

"Commendable, yes. Excellent job at Mount Rushmore. Your country is indebted to you. Unfortunately, even with the Bomber out of the way, the country is still in danger."

The Speaker paused and picked up a pipe from his desk. He didn't light it but passed it back and forth between his hands with an occasional brief stop between his teeth. He then said, "I think the country is in more danger under current circumstances than with the Bomber doing his dastardly deeds."

Someone actually used the phrase *dastardly deeds*,

Rigby marveled.

"If we can't get past this constant political bickering, we won't be working on solving our problems. I believe my idea will get us started. Embarrass my colleagues."

While getting a few kudos for yourself, Rigby mused.

"If I go forward and whatever Paul Mallory was referring to arises—well, then we fall off the cliff in my estimation. You've got to discover what Mallory knew."

Without an invitation, Rigby moved to a chair in front of the Speaker's desk and sat down. He considered the problem and found himself in agreement with the Speaker. He wanted to help; he just didn't know how. He had been to the island and found nothing of interest about Roosevelt, specifically. The map that led to the bones of the Bloody Sword was interesting. Danni Warren, whom he found on the island, was more than interesting. Orville Randolph, might be a key to something. But what? There seemed no obvious connection to what FDR might have done.

Perhaps if he had more time on the island, he thought. Although, given the circumstances of him running out before the court hearing, he doubted the government of Costa Rica would permit him back there. His first visit was cut short by the assassin.

Assassin. He sat up in the chair and stared right past the Speaker without looking at anything, juggling the pieces in the evidence pouch he stored in his mind.

"What is it, Agent Rigby?" the Speaker said, noticing the change in Rigby's demeanor.

"A phone?" Rigby said.

Nolan, the aide, directed Rigby to a telephone on a side table next to a stuffed chair.

Rigby called the Deputy Director of the FBI and made a request for forensic assistance.

When he was finished the Speaker asked, "Will this lead to the answer about Roosevelt?"

"I don't know. It might help."

Irritated, the Speaker of the House raised his voice: "You're with the FBI, the greatest investigating force in the world. Don't you have any leads?"

Rigby knew even the greatest investigative force in the world couldn't cover every angle.

Just then his cell phone buzzed. He removed it from his pocket and looked at the text message from Smitty.

Sometimes it was the lone researcher or the lone inventor that found the key to a puzzle. He had a lone ranger working for him.

"I have one lead now," he said holding up the cell phone. "But it means a long trip."

Chapter 41

The old lady with distinct Polynesian features wearing a flower in her hair placed the tray containing glasses of juice and water on the coffee table separating her husband and FBI Agent Zane Rigby. The old man, his face marked with more lines than a Rand McNally map, sat in an electric wheelchair. He wore a heavy sweater despite the heat turned up in the house. Outside a large picture window, Rigby watched some dolphins playfully arch out of the blue Pacific off the Poipu beach area of Kauai.

"Isn't she a pip," the old man said indicating his wife, who had left the men to talk. "Gorgeous as the day I met her. Course, I wasn't much to look at when we met. Bones nearly poking out of my skin. Aolani was my nurse at Pearl when they brought me out of the camp at the end of the war."

With a shaky hand, Clarence Underhill reached for a glass of orange juice and moved it slowly to his lips.

"You survived the sinking of the USS *Houston* and the prisoner camps." Smitty had given Rigby the information about the association that kept alive the memory of the *Houston*, Roosevelt's favorite warship. The cruiser had taken the president to Cocos Island three times in the 1930s and was lost to the Japanese in 1942.

Smitty turned on her investigating and interviewing skills and Rigby found himself following the only thread she had come up with—a thin thread at that. It had brought him to the Garden Isle of Kauai to meet Clarence Underhill.

When you had nothing to go on, even a thread looked thick as a rope, Rigby figured.

"You come a long way to talk to me. Can't imagine what the FBI needs to know about FDR from the 1930s. You can't tell me, I suppose."

Rigby shook his head.

"Figured as much. I just don't know if I should tell *my* story to you since you won't tell me *your* story. Hardly seems fair." The old man's laugh sounded more like a cackle.

Rigby gave a bemused smile and appreciated the man's sharp retort for someone he guessed was over ninety. "I'm working on a mission that requires only a need to know basis. I'm sure as an old military man, you understand orders."

"Orders," Underhill said so softly that Rigby barely heard the word. "I like *order* in my life. Predictability. The way things ought to be. I've had the unpredictable in war and prisoner camp. I had enough for a lifetime in just a few years. They weren't short years, mind you, like the saying goes, *a few short years*. No sir. They were the longest years a man can live."

"I've read some of the stories about the *Houston* and its crew. Very rough."

"Much more than rough, I can tell you. Touch and go for a lot of us after liberation. I was brought to Hawaii to recuperate. Fell in love with the place. The same will that kept me alive in the prisoner-of-war camp kept me going, helped me recover. That and a beautiful nurse." The old man winked and jerked his thumb in the direction his wife had departed.

Rigby smiled.

"Got married and stayed here. What fool wouldn't if he had the chance?"

Rigby thought of his lonely apartment in the middle of a crowded city and knew the old man made sense.

"So you can't tell me what you're all about but you better tell me what you need to know so we can make sure your trip here was not just an excuse to visit paradise."

Rigby said, "You responded to the USS *Houston* Association request saying you knew a Marine who was

175

aboard the ship when President Roosevelt was also on board."

"That's right. Sergeant Tony Spontelli. Not a big guy, but tough. Don't know how long he served on the Old Girl, but he was there when the president made his last couple of visits. FDR kind of adopted Sergeant Tony, so I was told. Something to do with the New York connection. Tony was a Brooklyn boy and he told FDR that he had voted for him— what was it, four, maybe five times by then. The man's two terms as New York governor and a couple of terms as president at that time and one more when he ran as vice-president."

"FDR was vice president?" Rigby said in surprise.

"Ran for vice president. Didn't win. When was that? Sometime in the 1920s, I guess. Anyways, Sergeant Tony, when he gets the chance to say a few words to the president, he tells him he voted for him all those times. The president eats it up, you know? He invites Tony on one of his fishing trips when they lower the longboat off the cruiser. Must have hit it off pretty good 'cause Tony is at the president's side during all his trips on the *Houston* thereafter."

"He told you about his conversations with the president?" Rigby leaned forward in anticipation that Underhill would have some information that could point him toward what Paul Mallory was after. He knew that if this expedition was a dead end, he had no other avenues to pursue.

"He told us stories. Went fishing with the president off the ship. Went ashore with him on that island...Cocos I think the name was, when the president decided to have lunch on a beach—"

Rigby interrupted. "Was the presidential party looking for something on the island?"

"Maybe a coconut to have with their lunch. He said they went for lunch on the beach and spent the afternoon there. Never mentioned that the party went beyond the beach. I think that would have been hard. The president couldn't walk. I suppose you didn't know that."

Rigby nodded. He sat back in his seat.

"Did Sergeant Spontelli ever say that President Roosevelt mentioned a treasure?"

The old man paused a moment then turned to Rigby with a hint of a smile and a face lit up by a revelation. "Is that what this secret mission is about? A treasure hunt?"

Rigby considered his answer. The treasure hunt was not what his investigation was about. The treasure could lead him to what he needed to find out. He decided he could share that much with Underhill.

"If a treasure hunt happened it leads me to what I need to know. I'm not sure there was a treasure hunt. Did Spontelli tell you there was one?"

"Nah," Underhill responded with a touch of disappointment. "He did mention the president meeting with a couple of British treasure hunters working the island. They had lunch aboard the *Houston*."

Rigby remembered that Smitty had told him about that lunch. She found a reference to it with the treasure hunters in the ship's log.

"Did the Sergeant say what they talked about at the lunch?"

"No. It was some hush-hush thing I guess. Led to some paper being signed, I think it was."

Rigby tried to make sense of what Underhill was telling him. "The president signed some document there?"

"Don't know about that," Underhill said. "I think it was the next time FDR was aboard in the late thirties that he signed something. Spontelli hinted something important happened. Top Secret important. Walked around proud as the cock on the walk like these roosters around here on the island 'cause he was part of some secret."

Rigby wondered about all the roosters and chickens freely roaming around Kauai. At the moment he was more interested in Spontelli acting like a rooster, as Underhill put it.

"He never revealed the secret, I suppose," Rigby said.

"Got himself killed. We lost so many good men the day the Old Girl went down."

There was something in Underhill's story that intrigued Rigby. He wanted to push the old man to remember.

"You said Sergeant Spontelli died protecting some Top Secret document signed by FDR."

Underhill looked out the great picture window at the vast ocean. Rigby could tell the mood had changed in the room. Underhill became quiet. He was not looking at the ocean but at the ghosts that lived there. Ghosts of the men who sailed with him on the USS *Houston* and did not come home. When Underhill turned back to look at Rigby his expression was solemn.

"It was terrible, terrible the night the ship went down..."

**

Seaman first class Clarence Underhill felt a tremor shimmy through the ship. The Old Girl lurched toward the starboard, the hull lifting from the water on the port side. Torpedo hit, Underhill thought. Must have been.

Underhill grabbed hold of a rail to stay on his feet. His mouth was dry. He tried to swallow saliva but could produce none. Strange, he thought. He was sweating profusely, his shirt soaked with perspiration.

Another star shell burst overhead, adding to the brightness of the night sky. Midnight had passed only minutes before yet the sky was illuminated like a Christmas tree with star shell bursts, the glare of searchlights and big and small gunfire. Tracer ammunition stitched the sky and ships on fire added more light.

The Houston *took another hit. Underhill toppled to the deck, ended up on his back looking to the sky. A moment ago he thought of the sky lit like a Christmas tree.*

Images of that holiday flashed through his mind. The family gathering around the tree on the California ranch. Christmas and peace were so far from this place. Now past midnight, the calendar had turned the page to March. Christmas 1942 was many months away. He doubted he would ever see it.

Underhill tried to gain his footing. Get back to his mates at the gun turret. He looked toward the forecastle but could see only a curtain of smoke from the fire that raged in the forecastle's paint locker, which had taken a direct hit.

Shouts of defiance mingled with cries of anguish and pain. A man was sobbing nearby. Underhill tried to see who it was. He could not see the man's face, only his legs, the left one nearly severed below the knee.

Machine gun fire drowned out the wounded man's cry. The flash of a bomb bursting overhead forced Underhill to turn his head and close his eyes.

The enemy tin ships were so close that gunners from the Houston *were having trouble training their weapons on them.*

For weeks the Allied Navy had been looking for the Japanese fleet. Now the Houston *and Australian cruiser, HMS* Perth, *had the bad luck to stumble onto an attack force after the two ships had finished a round in the Battle of Java Sea.*

The Allied ships had come across a Japanese army moving ashore. The troop transports and supply ships made inviting targets but the accompanying three cruisers and squadrons of destroyers presented a problem.

The Japanese continued pouring fire at the Houston. *Underhill scrambled to get back into position when another torpedo blasted into the side of the hull. Underhill bounced* against the rail and held on. The body of a shipmate came flying past, falling from a position above him to the churning sea below.

Through a swirl of smoke Underhill could see Marine Sergeant Tony Spontelli heading toward him with a determined look on his face. Underhill had spent some time with the veteran Marine. Spontelli told him stories about some of the exotic places he visited aboard the Houston and the times President Franklin Delano Roosevelt himself had accompanied the crew.

Spontelli moved past the hunkered down Underhill but stopped short when he saw the Captain emerging from the bridge and heading one deck below toward the armored conning tower.

Spontelli instinctively helped Underhill to his feet without saying a word and headed to meet the Captain. Underhill followed.

Screaming over the gunfire and the cries of men, Sergeant Spontelli told the Captain, "The ship's confidential papers are all together. Shall I throw them overboard, Captain?"

The Captain nodded. "I'm ordering 'Abandon Ship'. They'll be destroyed."

At that moment, a Marine lance corporal with a bugle in hand ran up to the Captain.

"Do as I ordered," the Captain said, "sound 'Abandon Ship.'"

The bugler moved off hoping to find the ship's communication system still in working order, and in a moment the clear sound of the bugle call added to the noise and confusion aboard the USS Houston as she listed farther to starboard.

Underhill scurried to find a life vest when he heard the Captain call to the retreating Spontelli. "Roosevelt's papers in the waterproof safe in the bridge."

"Going now," the Sergeant said.

The whistle of a flying bomb was audible for only a couple of seconds before a terrible explosion tore up the deck, sending pieces of the bomb and shrapnel flying through the air, cutting Spontelli in so many places that his shirt turned instantly a brownish red, fountains of blood spurting from his head and neck. He dropped to the deck dead right next to the fatally wounded Captain. The explosion had sent Underhill sprawling on the deck.

Underhill could feel the fire caused by the explosion burn the back of his neck. He jumped up and hurried to claim a life vest, pulling it tight around him. He heard an officer order the engines left running at half-speed so that the ship wouldn't take anyone down with her. He didn't understand; did not try to figure out what the order meant. He saw life rafts bobbing in the sea and focused all his energy on getting to one.

Underhill managed to find the stairs to the lower deck through a screen of smoke. He climbed the rail on the ship's port side and, with the ship tilting starboard; he used the hull as a slide to drop into the sea.

He splashed into the water, plunging below the surface and swimming back up. He broke the surface of the water next to a fellow sailor, lifeless and floating only because he wore a life vest.

Underhill saw dead fish all around. He knew there were sharks in these waters but did not worry about them. They would be dead like the fish, too.

Underhill searched the sky for the six bright stars that made up the Southern Cross hanging over a strip of land. He would follow the stars to survive and to find cover.

After only about two dozen strokes, Underhill felt a tremble surge through the water. He stopped swimming and turned back toward the ship. The USS Houston, *its Stars and Stripes flying boldly in the breeze, machine guns blazing, slipped beneath the waves, going down fighting.*

Underhill took no time to consider the ship's fate. He

181

wanted to survive. To live to fight on and avenge the death of his good ship and all the good men who lost their lives this night. He pushed on.

He never made it to shore.

A Japanese motorboat manned by armed soldiers pulled alongside him. Underhill expected to be shot in the water. He started to mutter a prayer asking forgiveness for his sins.

A heavily accented voice speaking English came from the rear of the craft. "Hands up, American sailor. If you want live this night, hands up and my men will pull you in."

Underhill saw the officer speaking to him, gesturing with his hands for Underhill to comply by raising his arms.

He saw no alternative. If he resisted he would be shot dead. If he tried to swim away he would be shot dead. Underhill raised his hands. As soon as the soldiers saw he was unarmed they pulled him aboard.

Panting and dripping wet, sprawled in the hull of the motor craft, Underhill looked up at the officer sitting aft.

"Why didn't you kill me?"

The officer looked down at him and said, "Enough killing. The Emperor needs manpower."

**

"Manpower." The old man shook his head. "Manpower, he said."

Underhill looked at Rigby and the FBI man could see tears in his eyes.

"What he meant was *slave* power," Underhill continued. He paused a moment, composing himself. "To build their damn railroad. Enough good men died that night the Old Girl went down but more deaths were to come. Yes indeed. Terrible deaths by disease and starvation and brutality."

"You've sacrificed a lot in service to your country,

Mr. Underhill. This country owes you a great deal."

"Thank you son, but no thanks are due. I knew what I was doing and I knew why."

"That document you mentioned, President Roosevelt's paper. The one the Sergeant was after when he was killed. Did anyone retrieve it?"

"Doubt it. Don't see how. Sergeant Spontelli and the Captain were killed. The ship didn't go down too much after. No one could have gotten it."

"Could it still be there?" Rigby asked more to himself than to Underhill.

"Seventy years under the sea. Wouldn't matter if it were. Be nothing left of it."

"The captain said it was in a waterproof safe."

"Seventy years," was all Underhill said.

Despair wrapped Rigby in a tight grip. He could see no path to follow; no way to uncover what Paul Mallory was after. Rigby wanted to help solve his country's problems just like Seaman Underhill had contributed in America's time of need. Yet, he didn't see how he could find the answer.

He looked at the withered old man who stood for something important: perseverance and guts. For carrying on.

Rigby would take inspiration from the old sailor. He, too, would find a way.

Rigby rose, squared his shoulders and snapped off a sharp salute to an American hero, Clarence Underhill, United States Navy, retired.

Chapter 42

The Judge stared across the desk at Rigby with a look of dismay. "You want to do what?"

"Find the document President Roosevelt signed and hid away."

"The one on a ship sunk during World War II?"

Rigby could see from the Judge's expression that she thought he lost a few screws. "Yes. I want to go after the document in the waterproof safe on the USS *Houston*."

The Judge laughed. Rigby was certain that hearing the Judge laugh after he made an unusual proposal was not a good thing.

"The Navy doesn't like spending money on wild goose chases."

"You mean they want to save it for $800 hammers." Rigby thought how that comment dated him back a couple of decades.

The Judge dropped her smile. She wasn't interested in his smart-aleck responses. He knew she wanted Rigby to complete his assignment so that hopefully the Speaker could end the squabble between the president and the leader of the Senate. If the argument continued, the Director had warned, she would be required to cut her staff to the bone by the end of the week.

"I don't care how waterproof a safe was supposed to be in 1942, by today's standards it probably wouldn't even qualify as waterproof. A piece of paper even wrapped in oilskin wouldn't survive. That's assuming it even made it through the battle without damage. A shell might have hit the safe. No, Agent Rigby, that paper, whatever it was, is gone. Blown up, deteriorated, or fish food. One way or another it's gone."

Rigby threw up his hands. "Then I regret to inform you the search seems to be at an end. Detective Denver has no leads to Mallory's killer. There's nothing more to follow about Mallory's supposed evidence that FDR was up to something that might disqualify him from being placed on Mount Rushmore. There's nothing to go on, Director."

"Are you quitting the investigation on me?" She seemed genuinely surprised at the prospect. "Whatever Mallory had, I can assure you, he discovered without having the document from a sunken ship. If you quit, when I start laying off personnel at the end of the week, you will be the first to go."

They stared across the desk at each other, their idle threats doing little damage to their defenses. Rigby was tired. The flight from Hawaii to Washington drained him and he had come directly to the Bureau after he landed.

The Judge broke the silence first. "One thing I know about you, Rigby, is that you're not a quitter."

Rigby shrugged. "You're not going to fire me because you know that."

"So where does that leave us?"

"I need you to back my play. I contacted the Navy about sending divers down inside the USS *Houston* to find the safe. I got pushed back. They cited something called Title XIV, the Sunken Military Craft Act. The ship is a gravesite and must not be disturbed without permission. You've got to go higher up to get permission."

"Higher up?"

"I was directed to the Naval Historical Center when I asked about the safe. A captain there turned me down based on the regulation. That Sunken Military Craft Act. She read me parts of it. Under the law, permission to remove something from a sunken craft can be granted by the Secretary of the Navy. The Secretary of the Navy would grant a request from the Director of the FBI."

The Judge thought about Rigby's request. Then she

said, "He would grant the request with no questions asked, I wonder? Remember, this mission has a tight lid on it. The Speaker doesn't want word to get out. I don't want to have to explain things to the Secretary."

"The Secretary will take your word. Clear it with the Speaker first. I'm sure he'll go along."

"I'm not so sure. I'm going to be asking him to reveal his plan to the Navy Secretary, who works for the president. I'm taking this gamble and releasing the Speaker's secret with very little upside. Securing an unknown document that has been in seawater for seventy years is unlikely to happen."

"It's the only lead we have."

A knock on the door interrupted the conversation. The Director's assistant entered with a piece of paper in her hand. She handed the Director the paper and said, "Deputy Director Duncan wanted you to see this right away."

The Judge looked over the paper as her assistant exited and closed the door. After a moment the Judge looked up from the paper.

"Interesting. A ballistics report on the bullet that killed the Monument Bomber."

"I requested it. I'm guessing a rifle. He was shot from a distance."

"Yes, a rifle. That wasn't what I was referring to. The bullet that killed the Monument Bomber was fired from the same weapon that killed Pedro Campos on Cocos Island. The gunman could have been gunning for you."

"Just as I thought," Rigby said.

Chapter 43

"Look at it this way." Danni Warren brushed a strand of hair off Zane Rigby's forehead. "You have more time to spend with me."

The encouragement did not bring a smile to Rigby's face. He sighed and took a long pull from the beer bottle. They had met at a Georgetown bar after the Judge refused to speak to the Navy Secretary about the sunken ship.

"Seems to me that treasure, if there is one, is all that you're concerned about."

"My, is that showing," Danni said with a faux expression of embarrassment. "I can't keep any secret from you." She gave a throaty laugh to let him know she was in on her own joke.

"You've been to the island twice," Rigby said. "No treasure."

"You're giving up too easily. You just told me your boss said you were no quitter."

Rigby answered this slap at his ego with another long pull on his beer bottle.

"Let me try to convince you to take me back to the island. What do you say, your place or yours?" She smiled coquettishly.

Why the hell not? Rigby decided. Being fawned over would help ease the pain of having his opinions rejected by the boss.

They walked back to Rigby's apartment and although he had his arm draped around Danni's shoulders, his concentration was elsewhere.

Who was the gunman who killed both Campos and the Bomber?

Rigby wondered if the shooter was an accomplice of

187

the Monument Bomber. Maybe there were two shooters. The Monument Bomber himself was shooting at Rigby on the island. When he failed to kill Rigby on the island and failed to destroy Mount Rushmore, the Bomber's contact got his rifle and punished him for his failures.

Rigby understood there were many possibilities and he was no closer to solving the problem. Looking at the attractive woman who accompanied him up the stairs to his apartment, he decided to let it go for a while.

They entered the apartment and Rigby thought he saw disappointment on Danni Warren's face.

"Not the Taj Mahal," he admitted, "but then I'm not here that much. A place to sleep and have breakfast."

She looked around corners and ran her finger over the furniture, noticing that he was behind in his dusting. "I assume if you weren't sleeping and eating breakfast alone you'd look for an upgrade."

Was that a putdown of his living arrangements or a question with deeper meaning? And future possibilities?

She didn't give him time to think about it.

"So there's no misunderstanding about my intentions." Danni dropped her purse on the sofa, took off her light jacket, and after the shortest pause pulled her tangerine orange, scoop neck top over head and tossed it aside, standing there in the blue bra that matched the color of her designer jeans.

"This is the first time we've been alone with a little time on our hands since the South Dakota forest and I don't want another missed opportunity." She smiled at his appreciative stare. "Hurry now before your FBI boss changes her mind or some admiral calls."

Rigby's hands were working the buttons of his shirt as Danni talked about the possible interruptions. He stopped.

Of course, why hadn't he thought of that before? He didn't have to go to the Java Coast. Not if someone he trusted could see the dive done in the next day. Someone

188

who could make it happen.

He held the index finger of his right hand up indicating he needed a minute and fished his cell phone from his pocket. Danni crossed her arms over her chest in a manner that left no doubt she was not pleased.

When the person on the other end of the call informed him that he reached the Pentagon, Rigby asked for Admiral Rosshowe.

The admiral was tracked down and pulled out of a meeting.

"Thanks for rescuing me, Rigby," the admiral said when he took the phone. "I was in a goddamn meeting deciding which important defensive resource we'll have to close if the politicians don't get their heads out of their asses and the government shuts down. That's one duty I want to avoid."

"Good. Now you can do me a favor."

"I thought I did that at Rushmore."

"Same team, different game," Rigby said, throwing the admiral's favorite analogy back at him.

"What is it this time?"

Rigby explained that the mission that sent him to Cocos Island led him to a sunken U.S. warship in Southeast Asia. He explained he was looking for a document in a waterproof safe that was aboard the USS *Houston* when the Japanese sank it during the war. He understood permission was needed to dive onto the ship.

"You want me to get you permission to do the dive?"

"More than that, Admiral. Time's short. I need you to get permission, order the dive and get it done ASAP."

"With Navy divers?"

"The best," Rigby said, pouring on the flattery.

"You want to tell me more about this mission of yours that it has to be done in an all fired-up hurry?"

"Let's say it has to do with the agony you're going through with your meeting. Maybe we can stop that."

189

The "harrumph" came over the phone loud and clear.

"I'll get back to you," the admiral said.

"How long?"

"Would an hour be quick enough?" the admiral said with sarcasm.

Looking at Danni Warren, Rigby said, "That should be perfect."

He turned off the phone and approached Danni, who still wore a scowl, and gently uncrossed her arms.

"Now, where were we?" he said, reaching around her back for the bra clasp.

Chapter 44

The first thing Rigby saw on the television monitor was a pair of diving fins being pulled over a diver's boots at the edge of a platform. When the diver finished his task and looked up, the camera attached to the top of his mask moved along with his head, catching the expansive sea before him.

"Testing, testing. This is ND Master Diver Erik Swenton attached to the Military Sealift Command. Prepared to dive Banten Bay, Sundra Strait. Can you read me on the *Maritime Salvage?*"

The diver turned to look at the nearby ship. It was a large vessel. Rigby guessed it was about 250 feet in length, maybe fifty feet at the beam carrying fore and aft booms for heavy duty salvage work.

A confirming response to the diver's test call came from the ship.

"Repeating test. Master Diver Erik Swenton prepared to dive to the USS *Houston*, Sunda Strait. Can you read me, Command?"

Halfway around the world at the Pentagon, in a small room filled with electronic equipment, Admiral Andy Rosshowe turned to his aide and said, "Tell Master Diver Swenton we can read him loud and clear."

The aide passed on the confirmation to the diver.

"Give him the go sign." Rosshowe turned to Rigby and added, "Make yourself comfortable, Agent Rigby. I've got two divers ready to go down to the *Houston* and find your safe."

Rigby nodded as he sat in a desk chair. "What are the chances they find it?"

"Slim. I hope to hell it's there and it's got whatever the hell you're looking for and whatever the hell you're

191

looking for is important to the security of the United States. It ain't cheap sending a Navy salvage ship out."

"Same team," Rigby said to Rosshowe, Rigby's way of asking the admiral to trust his play.

Rosshowe offered a crooked smile.

Rigby turned his attention to the fifty-inch video monitor in the small, windowless room. The lead diver wore a full diving mask, which had room for a communication microphone, and carried a video camera on his head. What he was seeing was projected via satellite to the Pentagon command post and aboard the salvage ship. The divers were in the water now. Rigby could see the second diver when Swenton turned to look at him.

Fish flowed with the current in front of the divers. Swenton called to his partner, "Watch the school of lionfish following us like we're their mamas. They got sharp fins."

The second diver nodded and headed down toward the ocean floor.

"Ten meters," Swenton said. "Current's moderately strong today. Kicking up some dust. Visibility poor."

"Roger that," came a voice over the communication system from the team monitoring the dive aboard the USNS *Maritime Salvage*.

The divers moved slowly through the drifting sand. Stingrays were all around them, flapping their oddly shaped, wing-like fins.

"Stonefish," called out the admiral's aide when the diver looked at one in the face. The creature appeared as if it could be mistaken for a stone if it were still and not swimming about. "Poisonous," the aide said. "I hear the pain from the poison's so severe that people want their legs amputated if they step on one and take in the venom."

The diver must have been aware of the danger because he carefully moved around the stonefish and propelled himself deeper into the bay. "Twenty meters," he reported.

Suddenly, the divers broke through the veil of drifting sand and there she was: the USS *Houston* lying on her starboard side. Now an artificial reef covered with coral and the home for thousands of fish swimming around and through openings on the ship.

"We have visual. Do you copy?"

Both the ship and Pentagon responded in the affirmative.

"Skip," Swenton called to the second diver, "careful of the fishing lines and nets. The ship's draped with the stuff. We get caught we'll have to cut our way out."

The diver named Skip gave a thumbs-up. On the monitor Rigby could see the fishing nets wrapped around the barrel of one of the cannons on a rear gun turret.

The ship was so covered with corals and mud and underwater sea plants that it was difficult to see the lines of the old vessel.

Rigby pointed at the screen. "Look at that black glob by the plant."

"Oil," the admiral said, "still leaking from the ship after all these years."

"Moving toward the bridge," Swenton called.

Bubbles created by Skip floated up in front of Swenton's mask, the camera capturing the picture of the great ship screened by a set of bubbles. Rigby leaned forward in his chair as the outline of the *Houston* grew clearer on the big screen.

When the divers reached the port side, Rigby could see a terrible gash in the hull surrounded by undersea growth.

"That's where a torpedo ripped her open," Admiral Rosshowe muttered, "poor bastards."

The divers crossed the rail and moved along the superstructure of the vessel lying on it side. An opening in the bed of coral proved to be a hatchway. Skip used his light to peer into the opening.

193

At the rail near the bridge, Swenton looked down away from the bridge toward his fins. He reached down and Rigby could see the diver's gloved hand come into view on the screen. As Swenton reached toward the boot, Rigby noticed a small sack that the diver had attached to it. He grabbed the sack, undid the attachment, and pulled it toward him.

"What's that?" Rigby asked.

"You'll see," the admiral said.

The camera followed as the diver turned his head, focused on the sack. His hands pulled it open and reached into the sack pulling out and unfurling an American flag.

He kicked toward the rail and wrapped the flag across it. Both divers held still for a moment in the mild current and raised their hands in salute, Rosshowe also offered a salute.

Swenton said, "To honor the memory of those lost on the USS *Houston*."

As soon as the short ceremony ended, the divers continued their journey to the bridge. The windows were long gone and the divers could look inside at the rusty equipment and the fish that called this place home.

"No safe visible. I'm going in."

"Careful down there," came the voice from the salvage ship. "All kinds of traps."

"Roger that."

Bubbles crossed the camera's eye and Swenton proceeded through the opening into the command area. The second diver aimed his high-powered light into the bridge.

Sand, mud and coral covered the rusted equipment. Swenton scanned the area floor to ceiling. With the ship lying on its side, the safe could be anywhere. Except it was nowhere.

"Wasn't the safe bolted down?" Rigby asked.

"Pieces move in battle, tied down or not," Rosshowe said as he studied the monitor.

"I don't see how you can make out anything in

there," Rigby said, disappointment in his voice.

The admiral did not reply. He watched the Master Diver work his way carefully in the space made smaller by the mud and coral growths.

"Over this way, Skip," Swenton called.

Skip moved the light toward the corner. Coral covered some piece of equipment. Swenton pulled out a knife and probed. No safe.

The Master Diver took another look around and said, "Not here."

Rosshowe sighed. "Okay, son. Get out of there without getting hurt."

"Aye aye, sir."

The admiral turned to Rigby. "No go."

"Now what?" Rigby said more to himself than to the admiral and he leaned forward in his chair. The hope of finding something on the *Houston* was a long shot but he had no trouble following up on it because a long shot was better than no shot at all. That's what he felt he was left with now.

With nowhere to turn, Rigby felt he failed his mission. He convinced himself if he could succeed, solve Mallory's mystery about Roosevelt, he could help heal the bipartisan bickering in the government. No small contribution to what the constitution called *Domestic Tranquility*.

Now that small hope was lost.

"What's that?" Rigby heard Swenton say. He looked up at the screen. The divers had moved from the bridge area toward the seabed on the far side of the sunken vessel. The light played over a box-like object partly buried in the sand that had lost any definition because of a growing coral mask. The object lay below the area of the bridge covered from view by the ship's superstructure.

Both divers kicked toward the sunken object.

Rigby stood and moved next to Admiral Rosshowe in front of the large monitor.

The Master Diver reached the object and directed his partner to place the light on the coral crusted top of the box. With his knife, Swenton scraped away some of the coral over the rusted and faded lettering.

"What's it say?" came a voice from the *Maritime Salvage*.

Swenton moved toward the unit and Rigby could see he was waving the light closer.

Swenton began to spell out some letters. "J-E-D..." He paused. "Can't read the next couple. Then there's a Y. Then there's an...what do you call that thing? The symbol for the word *and*?"

Someone on the *Maritime Salvage* told him, "It's called an *ampersand*."

"OK," Swenton said. "J-E-D, a space where more letters were worn away, a Y and then an ampersand, then more letters. An M—more worn letters, then an E. Another space and then W-E-I-N-T then more scarring that covers the metal surface."

Rigby said, "The letters could be the manufacturer."

"Yeah." The admiral ordered his aide to get on the Internet and see what he could find.

The divers continued to examine the object.

The aide took little time in reporting back from his Internet search. He said excitedly, "Sir, the Jedrey, Mone and Weintraub Company was a safe builder that supplied the Navy before WW II, including waterproof."

The admiral snapped his fingers. "That's our baby. Inform the divers."

The aide relayed the message.

After watching the divers examine the old safe for a few moments, the admiral took the microphone from his aide and asked, "What kind of equipment will you need to get it open?"

The Master Diver started, "Well, sir..." He paused and worked his knife through the coral and mud that had built up over the years. "Hang on a second."

He pushed the knife through a particularly hard piece of coral and saw the lid of the safe lift slightly.

"I think my knife is all I need. The lid is unlatched. Hold."

Admiral Rosshowe looked at Rigby. He said nothing but both men knew what the diver's report meant. The safe was no longer waterproof, if it ever really had been, especially sitting in the ocean for seventy years. Anything inside would be destroyed.

"Got it," Swenton called.

Using his knife like a crowbar, Swenton popped the lid free. He grabbed it with one hand, sheaved his knife, and then with both hands threw the safe lid open.

Skip aimed his light into the safe.

Empty.

"Nothing in here," Swenton confirmed. "Some water, of course. Nothing else. No objects, papers, oilskins. Not even fish."

This makes no sense, Rigby thought. A Marine gave his life during the battle trying to secure whatever document was in there. Had the old man in Hawaii remembered the battle wrong?

For Rigby it was another dead end. The dead end of dead ends.

"Put the light here," Rigby heard Swenton say.

Rigby looked back at the screen. Skip focused the light on the back of the safe door. Swenton moved close to the door so that the image would be clear to the Command Center and the monitors on the *Maritime Salvage*.

Scratched on the back of the safe's door, probably with the point of a knife, were characters and words. Swenton read them aloud as he traced them with his finger: *"BK was here 10/11/1945."*

Chapter 45

Rigby sat across a conference table from Admiral Rosshowe in a small room not far from the Command Center. Neither man had an explanation for the markings on the backside of the safe's door.

"This tells me one thing," Rigby said. "There was something important in that safe. If Sergeant Spontelli died trying to secure whatever it was before the *Houston* went down and someone went to all the trouble to dive down and look for it a few years later, it was important or valuable."

"To someone," Rosshowe said. "Maybe personally or historically, but maybe nothing to do with your assignment."

Rigby pondered that thought for a moment but dismissed it. Too much activity focused on the contents of the safe for whatever was inside not to be important to his search.

A rap sounded on the conference room door. The admiral's aide entered the room. He carried a file.

"I thought you'd like to know, sir, I was just looking through the file we put together in preparation for the dive to the *Houston* and I found something odd."

"What's that?"

"Sir, the date scratched on the back of the safe's door was October 11, 1945."

"That was pretty clear."

"Sir, according to records, the USS *Houston's* resting place was not discovered underwater until the early 1970s."

Rosshowe turned to Rigby and both exchanged puzzled glances.

"A chance discovery?" Rosshowe wondered aloud. "A treasure hunter looking into a safe on the bottom of the ocean?

"Or a secret mission to recover something important?" Rigby said. "A mission never reported, so the remains of the *Houston* were not disclosed. That sounds like a Navy mission to me."

The admiral nodded. He turned to his aide and said, "Get on it. Old reports. I'll secure clearance for Top Secret matters. See what you can find out."

Chapter 46

Danni rolled to her side leaning on her elbow and kissed Zane Rigby on the cheek. He lay on his back in the bed staring at the ceiling of his room. The soft kiss did not even bring the slightest smile to his lips.

"You did all you could, Zane," she said in a soothing voice. "Don't be so hard on yourself. Some mysteries of life are not meant to be uncovered."

He shook his head, unable to accept that philosophy. Too much was at stake. He felt an obligation to help heal the country. He needed to know why Paul Mallory and Pedro Campos were murdered. He wanted to honor the memory of those American sailors lost on the USS *Houston*. Beyond all those noble pursuits, he wanted to keep his job.

If the partisan bickering continued and the government shut down, the Judge was going to have to cut way back. It only made sense that an agent in the twilight of his career who could not bring his assigned case to a satisfactory conclusion would be on the chopping block. Besides, in the FBI hierarchy of responsibilities, the Office for Cases of Historical Significance ranked at or near the bottom.

He wondered if his time had come to move on. He felt Danni's hand massaging his arm, trying to comfort him. He wondered if he could lead a settled life. He wondered if this woman could be part of that life. He really didn't know a lot about her other than she was adventurous, attractive and fun to be with and had a unique pedigree that probably wasn't going over well at the Bureau. What more should he be looking for in a companion? Especially at this stage of the game.

Danni had become a roommate of sorts. Her stay at a

local boutique hotel came to an end after a couple of days, the hotel having committed all its rooms to previous reservations. By then Danni's visits to Rigby's apartment had occurred more frequently, and neither objected to the idea that she set up residence for whatever time she would remain in America waiting to hear from the English court while helping Rigby work through his puzzle. She made no secret that she still wanted to uncover the treasures of Cocos Island.

"What's that expression—a penny for your thoughts? How about I offer you a dollar?"

He smiled at her, the first time he had smiled all morning, and was rewarded with a gentle kiss on the lips.

Rigby decided not to tell her what he was thinking. He did not know how she would react, if it would put her off somehow. He didn't know how he felt about what was going through his mind about her and his future. He needed to think more on it. He did know how he could steer the conversation away from that.

"I was thinking about the empty safe. There are so many possibilities. If some treasure hunter opened the safe and found something valuable, he would have ignored whatever else was in there. Either way, it would be no more. Just leaving a document exposed to the water all that time would have destroyed it."

"I thought you said it was probably some Navy diver that opened the safe. If that's the case, they would preserve what was in there, wouldn't they?"

"Maybe. We're trying to track that down. Who knows what we'll find from seven decades ago? Probably nothing. Even if they did find the reason for the dive, where would the thing be?"

Danni rolled onto her back. "Depends what was in the safe. Something valuable to anyone who came across it, then it would be hidden away. If it had no intrinsic value—if it was important, say, but a man on the street wouldn't see

201

where he could make a nickel from it—then it could be anywhere. It could be hidden in plain sight. That's the best place to hide things, I think."

"If that's the case," Rigby said, "it's been hidden pretty well because no one has seen it in seventy years."

The telephone rang. Danni reached for it.

"Don't answer!" Rigby snapped.

Danni looked at him with a devilish smile. "Why? You embarrassed for people to learn 'bout me?"

"Not people," he said defensively. "Smitty. I don't need the headache."

Rigby reached across Danni and picked up the phone. "Hello."

He listened for a moment and nodded at Danni, indicating that his guess was correct. Smitty was on the line. Danni smiled, pinched his arm and slid out of bed, heading for the bathroom.

Smitty said, "I followed your suggestion. If Mallory had uncovered something about FDR he must have been digging into files and reading old manuscripts. Nothing at the Smithsonian and the Library of Congress but I made a couple of hits."

"What was he researching?" Rigby asked, sitting up.

"I don't know what but I know where."

"Okay," Rigby said impatiently, "where?"

"Mallory's been up to New York at the Franklin Roosevelt Presidential Library in Hyde Park—but that's not all."

Rigby wondered why he had to wait through a pause for Smitty to finish the thought.

"Mallory also made a Freedom of Information request for old records at the FBI."

Chapter 47

The FBI reports from the 1930s were crude typewritten documents with smudged, uneven lettering, often covered with handwritten notes and other assorted marks. A date stamp had been used to identify when the document was received. Names and even paragraphs were blacked out to keep confidences. Zane and Smitty sat at a table at the archives looking through the files that Paul Mallory had requested under the government's Freedom of Information Act.

Two files were spread out before him, although not all the pages existed in the files. On the top of one page, Rigby read:

Federal Bureau of Investigation
FOIPA Deleted Page Information Sheet.

Under the title was a list of reasons for the deletion of the pages. The box checked was the fill-in-the-blank line with no helpful reason listed. What was written would make a bureaucrat cry with joy: *The following number is to be used for reference regarding these pages: 99-87659-3 and 4.*

At the bottom of the page was a stamp that informed the reader the missing page would not cost:

Deleted Page(s)
No Duplication Fee
For this page

File number 65-53615 was an assortment of notes and letters dealing with a reported plot to assassinate Adolf Hitler in 1933. The file was not thick and Rigby made short work of going through it.

A letter sent to the German Embassy in March from someone named Daniel Stern said that if the persecution of German Jews did not stop, he would assassinate Hitler. The embassy forwarded the letter to U.S. Secretary of State Cordell Hull along with a demand for an investigation.

Hull turned the letter over to the Department of Justice, which in turn requested its investigative branch to follow up. Documents indicated searches in Philadelphia, the city from which the letter was sent, and Phoenix, where a second tip came in, turned up nothing.

The Philadelphia consul for Germany dismissed the threat. *Hitler gets threats all the time from cranks of the Jewish element*, the reporting agent wrote, quoting the consul.

A final letter-report issued in September 1933 closed the case. Daniel Stern was not found and no threat was uncovered.

The second file, 99-87659, revealed only that another plot to assassinate Hitler was briefly investigated in 1937 by the FBI. There were few details. A short memo revealed the plot was traced to an American official and then the case was closed. A note indicated a letter was in the file but the letter was missing.

"Crazy Hitler stuff," Smitty said, running through some other sheets of paper Paul Mallory had requested. "Sightings of Hitler in New York City and Wisconsin; getting off a submarine near Argentina—all after he was supposedly dead. Here's a newspaper clipping of a Damon Runyon article about the possibility of Hitler living in New York. Runyon writes, *"You can live and die in New York City without your next door neighbor giving you a second glance"*. Funny. Why would the FBI keep all of this weird stuff?"

"The bigger question is, why did Mallory want to see it?" Rigby said. "This may have nothing to do with

Roosevelt's treasure. Maybe Mallory was writing a book. He's written about Roosevelt and Hitler before. I saw a framed magazine article on the two mounted on his office wall. He won a prize for it."

"You know Roosevelt and Hitler both become top dogs in their countries that same year, 1933."

Rigby shrugged. "Yeah."

"You seeing her?" Smitty asked.

"Seeing what?" He looked over at the paper Smitty was examining.

"Her. Not what. Are you seeing *her*?"

Rigby looked at Smitty, his mind shifting away from the FBI files.

Yes, he was seeing her. He knew Smitty was jealous but it made little sense to deny it. He would have to let Smitty know the truth, especially if the relationship deepened, and Smitty would have to deal with it. He thought having a solid relationship with this new woman would hopefully end Smitty's infatuation.

Now was definitely not the time to have the conversation. He said nothing.

"She's related to a famous gangster, you recall. Not good for an FBI man to be seen with a gangster's relative."

Time to change the subject.

"This file with the missing letter…" Rigby lifted the file from the desk. "You got any ideas?"

She did not immediately answer and he wondered if she were ready to move on.

"Nothing to go on," Smitty finally said as she shuffled through the pages again then took the old manila file folder from Rigby and examined it. Turning it over to look at the back of the folder she said, "There's a faint note here."

Rigby looked closely to where Smitty was pointing. The notation, written in pencil, had faded over time.

"What do you think it says?" He pulled reading

glasses from his pocket. "You got better eyes."

"I think it says, *Copy of FBI letter to*...looks like *HP*."

Rigby focused on the markings and said, "Yeah, I think so. Who's HP?"

"You're asking me?"

"No, I'm asking the God of All Knowledge but he or she never answers. You're the closest person who sits near the God's throne."

Smitty broke into a smile. "Thank you, Z. That's the nicest thing you've said to me in a long while. You do care."

Time to shift gears again, Rigby thought. "Aggravating, this alphabet soup. BK under the sea. HP on the file. Who do you suppose wrote that note?"

"My guess," Smitty said, "it was written by a long-ago archivist or librarian trying to keep track of files in a less structured time."

Rigby could buy that. Since the archivist was not identified it did not help any. He worked his way back through all the papers before him but could not guess what secret they might hold.

He leaned back in his chair and blew out a sigh of frustration.

"Means nothing to you, huh?" Smitty said. "Well, let's go to dinner and talk it over. We'll come up with something."

Rigby smiled at her while trying to figure out graciously how he could avoid the invitation because he already had dinner plans with Danni...

Saved by the bell, or at least the buzzing sound his cell phone made when it vibrated. He held a finger up to Smitty asking her indulgence and answered the phone.

"Rigby."

"Rosshowe here. We got a hit from our Navy diver files after the war. There were not many of them; the service was relatively new."

Rigby looked around and saw there was no one else in the archives room to disturb.

"I'm putting my cell on speaker," Rigby said, "Ms. Wong is with me."

He clicked on the speaker button and placed the phone on the table as he said, "Admiral Rosshowe with a report on the diver."

"We found the records as you suggested, Ms. Wong. Thank you. There was a separate file on early Navy divers. One diver was named Brian Kelly. He was from Rhode Island. Served from 1944 to 1964, a lifer. He was a deep sea diver and also worked with the new aqualung following the war."

"Would there be orders in his file? Orders to dive to the USS *Houston*?" Smitty asked.

"Nothing like that. Bunch of reports on his diving experiences. Lots of new technology at the time. The Navy wanted to know how it worked."

"Is he still around?" Rigby asked. "Can we talk to him?"

"Long gone I'm afraid. Passed in 1975. Only forty-nine."

Rigby massaged the back of his neck. Stress from the situation was building up. Hearing that someone passed away and was younger than him didn't help.

Smitty said, "What unit was Kelly attached to? Was there a special diver's unit?"

"Hold on," Rosshowe said and they could hear him conferring with someone.

Smitty whispered, "We don't even know if this is the guy. There could be a thousand BKs in the Navy. Might not have even been a Navy diver."

Rigby nodded. "True. But where else do we look?"

Rosshowe's tinny voice came back. "Got his record. Seems that during the fall of 1945 when that date was scratched on the safe, Seaman Kelly was borrowed from his unit and did a stint in the Pentagon."

"Why would they want him at the Pentagon?" Rigby asked.

"Don't know. Does seem peculiar but it could happen. He was there only until the end of the year then sent back to his assignment in Florida."

"The Pentagon is a far piece from the Java Coast." Another sigh of frustration escaped Rigby's lips.

Smitty asked, "Anything at all in his record about his Pentagon assignment?"

"Nothing," Rosshowe said. "All we got is a record in the file that he spent a few months in the Pentagon assigned to the office of Marine Corps General Orville Randolph."

Chapter 48

"General Randolph's the fellow we need to chat with," Danni said, trying to start a conversation at the restaurant chosen by Rigby and Smitty for dinner. Rigby figured the best way to deal with Smitty was to ask her to join the party.

"He's long dead," Smitty said in a way to make Danni feel stupid.

Rigby thought, he may be long dead but Randolph was very much alive as the central character to whatever happened on Cocos Island and the USS *Houston*. It was Randolph who left the map for Alvin Warren with the initials Col. O. R. written in the corner. The diver, Brian Kelly, was assigned to Randolph when the date on the back of the door of the safe was carved.

Rigby knew Danni was correct. They had to *chat* with Randolph. He could connect the pieces in the evidence pouch Rigby kept in the part of the brain that worked through his puzzles. Randolph had been dead for thirty years. Alvin Warren was dead. Paul Mallory was dead. No one left to tell the tale.

Rigby folded his hands on the table as if saying a prayer. He saw no clear path to what Mallory was after.

"Damn it," he said. "We need a séance. Dig up the old general's bones and ask him what this is all about."

"We already found bones and that didn't help us." Danni smiled. "On the island, remember?"

Smitty slammed a fist on the table. Both Rigby and Danni jumped.

"I'm thinking...if the general...Randolph...if he found the treasure. He's probably rich. Or was rich. Maybe the family's rich. Maybe that would tell us something."

"Maybe," Rigby said with no conviction. "Maybe not."

He stared down at his drink. Their table fell quiet as the hubbub from the bar enveloped them. They had no leads. None. It was more than frustrating. He wanted to stand up and scream. Let the tension out. He wouldn't do that. Thinking about what Smitty said, Rigby muttered, "Where did the general retire to?"

Smitty dug into her large purse and pulled out an iPad. Her research notes were stored on the tablet. With a few taps of her finger she brought up her notes and quickly scanned the page.

"Well, maybe we *can* dig up his bones. I have it that he's buried in the town where he retired after his army days."

"Where's that?" Rigby asked.

"Hyde Park, New York," Smitty said. "Interesting. Same town where FDR is buried and where his library is."

They were silent for a moment then Rigby jumped from his chair and Smitty looked at him with excitement.

At the same time they shouted, "HP!"

Chapter 49

"**Y**ou might as well ask me to find a needle in a haystack," the archivist said, hands on her hips. "Except in this case we don't know if this is the right haystack and we don't know if a needle even exists."

Rigby sat down on the bench next to Franklin Roosevelt. He had to admit the archivist summed up the situation pretty well. Rigby looked to his right at the bronzed, life-size Roosevelt statue. The president smiled as he looked straight ahead. His wife, Eleanor, was also smiling as she sat at a small table across from FDR. The bronze sculpture was perfectly set up for visitors to the Franklin Delano Roosevelt Presidential Library and Museum to sit on the bench next to the president and get a snapshot with their hosts.

FDR's library and home were located in New York ninety miles north of New York City along the Hudson River off Route 9, the Albany Post Road. The original library building was set back a short walk from the newer facility that housed the ticket booths, gift shop and reading room, where Rigby could look through old records connected to Roosevelt's voyages on the USS *Houston*. The statue stood just outside the new building on the pathway to the old.

Rigby was interested in just one FBI letter: the one that had disappeared from the FBI archive with a copy sent to *HP*.

Julianne Lang, the senior archivist assigned to Rigby, reminded him of a character actress from mid-20th century movies. He couldn't remember her name but she always seemed to play the spinster schoolteacher or the henpecking wife. Julianne Lang was dressed for those roles this day, wearing a plain flower pattern dress with her hair swept up

211

and clipped together above her neck by a massive hair clip.

"HP is all I got," Rigby said. "A pencil notation on the back of the file."

"Could be a name," Lang suggested.

Rigby gave her a look. Yeah, he'd thought of that.

"What was the file concerned with? That might offer some direction."

"Something about Hitler. What do you have about him here?"

Lang looked at Rigby as if he said the dumbest thing in the world.

"Ever hear of World War II? FDR had a tiny bit to do with it. We have, oh, maybe, two or three pages on it here."

To make her point when Rigby did not react, Lang added, "Two or three million!"

Rigby's voice exploded with frustration. "Yeah, I know. I know. Needle in a haystack. I don't have anything else to go on. Where do you suggest we start?"

He thought of Smitty's research acumen. Despite offers of help from both Smitty and Danni, Rigby traveled to Hyde Park alone. He didn't need the distractions that either lady would bring. He hoped to finally have a breakthrough in solving the Mallory case; get the Speaker of the House and all the pressure he could bring off Rigby's back.

Deadline for the government shutdown was a day away. Lang told him that she couldn't find the impossible in one day and the library was sure to be shut down tomorrow.

He had to admit, despite Danni's allure, he would have preferred Smitty's company to help wade through old papers. He had asked Smitty to take on an unenviable project. To see if she could find the document from the safe opened underwater by Navy diver Brian Kelly while he focused on the missing pages from the FBI file.

"You said this has something to do with the president's trips on the USS *Houston*. We have papers from the voyages. Copies of the ship's logs. Copies of messages received by the president. Day-to-day activities."

Rigby groaned. He did not want to spend the day working through papers, not knowing what he was looking for. Besides, he reasoned, whatever was in that purloined file would not likely be anything that qualified as a day-to-day activity. It would have to be something special. Something important. Something that maybe should not see the light of day. Something…top secret!

Rigby snapped his fingers, startling the archivist. "Do you have a classified document section here?"

Lang crossed her arms in a defiant motion as Rigby imagined that actress playing a long-ago schoolteacher would and stared at him with cold eyes. He wondered if she thought she was personally protecting FDR by not answering. He imagined anyone spending a lifetime at a presidential library would consider themselves a confidant of the president, a loyal friend and supporter.

The woman said, "Executive Order 12958 issued in 1995 required the archives to declassify many, many papers and records over twenty-five years old—"

"But not all," Rigby interrupted.

Lang paused before saying softly, "Not all."

"Then let's start there. This letter may be classified. Must have been important."

"If it's still classified, you'll have to request it. There are procedures in place for declassifying documents. The Archivist of the United States can work with other agencies like the Department of State and the National Security Council to declassify documents."

"How can I request it if I don't know what it is?" Rigby stood and raised his voice. "Ms. Lang, let me remind you I'm an FBI Special Agent investigating a murder that has direct impact on the functioning of the United States government. I'm asking for a little cooperation."

"I'm trying to cooperate," Lang retorted, not giving any ground. "I don't know what you're after."

Rigby did not know what he was after either, so how could this woman know? He wondered if there was another way to dig up the truth. Smitty said Paul Mallory conducted research at the Roosevelt Library.

"Let's try this." Rigby lowered his voice in what he hoped sounded like a conspiratorial whisper, making the archivist believe she was an insider, part of the team looking for the truth. "Can we find out what Paul Mallory, the journalist, was searching for at the library and what documents or letters he looked at?"

"The murdered journalist?"

Rigby nodded. "Can we find out if he wanted to see a classified FBI letter?"

"Yes, I can do that."

She didn't move.

"Will you?" Rigby asked impatiently.

"It might take a while."

He told her that he would walk over to the museum in the adjoining building.

Rigby breezed through the museum, spending a little extra time on the World War II exhibit, taking in Roosevelt's office, dominated by a picture of FDR's mother, the office said to look exactly as the president left it, and checked out a display on Social Security. It amused him to learn that Roosevelt had the sobriquet of *feather duster* placed on him when he first ran for political office because he was considered such a lightweight. Roosevelt drove around the county in a red Maxwell and called himself a *farmer*, of all things. He won the state Senate seat by just over a thousand votes.

Rigby's tour ended when he came across a display that said FDR was a member of the Harvard Republican club and campaigned for the Republican McKinley-Theodore Roosevelt ticket.

Rigby's mission was to find out why FDR shouldn't be put on Mount Rushmore along with Ronald Reagan and help end the partisan bickering. It would be an interesting tag-team to try and achieve that goal: a solidly liberal Democratic president who had started out as a Republican and a solidly conservative Republican president who started out as a Democrat.

Rigby went searching for Julianne Lang. He found her as she was hanging up the telephone at her desk. He did not like the expression he saw on her face. Disappointment? More than that: concern? Even anger?

She rose to greet him. "Follow me."

They walked down a hall to a small conference room. She closed the door behind them. Neither one sat.

"What is it?" Rigby said.

"Mr. Mallory was at the library. He requested the copy of an FBI letter that came to us from Washington years ago. He was refused because of the letter's protected status and was told he had to go through proper channels if he wanted to see it."

"And?"

"He began the request process."

"And what?" Rigby did not hide his impatience with the woman.

"He never came back, Agent Rigby. He was murdered and he never came back."

"Then let's take a look at the letter he wanted. No *request process*. I want to see it now."

"You can't."

"Yes, I can. I'll have the head of the FBI and the Speaker of the House all over the Archivist of the United States in ten minutes cutting the red tape. Let's just save a lot of time and you get me the FBI letter."

Julianne Lang shrugged. "I cannot get you the letter, Agent Rigby, because it is not there. It's missing."

Chapter 50

"Missing?" Rigby said. Though angry, he admitted to himself that he was not surprised. There was a fallen tree across every path he'd followed in this investigation. "Don't you have procedures to protect classified documents?"

"Of course we do," Lang said, showing anger of her own. "The FBI should have the original—"

He cut her off. "No. No copy with the FBI. When was the last time it was seen?"

"Let me finish," Lang said. "In looking for the letter for you, I learned that someone was asking for the letter after Mr. Mallory."

"Who?"

"They said an FBI agent asked for the letter. Now, no one can find it."

"FBI agent?"

"A man with FBI credentials."

"What was the letter about?"

"The record's not clear. It's identified in our catalogue as a letter to J. Edgar Hoover from a field agent closing an investigation dealing with Hitler. That's all I have."

At least there was an easy path to follow. "Give me the agent's name and I'll contact him or her."

Lang blushed. There was no anger or defiance now, just regret. Softly she said, "I'm afraid I can't do that. I don't have it."

Rigby waited for more information. Lang obliged after taking a moment to swallow her pride.

"We do things right here. We are proud of being the first presidential library setting the standards for all that follow. But sometimes young people make mistakes. I was not on duty the day the agent came in. A young lady fairly new to our team was assigned to him. Apparently, from what I learned from my telephone inquiries, the agent bullied his way around, talked about national security and had Ms. Littlehorn produce the document he wanted. When she left him for a moment he walked out of the research room with it, apparently folded and placed inside his laptop case. That's the way it figures, anyway."

Rigby wished the inexperienced librarian was assigned to him when he arrived. It would have made his investigation easier.

"The name of the agent?" he asked.

Lang blushed again. "Ms. Littlehorn did not record it. She said he was acting like it was a national emergency and things had to happen instantly."

Rigby nodded calmly, as if this turn of events was all in a day's work. Nothing new he thought. "Let me talk to Ms. Littlehorn."

Lang nodded and told Rigby to follow her.

Carol Littlehorn was a tall woman in her mid-twenties with yellow hair and the lanky look of a beach volleyball player. Her blue eyes revealed insecurity.

Julianne Lang introduced Rigby, who pulled his credentials out and presented them to the young lady. He considered for a moment that he was humiliating her because she had not been so careful with the first FBI agent to see his credentials, and Rigby's action was driving that fact home.

"What did the agent tell you about the FBI letter?" Rigby decided there was no reason for small talk.

"He said nothing, Agent Rigby. He flashed his ID at me and said he knew Mr. Mallory wanted to see a certain letter. He demanded to see it. Right away, he said."

The woman looked at the senior archivist and Rigby understood that Carol Littlehorn was worried about her job. He knew the feeling. He'd made enough screw-ups in his career to fill a book. He wasn't interested in causing the young woman grief.

"Nothing we can't fix," he said. "I understand you don't recall the name."

"I just...don't remember."

"What'd he look like?"

"Older gentleman. His ID was a little different than yours."

"Different? Different how?"

"I don't remember exactly. It said Federal Bureau of Investigation. It just didn't look like the one you showed me."

Rigby tried to understand. A fake ID, no doubt. He thought about the young woman's description of the agent. He was aware that to young people anyone over forty looked old.

"How old? And again, what'd he look like?"

"Shorter than you. Shorter than me, too. Whitish hair, mostly, white thick eyebrows, a little stooped at the shoulders."

Sounded like a senior citizen, Rigby mused. FBI agents didn't stay on the job that long.

Lang stood by while the interview proceeded, rubbing her hands in an agitated fashion. Finally she said, "I don't understand how you could leave the man alone with a classified letter. Even if he did bully his way in here. Didn't we train you that we never leave anyone alone in the library?"

"Yes, Ms. Lang. I'm sorry. It's just that we were in a research room. There were no other documents—"

"Except the one he was inspecting," Lang snapped.

"Yes, but I thought it was okay because Brad already scanned it."

Rigby held up his hand and looked at Lang then back at Littlehorn.

"Brad *scanned* it?"

Lang stepped in front of the young woman. "He did? Under whose authority?"

"Well, I…" Littlehorn shrank back a bit. "I knew we were scanning the documents in the library. Turning all the documents into digital format. This one was old. When I retrieved it I had to sweep a layer of dust off the file. I figured while it was out, I'd ask Brad to scan it for me."

"And he did?"

The young woman smiled, relaxing for the first time. "Why wouldn't he?" she said.

Rigby thought, she is going to owe him big time for this—lucky Brad.

Chapter 51

B rad sat at his computer terminal in an area close to the library's research room staring at the screen. Julianne Lang did not bother with introductions this time. She ordered him to find a document that he had scanned into the computer files for Carol. Brad remembered the letter immediately.

"Yeah, weird, man. Hitler stuff."

He adjusted his glasses, clicked his mouse a few times and rolled his chair back from the terminal.

Rigby leaned forward to read the letter that filled the screen.

Federal Bureau of Investigation
311 Hurley-Wright Building
Washington, D.C.

August 25, 1937

The Director
Bureau of Investigation
U.S. Department of Justice
Washington, D.C.

Dear Sir:

Re: Marine Corporal Myers—Threat to Assassinate German Chancellor Adolf Hitler

With reference to the above entitled matter, please be advised that all outstanding leads have been followed. Marine Corporal Joseph Myers was overheard conspiring to

220

be part of a team to assassinate the German Chancellor. This was reported by an observer to authorities who brought it to the Department of State. The Department sought investigation from the Department of Justice.

Our investigation determined that said corporal was not sober when he made the comment and that military authorities reprimanded him. Further investigation was terminated at the request of the President of the United States.

Accordingly, the Washington Field Office is closing this case.

Sincerely,
Bertrand Oliver, Special Agent in Charge

Chapter 52

Aprinted copy of the letter from Special Agent Oliver to Director J. Edgar Hoover sat on the small desk under the burning desk lamp in Rigby's motel room. Julianne Lang had printed the copy of the letter and handed it to him, clipped to her business card. Tie off, collar button open, Rigby had been staring at the letter for over an hour. Occasionally, he would take a sip from his tumbler filled with the Scotch he had bought at a local store.

With the letter in hand and the description of the FBI man who had claimed the original from the FDR library, Rigby now knew where the leak came from on this investigation.

The Director of the FBI herself—the Judge—had spilled the beans.

Not on purpose, of course. She was not an accomplice to murder. But he knew who probably pulled the trigger. He just didn't know why.

He saw the man standing in the group of retired operatives at the Society of Former FBI Special Agents annual meeting. The Judge was telling the men about Mallory and his investigation. Retired agents had identifications with FBI logos. Good enough to fool a young, nervous librarian.

One of those agents in the group had bushy eyebrows—white bushy eyebrows. That feature belonged to the one who stole the letter from the FDR Library.

He remembered the old agent's name: Jones.

Rigby hadn't called in his conjecture to the Bureau. He first hoped that relaxing with the Scotch would help him clear up the puzzle. After tipping the glass a while and not coming up with one logical explanation for why Jones was

222

involved—it had to be Jones, he was sure—he started hoping the liquor would wash the problem out of his head so he could get some rest.

The government was closing down tomorrow. He'd be out of a job along with a million other poor slobs. But then, he never did this job for the money. He did it because he wanted to help set things right.

Maybe he could set things right once he took down Jones.

Through the initial fog that the liquor brought on, Rigby struggled with the question of why the president of the United States would be directly involved with an investigation of a Marine corporal and what that might have to do with former FBI agent Jones.

The letter was written in 1937, after Roosevelt had taken a couple of trips to Cocos Island aboard the USS *Houston*, but before his last trip to the island aboard that ship. Rigby wondered if Corporal Myers served on the *Houston* when Roosevelt was aboard. Specifically, he wondered if the corporal was in the unit commanded by Colonel Orville Randolph. He had to be, Rigby figured. There had to be a connection. There *had* to be. He just didn't know how to make it. He rolled his glass gently across his forehead. A headache was coming on.

Perhaps the easiest route to the answer was to let the Judge know his suspicions and then round up Jones for questioning.

There was a knock on the hotel room door.

Rigby started, the interruption surprising him. He expected no one and had not left word where he was staying in Hyde Park. He had chosen a motel on the Albany Post Road near the entrance to the Roosevelt estate.

Rigby walked toward the door but stood off to the side and called out, "Who is it?"

"A surprise!" the excited female voice exclaimed from the other side of the door. Danni!

Rigby yanked opened the door and Danni Warren rushed in, throwing her arms around his neck and planting a long kiss on his lips. "Surprised, right?"

"How did you find me?"

"Easy. Nothing, compared to tracking you down in South Dakota. You told me you'd be at the Roosevelt Library and there aren't a lot of places to hide up here. Not a whole lot to do at night, either, except be in your room. I have something to get from the car for you to see. I'm so excited! Be right back."

As quickly as she had charged into the room she was gone again, running through the open doorway and pulling the door closed behind her.

Her excitement was infectious. He was happy to see her. The feeling that gripped him was more than excitement, more than playfulness or escaping the drudgery of his research and his seemingly unsolvable puzzle.

A stronger feeling was involved. Affection? More.

Companionship. Wanting to be with Danni. He had not had this kind of feeling for a woman in a long time. He wondered if it were destined to last. He knew he wanted to find out. He could hardly wait for her to come back.

Again, a knock on his door. Danni had locked herself out when she rushed off. She said there was not much to do at night in Hyde Park *except in your room*. The possibilities excited him. He imagined that what she wanted to show him was sexy lingerie and eagerly anticipated seeing her in it.

Rigby opened the door. A rifle butt thrust through the opening caught him full in the chest and knocked him back. He stumbled, trying to keep his footing, lost it and fell backward onto the bed.

His assailant now pointed the rifle straight at Rigby. Holding the weapon was a man about five-nine with white stubble on his chin and a fedora pulled low over his eyes. The eyebrows were bushy and white.

Jones.

"Up and face the wall," Jones said.

Rigby pushed himself off the bed. He eyed the firearm tucked in his shoulder holster out of reach on the bureau.

Rigby faced the wall and the man quickly and professionally frisked him before stepping away. "We're going out."

Where was Danni? Had he hurt her?

Jones opened the door, looked both ways down the corridor, and motioned with his rifle for Rigby to move. They walked down the corridor, though the rear door of the motel and into the dully-lit parking lot.

Rigby considered how to free himself from the armed kidnapper. He needed to know about Danni.

She wouldn't be there to rescue him *this time*. Twice he'd been kidnapped. On the same case. By two different guys. For a senior FBI agent, he was one hapless screw-up.

And Danni was around both times…

Two kidnappings, and Danni around both times. She had rescued him from the Monument Bomber and her timely intervention had helped him save Mount Rushmore. This time, he was expecting her return to the room. He was not ready for an assailant when he opened the door. Her unexpected presence had lowered his defenses.

He was being stupid. What would Danni have to do with this? Yes, she was interested in the treasure on the island…if there *was* a treasure on the island. But, how could she tie into Mallory's murder?

She had been to Mallory's place. She had been in his bedroom.

Jones directed Rigby to a late-model sedan in the back of the parking lot. It stood alone under a canopy of trees. Away from the motel and parking lot lights, it was extremely dark. The car beeped and the car headlights flashed on and off in response to the gunman's car remote.

"Open the driver's door and get behind the wheel."

Rigby looked back at Jones. He was going to let Rigby drive? A mistake. Rigby could crash the vehicle or run it off the road.

Rigby opened the driver's door and slipped in behind the steering wheel. He heard the rear door on the driver's side open and the man climbed in behind him.

Once inside, Rigby heard a muffled grunt. He turned but only saw his assailant at first. A second muted stream of words directed him toward the rear floor of the sedan. Danni was gagged, her hands tied behind her back. She was caught in an awkward position, her skirt hiked up all the way to her thighs, exposing white panties.

Jones leveled his rifle at Danni and said, "You'll follow directions exactly. Any false move or attempt to signal anyone will end this lady's life."

Chapter 53

"Drive. North on Route 9. I'll tell you when to turn. Obey the speed limits."

Rigby started the car, backed it out of the parking stall and headed out of the lot.

He wondered where they were going. Did Jones intend to kill them in some quiet place? He was taking a risk by moving them anywhere. Rigby was already figuring how to outmaneuver him; take him down. But he was concerned about Danni. She must not be in the line of fire.

Danni. Only moments before he'd been wondering about her. Questioning whether she was somehow involved in the mystery surrounding FDR on Cocos Island and the death of Paul Mallory. Were things different now that she was trussed up like a pig ready for the butcher? Or was that camouflage? A red herring to throw him off the scent?

He wondered if he should trust her. Wondered if he should spend time worrying about her safety. If she were in on this—whatever *this* was—he could make his move easier if he only had himself to consider.

"Left at the light," came the command from the back seat.

Rigby waited for the intersection to clear then turned. He followed the country road as it rolled downhill toward the Hudson River. In the darkness on his right he saw a wall running along the road, the border of a great estate. It must be the Vanderbilt Estate he had seen on a map of the area. With the help of a couple of on-site security lamps, he could vaguely make out the shape of what looked like a horse barn.

The car's headlights picked up the swirling mist of a light fog as the road turned to parallel the river.

"To the right, in here," the rifle-toting man said and

Rigby turned the car into a parking lot. The headlights caught a sign that identified the small building in the lot as the historic Hyde Park Railroad Station.

"Park it."

Rigby stopped the car and cut the engine. He heard the rear door of the sedan open and Jones slipped out, keeping his rifle trained on his captives.

"Help her out of the car and come with me. Hurry it up."

Jones kept his distance from Rigby but the rifle stayed on him as he circled around the back of the car.

"Take her out gently. Nothing stupid now."

He followed orders, lifting Danni out as gently as possible and standing her up next to the car. He untied the rope holding down the gag over the mouth; then he freed her hands.

Danni spat the handkerchief from her mouth. She tried to speak, emitting only a hoarse sound. She swallowed hard then managed one word: "Bastard!"

"Inside," the gunman said. "Quickly."

They walked to the door of the small station building. Jones carried a flashlight and a key. He handed the latter to Danni and told her to unlock the door then stepped back a safe distance from his captives.

Danni unlocked the door and pushed it open. She followed his instructions and found a light switch.

Rigby thought turning on the lights was a mistake. The train station was a museum. He saw the marker that declared it to be on the National Register of Historic Places. The station had obviously been refurbished to look as it had seventy or eighty years ago. Ticket booth, waiting room, baggage area, and benches had all been redone. A model train was on exhibit and historic pictures of the station in its heyday were displayed on the walls. There was no way the light should be on in the middle of the night. Even though the station appeared to be in a secluded part of town,

228

someone was bound to notice.

Jones motioned Danni and Rigby to a bench and they both sat down.

Rigby looked at Danni and gave her a reassuring smile. He wanted to show his concern. He wanted to comfort her. He also wanted to keep an eye on her. He wanted to see if any signal passed between her and Jones—a nod, a wink, or a change of facial expression indicating that Danni was not what she seemed.

"We've done a good job remodeling this old place," Jones said. "Only open one day a week, but the tourists come. Still, we've got work to do on it all the time and a lot of us work at night."

So much for it being unusual that the old station was lit up at night, Rigby thought.

Rigby said, "You're going to embarrass the Bureau, Jones."

"How nice, you remembered. Our introduction was so brief but then your old acquaintances, Adams and Hightower, were in the group."

"Along with the Director."

"Yes. And she was so full of information and merriment."

"Stop pointing that gun at us," Danni said.

"It's more effective if you point it where you intend to shoot," Jones said with a smile.

"What do you want from us?" she asked.

It was her tough voice. She showed no fear of their captor. Rigby still wondered if it was bravado or just an act. Maybe she had no reason to be afraid.

"This is a historical place. Yes, history happened right here. There was a railroad station here since 1851. This station was put up in 1914 when new track was laid. Designed by the same architects who did Grand Central Station in New York City. A historical association runs it now. We take care of the place. See the pictures on the wall?

229

One is the King and Queen of England visiting here. Another is the president's casket coming home."

Jones looked at the picture of the funeral train and snapped off a salute.

Something in the picture of FDR's funeral train caught Rigby's eye: the tall officer standing near the camera in front of the flag-draped casket. Rigby knew he should be looking for something he could use as a weapon, or figure out an escape route. But he saw something in the way Jones held himself when he saluted.

The officer's face in the picture wasn't clear.

"General Orville Randolph?" Rigby asked.

"Yes sir," the gunman replied. "The best general in the Marines."

The pieces in the evidence pouch started to fit.

"You were just saluting him, not FDR's casket."

Jones turned to look Rigby in the eye. "I have all the respect in the world for President Roosevelt. I won't let his reputation be hurt. General Randolph was my mentor. My father died when I was six. When I joined the Marines I was blessed because I ended up assigned as an aide to an old general finishing his hitch. I'd just earned my sergeant stripes. I spent two years with him in the service but he changed my life. Even worked for him when I got out—"

Rigby cut him off. "Colonel Randolph was in charge of Operation Bloody Sword."

"No," Danni said. "Bloody Sword was a pirate who buried his treasure on Cocos Island. You saw the map."

"The map to a graveyard for men who were part of the Bloody Sword operation," Rigby said.

Had to be, Rigby thought. It made sense. Bloody Sword may have been a pirate who roamed Cocos Island, but the military appropriated his name. Whatever the expedition was, Mallory thought it would sink FDR's reputation.

Now was the time to see if he was right.

"Bloody Sword was a military operation approved by

President Roosevelt. Right, Sergeant?"

"Haven't been a sergeant for years," the man said. "Or an FBI agent. Simply Mr. Jones now. Having a plain last name gave my mother permission to go extravagant, you could say, on the first handle. Harley. Never liked it but it is what it is."

Rigby concentrated on the name. Harley Jones. He did not remember hearing it before or seeing it in any of the research on the FDR case. He looked at Danni, who also showed no recognition of the name or the man. She stared straight ahead, giving no sign what she was thinking.

"You're not old enough to have served on the *Houston.*"

"I was born the same year it sank," Harley Jones said. His smile came back. He seemed to enjoy Rigby doing mental exercises.

"So General Randolph told you what happened on that island with President Roosevelt?"

Jones shrugged. He wasn't saying yes or no. He waited to hear more from Rigby. He wants to know what I know, Rigby thought. But he wasn't sure what he knew. There were a lot of items floating around in that evidence pouch in the back of his mind. Gut instinct sometimes brought them all together.

Rigby knew one thing. If he kept Jones interested in what he had to say, the old man wasn't shooting the rifle at him and Danni.

Rifle.

Rigby said, "It was *you* on the island. You shot Pedro Campos. It wasn't the Monument Bomber. Campos was shot from a distance. By a rifle."

Jones shrugged again. The slight smile had not left his lips. He was quiet for a moment but then, as if he had to acknowledge the statement, he said, "I was a marksman in the Marines."

This man killed Pedro Campos. Anger rose in Rigby.

231

Campos was not a friend, just an acquaintance, and he'd held a grudge against Rigby for years. Yet, Campos was working with Rigby when he was killed. The reason Rigby joined the FBI was to stop senseless crime. Campos's death was more than senseless. In fact, Rigby realized, it was unintentional.

The question that seemed unexplainable was why a former FBI man tracked him.

"Not much of a marksman," Rigby said. "You were aiming at me."

The smile fell from Jones. He stiffened. "Still a marksman. You should be grateful."

Grateful? For Campos being killed? Why should he be grateful for that? Rigby shook his head.

Then he understood.

Rifle.

"You shot the Monument Bomber. He was shot from a distance."

The smile returned. "Probably saved your life there," Jones said. "You should thank me."

"Not if you're planning to take it now."

Jones said nothing. Rigby thought he now understood the expression, *eerie silence*. No one made a sound, yet it was spooky, knowing that Jones probably intended to kill them.

"You were in the neighborhood because you were following me. To kill me because you missed on the island. Why didn't you let the Bomber take me out and save you the trouble?"

"We're still on the same team when it comes to America's enemies."

The same team. That's what Admiral Rosshowe said to him. The admiral and Rigby both worked in defense of the country. Harley Jones was a killer with an agenda. But he was on *the same team*. Did he kill to defend the country? He hadn't been military for a long time.

"I see the wheels turning there, Agent Rigby."

"You're an FBI man," Rigby said. "Now you're turning against the country you defended."

Jones became angry. "I'm still defending this country! I've always defended this country. After I finished my military service and went off to help the general he returned the favor and saw to it that I got an appointment to the Bureau. You had to be a lawyer in those days but the general spoke up for me directly to J. Edgar, himself."

"You still have credentials."

"Alumni stuff. You'd be surprised how many sentries don't inspect them closely. My old friends in the bureau still tell me what's happening. Feels like I'm still on the inside."

Rigby remembered the Judge laughing about the Speaker's Mount Rushmore plan with the former agents, including Jones. The Judge was the leak. This was a needle he could drive into her—if he lived.

"My creds are pretty effective when flashing 'em at a young researcher at the Roosevelt library and asking her to give me a heads up when someone comes looking for certain documents."

"The kid believes she's doing her duty by tipping off someone she thinks is in the FBI."

"She's doing her duty," said Jones.

Danni spoke up: "I don't know why you're doing this, but it's time to let us go. Is it money you want? I have plenty."

"Bribery?" he scoffed. "I don't serve to make a buck."

"You don't believe me. I *do* have money. I'm rich. I'll give you what you want. Just let us go." She looked at Rigby, probably figuring he didn't believe her. "It's true. I'm rich. It's what I was going back to retrieve from my car to show you: a message from my solicitor. I won the case brought by Alvin's children. The inheritance is mine! All of it."

She smiled at him weakly. She had a lovely smile.

Oddly, what flashed through his mind was a saying his mother always told him. It was just as easy to fall in love with a rich girl as a poor one.

Danni was a rich girl, or so she said. Was he falling in love with her?

Considering the rifle pointed at them, this was not the time to worry about that. Especially since he had not cleared his mind of his suspicions about her.

"Alvin?" Harley Jones said. "You were on the island. I remember. Newspaper stories. You were the young actress who walked to the altar with the old industrialist, Alvin Warren. Dimes Rothman's niece or something."

"Cheap journalism, that's all that was."

"Small world. My old boss knew Mr. Warren's brother, Robert."

Orville Randolph was his old boss. Rigby thought of the connection to Alvin Warren. Randolph's initials were on the map leading to the Cocos Island cave. Danni told him Randolph's calling card was clipped to the map and Warren's older brother's picture in his desk drawer. The cave contained no treasure but two skeletons.

"Why did General Randolph visit Alvin Warren and give him the treasure map?" Rigby asked.

Jones said nothing.

Turning to Danni, Rigby said, "You said Alvin's brother was older. I think you said about fifteen years older than your husband."

Danni nodded. "Alvin was always proud of his brother. He was a bit of an adventurer. Died before the war but Alvin still talked about him all those years later."

"Did you and your husband ever visit his brother's grave?" Rigby asked. He was no longer looking at Danni. He asked his question of her but now looked at Jones, measuring *his* reaction. Jones stood straight and took a step toward the bench where they sat.

"No," she said.

Rigby nodded. "Half right. Your husband didn't, but you did."

"What are you talking…" She stopped and gasped, a hand covering her mouth.

Rigby could see in Jones's reaction that he was right.

"Robert Warren's skeleton was in the Cocos Island cave. Colonel Randolph put it there. He left the map with Alvin Warren to show him his brother's final resting place. Did Randolph kill him, too?"

"He *honored* him!" Jones snapped, clutching the rifle tightly, his knuckles turning white. "He honored two brave men who died for their countries by returning them to the island where the plans were made."

Countries. The men were from different countries. Rigby felt the emotion churning in Jones. He might say more.

"Who was the other man?" Rigby asked.

"Corporal Joseph Myers, United States Marine Corps. You just read about him."

Yes, he had. The man discussed in the FBI letter who threatened to kill Hitler. The President of the United States ordered a stop to the investigation. The young woman at the library had done her job. She told Jones that Rigby inspected the FBI letter that closed the Myers investigation.

Rigby said, "Myers was part of on an assassination attempt on Hitler. Warren too, I guess. The president knew about it. They all got together on the island to plan. Randolph was in charge of the effort."

"You didn't think the British treasure hunters were really treasure hunters, did you?" Jones laughed.

Rigby had no idea, not until that moment, but he wanted Jones to believe he was following the thread of evidence the whole time.

"Of course not. It was a cover to meet with the president and ask for his help in killing Hitler. That was in 1935 during the president's second trip to the island."

235

"Roosevelt thought about it. He allowed planning to begin. Asked Colonel Randolph to draw up a concept."

"But something happened. Something went wrong."

Jones did not answer.

"The proof of what went wrong was in the safe of the *Houston*," Rigby continued. "That's why Randolph, then a general, sent a diver to retrieve it. So no one would ever see it."

"No one ever will," Jones said. "The general took it with him to the grave."

A car passed outside. Jones took a couple of steps back, keeping the rifle trained on Danni and Rigby. He peered out the window, turned back to check on them, repeated this a second time, looking through the window then turning back to his prisoners. When he stepped toward them he looked pale. The muscles in his jaw tensed.

"Time to go." Jones waved the barrel of his rifle in a circular motion.

Rigby knew if they went anywhere it would not be a good ending. He needed to keep Jones talking. Maybe the driver of the car that passed was already calling the police.

"What was in the safe?"

"Get up. You're both going for a swim."

Chapter 54

Jones had turned out the lights in the train station and locked the door behind them. The flashlight was the only illumination they had to cross the tracks and make their way to the river's edge. Jones had fixed the flashlight into a clamping mount on the rifle barrel. Where he pointed the rifle, the light would shine.

Rigby and Danni walked in front of him toward the river, stepping carefully over two sets of railroad tracks. Danni lost her footing once in the loose gravel. Rigby reached out and grabbed her arm.

Only a couple of yards separated the tracks from the river's edge. A rock outcropping extended into the river, with a wooden dock to the right. Danni started for the rocks but Jones ordered her to stop.

"The dock," was all he said.

They walked toward the dock, the wooden boards running parallel to the shore for a few feet before sticking out into the water. Rigby took in the dark surroundings. A few lights blinked from homes on their side of the river. There were some lights on the other side as well, but not many. The river itself, and the wooded areas on both sides, were black. Was there someone out for a midnight stroll who might be watching the activity on the dock? Even so, would they be able to see?

Rigby knew that if he and Danni were to survive the evening they would have to rely on themselves to escape. Swimming to freedom seemed the best possibility, a sudden jump into the river and below the surface. Jones kept some distance between himself and his captives so that they could not overpower him.

"Keep going right to the end of the dock," Jones

ordered. They obeyed, a few loose boards squeaking as they stepped on them.

At the end of the dock stood a small red wagon, the kind that kids pulled around with their favorite toys. Rigby had a Radio Flyer wagon when he was a kid and used to give rides to his little brother or the neighbor's cat. What was that cat's name? Why was he trying to remember the cat's name now with a rifle pointed at his back? Is that what he wanted to be his last memory, the neighbor's goddamn cat in the red wagon?

Concentrate on turning the tables on this bastard, he told himself.

"Take your choice from the wagon. There's a couple of different models in there," Jones said.

What was he talking about? Rigby looked into the wagon. Hard to see. Something black.

"Pick 'em up," Jones ordered.

Rigby reached into the cart and picked up what lay on top—*tried* to pick it up, at least. Heavy. Extremely heavy. He shifted his weight, used his legs and brought the object into the light from the flashlight.

It was a vest. A very heavy vest made of Cordura nylon with a series of pockets on the front and back filled with weights of some kind. Rigby was no gym rat but he guessed he had lifted eighty pounds, probably more.

"Put it on."

"What the hell are you doing to us?" Danni cried out.

Jones aimed his rifle at Danni and said in a menacing voice, "Put it on."

Rigby complied. Though heavy, on his back and shoulders it was a little easier to bear. At least for a while. He clipped the belt together on the front and it fit securely.

"Now, do you want one too?" Jones said to Danni.

A question, Rigby thought. He was *asking*? Was that a small laugh in his voice? Would Danni laugh, too?

"Of course I don't want one," she snapped.

Rigby turned to her, tried to catch the look on her face, but the light was not shining in her direction.

A moment passed and Jones said, "Ain't that too bad. Put it on. Rigby, you help."

"This thing weighs almost as much as she does," Rigby protested, realizing that relief washed over him because his suspicions were misplaced.

"Just do it!"

Rigby lowered himself toward the cart by bending at the knees so that he could handle both the weight on his back and the second weighted vest. He picked it up with a grunt and slipped it on Danni. Clipping the vest at her navel in front while standing between her and the gunman he whispered, "We'll be fine. Just don't lose it."

"Step away from her," Jones demanded.

Rigby did as he was told.

"Farther."

"Look, Jones," Rigby said. "Why are you doing this? We're on the same team. You said so yourself."

"Because the general would want it this way. He'd want to protect President Roosevelt at all cost."

"Protect him from what? He's dead."

Jones shoved the rifle in Rigby's gut. "And you soon will be because you won't let him rest in peace."

Then, in a lightning move the gunman freed his right hand from the trigger guard and pushed at the clasp on the vest's belt. Rigby stumbled back from the unexpected blow.

"A little adjustment I made to the weighted vests," Jones said.

Rigby looked down at the belt. Jones had put a padlock through a loop in the modified belt clasp and locked it.

The belt could not be undone.

Jones hurried to Danni and repeated the action with a second padlock.

"Now," Jones said, standing back and admiring his

handiwork. "Neither one of you are going anywhere. I'm sorry to do this, but it has to be. You're not going anywhere forever."

Chapter 55

"Time to go for a swim," Jones said. "Jump in."

"We don't stand a chance out there," Rigby protested.

"Better chance than you have here." Jones tapped the rifle.

"I'm not a good swimmer..." Danni began but realized any pleading would be fruitless.

"You have a chance in the water. I'm taking a risk giving you a chance. You just might make it." He smiled as if it were all a joke. He knew they wouldn't make it. "There's an upside for me, too. 'Cause if you don't make it, I don't have any cleanup. No blood, no bodies. You end up on the riverbed somewhere. The Hudson current can flow in both directions."

Danni cried out, "I don't understand. Why are you doing this?" Her tough voice was gone.

"I won't let anyone assassinate the character of the president. The general would want it this way. I'm also protecting *me*. I didn't mean to kill Mallory but he wouldn't stop his relentless searching. I had to stop him to protect Mr. Roosevelt and now I have to stop you, because if I don't then they'll come for me."

When Rigby and Danni did not reply Jones said harshly, "You don't want to take your chances, I'll end it right here."

"I don't think you'll shoot and bring out the neighbors," Rigby said.

Jones didn't shoot. He charged like a rhinoceros and drove them to the edge of the dock. Gravity grabbed hold and they both plunged into the water.

Rigby dropped like a stone. The weighted vest

dragged him down into the chilled, pitch black river. He could feel the disturbance in the water to his right. Danni was falling with him.

Rigby ripped at the coverings of the vest pockets that held the weights. They wouldn't budge. Jones must have sewn them or glued them down.

Got to swim, Rigby thought. *Must fight it.* He kicked his legs furiously. His hands shoveled water with powerful strokes. He felt his teeth chatter in reaction to the cold water embracing him. He started to move despite the weight of the vest.

He needed to get to Danni. She was a strong woman in good physical condition, but the weight would be more difficult for her to handle because of her smaller size.

She was next to him. He could feel her kicking and paddling furiously. She had hit bottom but was pushing toward the river's surface.

Rigby kicked harder. The cold water thoroughly soaked his clothes, adding more weight.

Placing his hands on Danni's hips he pushed her toward the surface as he kicked mightily, propelling both of them as best he could despite the weight.

Danni swam with all the energy she could muster. He saw her break the surface of the water. He was right behind her.

He cleared the water and sucked in a great gob of night air. It rushed into his lungs, paying back the oxygen debt in such a rush that it made him cough.

He saw Danni a couple of yards away, struggling to stay above water. She would start to slip under the river, paddle and kick back up, only to repeat the process seconds later.

He had to get to her.

Water splashed near Danni. Another splash next to Rigby. Then he felt something hit his neck, followed by a sharp pain. Rigby glanced toward the dock and saw Jones throwing something at them. Rocks? No, solid metal bars, probably like the ones fitted into the vest pockets. They rained down on Danni and Rigby. Danni cried out as she was hit. Another weight glanced off Rigby's shoulder.

They had drifted a few yards from the dock toward the center of the river, but that was not enough for Jones. He wanted them farther out, where they would sink to the deepest part of the river. Where their bodies would not be found.

As Jones reached down into the red wagon to pick up more weights, Rigby threw an arm around Danni's body and under her arms.

"Kick with me!" he exclaimed.

He kicked and paddled toward the center of the river. Danni obeyed, kicking hard.

He tired quickly and knew he couldn't keep it up long. As heavy as the weighted vest was when he put it on, it seemed to get even heavier with his exertion and the water-soaked clothes.

Then, he stopped. Exhausted, he could go no more. He looked back at the dock. Darkness had made it almost impossible to see. There was no light. Either Jones had turned off the flashlight or he had left the dock.

"Help," Rigby called out. "Help!"

Fighting the weight of the vest and his soaked clothes, trying to keep his head above water, his cry for help was not strong. He listened for a reply.

There was none.

Rigby doubted they could make it to the far shore with their weighted vests. He knew that Jones and his rifle awaited them on the near shore.

Given his exhaustion, Rigby realized they would drown soon.

He yanked at the padlock securing the vest belt. It did not budge. He had to open the lock to remove the vest.

He was getting tired, his fingers numb from the cold

water. The weight of the vest was too heavy. He could not make it to shore with Danni and he wouldn't leave her behind.

Rigby had to free himself of the vest. He had to remove the lock.

He looked at Danni and gasped, "Stay up. Hang in. I'll…get us out…of this."

He had to open the lock and there was only one way to do that without the key. Would he have time?

"Hurry!" Danni said through chattering teeth. Her mouth then slipped below the surface and she flapped her arms to rise up, spitting water as she did.

Picking a lock was not something they taught at Quantico. It was something he picked up working his short stint as a private investigator. The problem was, as a PI he had the tools to pick locks. He had neither a tension wrench nor a pick in the middle of the Hudson River.

He would have to improvise. But using improvised tools would be fine if he had all the time in the world. All the time he and Danni had in this world was running out fast.

He reached into his jacket pocket and removed Julianne Lang's business card, which had been clipped to the printed copy of the 1930s letter from the FBI agent. Removing the paper clip, he tossed the card aside.

He first pulled the paper clip open to expose the two-bar set of one loop of it, then pinched the metal strips as close together as he could, grunting and straining. He next bent the pinched bars at an angle. If he only had a pair of pliers to do the job right, he thought. This would have to do.

"Hurry," Danni said, her voice fading. He glanced over and saw that her body was weaker as well. She bobbed in the water trying to stay afloat but she was losing the battle. She would slip down, the water covering her up to her eyebrows before recovering.

"Hang on," he said as he kicked harder and splashed the water with his arm to stay afloat. Desperately, he reached into his jacket pocket and removed his FBI credentials. He opened the wallet that contained his badge and freed it from its holder. On the back of the badge was a straight pin held down by a clasp. Rigby undid the clasp and extended the pin. The edge of it had been turned up a bit during a raid when he was wearing it on his belt; it had fallen off and been stepped on. He hoped the bend in the tip would be enough to serve as a pick.

Rigby reached below the water and found the padlock at his waist. He would have to do this by feel—not an easy thing.

"Oh, Zane!" Danni cried out and she disappeared below the water. He let go of the padlock while still holding the makeshift tools and kicked over to her, grabbing her hair and pulling her face above water.

"Hold onto me," he said in short gasps. "Wrap your legs around mine. Put your arms around my neck."

She nodded weakly and did as he said.

He immediately felt the added weight pull him down. He kicked with his free leg and steadied his muscles to stay upright.

Rigby resumed working on the lock. With the bent paper clip he felt for the keyhole. He had to use the clip as a makeshift tension wrench, enter the keyhole and push down the plug inside the pin tumbler.

Jones's death trap was a simple padlock. Thank goodness for that. Probably just four or five pinholes in a rotating plug inside a cylindrical shaft. He had to put pressure on the plug with his tension wrench so he could use the pick to get under the pins and push them up and away from the plug. With the pins aligned above a certain point the plug could rotate within the shaft and the lock would open.

The paper clip tension wrench was holding. He took the pin on the back of the badge and slipped it into the keyhole.

Suddenly Danni sank down, pulling his head to the water. His hands let go of the lock. He desperately clutched the tools, the badge drifting away for an instant. He grabbed it.

Rigby wrapped an arm around Danni. Steadied her. Brought her back to the surface.

"Hold on!" he snapped. Frustration and fear had taken hold. "Hold on," he said again, more softly this time.

His hands went back to work. The paper clip went into the keyhole. The pin of the badge followed as he reached for the pins in the lock.

Danni's arms slipped away from his neck. She drifted below the surface. There was no fight in her this time. She slipped out of sight as her legs released from around his. She sank farther.

"Do this!" Rigby screamed at himself. He held tension on the plug, re-inserted the badge pin in the keyhole and lifted the pins in the lock. He felt them fall into place. He removed the badge, holding it tightly. He could feel the edge of the badge cut into the skin on his palm.

He twisted the padlock. Open.

Without letting go of his tools, Rigby pulled out the padlock, undid the clasp on the belt and shrugged the vest off his shoulder and back. It dropped away.

Pocketing the badge and paper clip, he dove below the surface into the ink-black water below. He could feel the bubbles from Danni's descent against his face. He went straight down, kicking and stroking, until a hand slapped against Danni's shoulder. He grabbed hold of her and pulled her to the surface.

Danni was unconscious. He needed to get her to shore. Rigby slapped her on the back, hoping she would throw up any water she swallowed. She jerked, water oozing from her mouth.

Rigby planted a shoulder in her chest and neck, keeping her head above water as he removed the clip and badge and worked on her lock. It opened, and he soon shed her of the weighted vest.

Rigby saw that they were closer to the Hyde Park shore than across the river. He did not know where the gunman was but would take his chances that Jones had run off. They would not go to the dock at the railroad station. He pulled her along, hoping to come ashore farther down in a wooded area between the Vanderbilt Estate and FDR's home. Minutes later he dragged Danni ashore, got on his knees and immediately began CPR.

Water drooled from her mouth. He clipped her nose shut and breathed into her mouth. She coughed, sputtering water into his face. Her eyes opened. She saw Rigby's face hanging over hers. She coughed again and said hoarsely, "Why, Mr. Rigby, it looks like you're about to kiss me."

And he did.

Chapter 56

Once they crossed the railroad tracks they were in a thick forest. Rigby knew that there were trails that led through the forest. At the presidential library, he had seen a map of hiking trails that ran between the Vanderbilt estate and FDR's home. He just didn't know where they were.

They plunged into the woods, carefully pushing back branches that grabbed at their wet clothes and threatened to scratch their faces and hands.

"What now?" Danni asked.

"Now we stay alert. Make sure he doesn't follow us, and we make our way out of here. The tables are turned. He'll be on the run. If he thinks we survived the river, he'll know we'll bring in reinforcements as soon as we can."

"He probably thinks we drowned."

"All the better. He won't run and we'll get him."

She nodded and kissed Rigby on the cheek. He squeezed her hand. Surviving danger would only make them closer, he thought.

All was quiet. No sign of Jones. They walked forward and waded through a small creek.

Something touched Rigby's leg. He jumped. His sudden movement caused Danni to gasp.

A large beaver scurried away; its slumber had been disrupted by the intruders.

Looking at the animal running away and the expression of relief on Rigby's face, Danni burst out laughing and quickly covered her mouth to restrain herself, her shoulders still jerking up and down in glee. Rigby offered a lopsided grin and tugged on her blouse to move her along.

Maneuvering through the forest was more difficult

than they imagined. The woods were thick and hilly. Little light penetrated the forest. They had to be alert that Jones was not following. They stopped often to listen for sounds. The going was slow.

When they stumbled across a trail they were not sure in which direction to go. Rigby tried to use the stars as a compass and head in the direction that would bring them toward the main road. A trip that would probably take thirty minutes in daylight with map in hand took nearly two hours. Finally, they came to a meadow and climbed a short rise toward a clearing.

At the top of the hill they reached the edge of the woods. Before them stood the stately home of Franklin Delano Roosevelt.

Rigby stopped before entering the clearing so that he could scan the area. The black night had become a silvery gray as day approached. How long had it been since they were kidnapped?

"I think someone lives in a building on the grounds," Rigby said. "A park ranger. Let's wake him up and get the word out on Jones."

Danni said, "Isn't the hotel just across the street?" Rigby nodded. "Can't we just go there and call the FBI or police and get out of these wet clothes?"

Rigby agreed, took her hand and led her down the long drive toward the Albany Post Road.

Behind the front desk a heavy-set young woman chewed on a Milky Way candy bar and read a magazine.

"You two go swimming this time of night?" she asked, disapproval evident in her tone.

"Yes and I lost my key. Could you please give me a duplicate to room 110?"

"You sure the extra key isn't for your lady friend?" the clerk said with a nod toward Danni.

When Rigby didn't answer, she said, "Got an ID? Can't give a key to just anyone."

"Lost it swimming."

"Then why should I give you the key?"

"Because I'm freezing and tired and ready to *explode!*"

"Don't get testy, mister. I'll call the cops."

"Do that," Rigby said.

"You think I won't," the clerk said picking up the phone and punching in some numbers.

A moment later, the clerk spoke into the phone, "This is Berta down at the Town and Country Motel. I got a crazy man here who claims he's a guest."

"Give me that," Rigby said and reached across the counter to grab the phone. Berta didn't resist.

"Who am I speaking to? Okay, listen close…no, *you* listen. I'm Special Agent Zane Rigby of the FBI. I need assistance." Rigby proceeded to fill in the officer on the phone about what had happened. He said Harley Jones had to be captured and detained. He offered a description of Jones and his car and told the officer where the old man was last seen. He told him to get word to the FBI and specified names and contact information.

When he finished, he handed Berta the phone as she watched him in stunned silence.

"The key," Rigby said, holding out his hand.

Key in hand, they detoured to Danni's car to retrieve her suitcase and went to the room. Inside, Rigby turned the heat on. He dumped his jacket off his shoulders and kicked off his shoes. When he looked at Danni she was stripping out of her wet clothes.

He stared for a moment and she noticed.

"What? You expect me to run into the bathroom? It's nothing you haven't seen before."

He smiled; she was stripping naked in front of him with no second thought, as if they were a married couple that did this sort of thing all the time. Married couple? It wasn't an objectionable idea. He could certainly get used to the view. She stood totally naked in front of him and walked over to the bathroom door to reach in and grab a towel.

"You're taking your time. Get out of those wet things," she said.

Danni finished toweling off and immediately dug into her suitcase and removed underwear, jeans, a long-sleeved shirt, sweater, and added a sweatshirt over the sweater. Rigby dried off and also got dressed.

She walked over and put her arms around him. "Hold me. As soon as I warm up, I've got a nice reward for my hero."

He reached beyond her to take up his gun and shoulder holster from the top of the bureau. "No, I'm going out." He strapped the gun on.

Danni said, "What is it?"

"Something Jones said. He may have told us where the missing document is. I've got to get there before he does."

Chapter 57

The chubby girl at the front desk was more cooperative when Rigby came by for directions.

"Tell me about cemeteries in Hyde Park."

"Yes, sir. What do you want to know?"

"Not historic ones that haven't been used for a century. Major cemeteries that have been around for a while and are still in use."

When the girl mentioned the Union Cemetery on Violet Avenue, Rigby knew that was his destination.

Rigby told Danni it was better if she stayed behind in the room. She was adamant. "Not with that creep around. I'm not going to be a victim of Jack the Ripper."

"Not very accurate or subtle but I get it," Rigby said. "Just stay behind me at all times."

They took his car and followed the clerk's directions. They had been on the same road just hours before when kidnapped by Harley Jones. Instead of taking a left on Route 9 toward the river, they took a right at the same intersection and came to the cemetery in under ten minutes.

Rigby drove past the entrance and parked the car on the side of the road. The sun was just brightening the eastern horizon, pushing away the gray sky and making it easy to see as they approached the cemetery boundary from the south.

They stood at the edge of the cemetery looking at the open fields of tombstones spread out before them.

"What are we looking for?" Danni asked.

"A grave." Rigby scanned the cemetery, which was surrounded by woods with a few trees mixed in amid the gravestones.

"Then I'd say we came to the right place," Danni said. "Whose grave and where is it?"

"I don't know where it is. I'm not even sure it's here. It just makes sense that it would be."

"We're going to look stone by stone?" Danni asked.

"If need be."

"For who? And for goodness sake, why?"

"You heard what Jones told us at the train station. What went wrong with the Bloody Sword expedition to kill Hitler would never be known because General Randolph took the proof with him to his grave. We're looking for the grave of General Orville Randolph."

Rigby suddenly stopped speaking and strained to listen. He heard it again. In the silence of the new morning a sound carried from the far corner of the cemetery. Metal hitting stone. He knew what it was: a shovel hitting a tombstone.

"Stay behind me and keep quiet," he said.

Rigby jogged ahead, picking his way through the headstones toward a stand of trees in the middle of the cemetery. Once he reached the trees he stopped. Using them as a shield, he peered into the cemetery grounds that extended to a pocket to the north. A few more trees were in this section of the cemetery, which was also bordered with trees. He could see the roofs of homes to the north beyond the tree line.

Toward the corner of the cemetery he heard the sound of metal on stone again, that same shovel turning up the earth.

The trees in the middle of the grounds afforded more cover. Rigby whispered to Danni to stay where she was. She refused. No time to argue. He pulled his gun and signaled for her to stay behind him.

He hurried toward the far trees, careful to stay on the grass and off the road to keep his footfalls silent. He stopped when he had no choice but to cross the pavement at intersecting roads that ran through the cemetery. After quietly stepping across the road he again jogged to the trees.

Danni came up behind him. Through the trees they saw the back of a man hunched over, shovel in hand, digging at the backside of a tombstone. The man paused and stood up, stretching.

Harley Jones.

Rigby hunched down behind a tree and Danni followed his lead. They waited and watched. From this position, Rigby could see Jones's rifle leaning against the tombstone.

Jones resumed digging at an angle to get under the stone. A few more shovels of dirt piled up behind him and he stopped. He dropped the shovel and got down on his hands and knees.

Jones reached into the hole and pulled out a round case. It looked to be about a foot-and-a-half long and four inches in diameter.

Large enough to hold a document, Rigby thought. He stood and released the safety on his gun. He held his hand up to Danni telling her to stay put, and stepped away from the tree into the clearing, inching his way toward Jones.

The old man rose to his feet, placed the cylinder on top of the gravestone and put his hands behind him on his lower back. He arched backward, stretching.

Rigby moved closer. Jones picked up the shovel and dug into the pile of dirt he had removed from under the headstone.

With Jones's hand occupied Rigby decided this was the perfect moment to announce himself.

Before Rigby could open his mouth Jones whirled and shoveled dirt into Rigby's face.

Instinctively, Rigby's hands flew to cover his eyes, his gun pointing to the sky. Jones tossed the shovel at Rigby. He ducked and took a glancing blow on his left shoulder. He stumbled to the ground and his gun flew from his hand.

Jones darted for his rifle that was leaning against the tombstone. He turned and pointed it at the fallen Rigby.

Chapter 58

Danni smashed into Jones in full sprint. They toppled onto the pile of dirt, the rifle falling to the ground.

Rigby grabbed his gun and scrambled to his feet.

Danni rolled away from Jones, giving Rigby a clear line of fire.

Jones reached toward the shovel.

"It's over, Jones," Rigby said. "Don't move."

Jones looked at the gun and leaned back against the dirt pile, covering his face with his hands, as if hiding in shame.

Rigby glanced at Danni.

"You all right?" he asked.

"Yes." She stood and dusted dirt off her jeans.

Rigby thought how much he liked and admired this woman. Sassy and tough.

He turned his attention to Jones. "You're under arrest for the murder of Pedro Campos and the attempted murder of Danni Warren and me."

"You forgot to mention the Monument Bomber. I saved your life."

"That too," Rigby said refusing to get into an argument with the man.

"Everything I did was about saving the country. Saving the reputation of great men," Jones said.

"Let's see what we got here," Danni said, picking up the case from atop the tombstone. "The real treasure map?" Excitement rang in her voice.

Rigby wanted to tell her to leave it for the professionals to open. The condition of whatever was in the case could be brittle, given its existence underground—even protected by the case. But he couldn't disappoint her after the brave action that probably saved the both of them.

Danni picked up the cylinder and twisted the cap. It took a couple of jerks and one strong grunt to get it to move. She unscrewed the cap and took it off. Looking into the cylinder she said, "A paper wrapped in plastic."

"From the USS *Houston's* safe," Rigby said with assurance. "No treasure map."

Danni reached into the case with two fingers and slowly pulled the plastic-encased document out. It had been rolled into a scroll to fit in the protective case. She peeled away the plastic and unrolled the paper while Rigby kept his gun trained on Harley Jones.

She looked at the document. To Rigby, it seemed an eternity before she revealed what she read.

"It's an order signed by President Roosevelt. The order overrides a previous one, which it says here was written in 1935. This one is dated in 1938."

"Two of the years Roosevelt was at Cocos Island aboard the *Houston*," Rigby said.

"This order cancelled Operation Bloody Sword." She looked up at Rigby. "You were right, Zane. Bloody Sword was the name of an operation, not the pirate."

"Does it say what Bloody Sword was?"

"Let me save you a lot of time," Jones said standing. "You won't find the whole story there. Maybe you'll come to your senses and let me do what I intended to do: destroy that document."

"An order canceling a military operation some seventy-five years ago. Why does it need to be destroyed?" Rigby asked.

"Because if the operation were completed, maybe millions of lives would have been saved. Look what's written there." Jones stepped toward Danni, extending his hand as if to take the paper.

Instead, with his right hand he pulled a knife from his pocket and placed the edge against Danni's neck.

"No more," he gasped.

Rigby tensed. The knife edged against Danni's neck. Jones looked ready to use it.

To Jones, Danni demanded, "Take that knife away from me."

"Not while your friend has the gun." He told Rigby, "Throw the gun over here or I cut her throat."

Rigby hesitated.

"Look," Jones started. Stopped. Started again with a softer approach. Rigby saw that he was trying to reason with him. "The fishing trip to Cocos Island in 1935 was a cover. The president was there to meet with British agents. Adolf Hitler had already become the Fuhrer, executed his enemies in the Night of the Long Knives and passed the Nuremberg laws one month before to deny the Jews all rights. Those who paid attention could see where this was going. They had a plan to kill Hitler. But, they needed military help. The United States was considered above the fray over the European concern for Hitler. There was no reason to suspect the U.S. would help in such an effort."

Rigby was frightened for Danni, but he forced himself to appear interested in Jones's tale to keep him talking.

"So these Englishmen disguised as treasure hunters visited with the president in a far-off place. Colonel Randolph was part of the meeting. The president agreed to consider their request for military help and ordered the Colonel to work with the Englishmen to put together a plan."

"One of those men was my husband's brother, Robert Warren?" Danni asked.

"Yes."

"Then the president had second thoughts," Rigby said.

"Stop moving, Rigby. I see what you're doing."

The edge of the knife's blade broke skin on Danni's neck. She cried out. A trickle of blood rolled down her neck.

257

Rigby took a step toward Jones.

"Back up or I'll finish the job," Jones warned.

"I wasn't up to anything," Rigby said standing still. "I was trying to understand, to hear what you were saying. To learn what Colonel Randolph was trying to do."

Jones hesitated. Rigby had given him a chance to speak up for Randolph and Rigby hoped he'd take it and buy some time.

"If you'd only understand," Jones said. "You'll see it my way. The plan was worked on and perfected over two-and-a-half years. It was set to go in 1938. Hitler was more dangerous then. He'd taken Austria. The assassination should have gone forward. But the president had a pang of conscience. He could not order the killing of another head of state. He was on the *Houston* again in 1938. He was supposed to give the final go-ahead for Bloody Sword. Everything was set. In fact, it was already in motion. Warren was in Germany and Marine corporal Myers, his American contact, was there too, ready to help him with the escape plan. The Marines would be part of the operation. That's when the president pulled the plug.

"Now you know what happened. You understand what I'm doing. Just go away. That's all. Forget about all this. Just make sure you leave the gun."

Rigby considered his next move. He did not want Jones to get the gun. Rigby was convinced he would use it to kill them both. Jones had already killed three. But Jones would soon tire of the cat and mouse game. He would cut Danni and come after him.

That's when Danni moved.

Her right hand came up across her chest, the index finger extended like a switchblade. She plunged it into Jones' left eye.

Jones screamed in pain as Danni twisted away from him, the knife slicing through her shirt.

One eye closed, Jones bellowed at the top of his

lungs and raised the knife high over his head, ready to drive it into Danni's chest.

Rigby's punch caught Jones squarely on the jaw and sent him sprawling. The knife fell from his hand. In a moment Rigby stood with the gun pointed at Jones, the man in a sorrowful heap with one eye closed, blood trickling, a deep red mark covering his cheek.

"Looks like I inherited something from my great-uncle," Danni said, standing next to Rigby and looking down at Jones. "Got a dime I can pop on his eye?"

Jones groaned. Even in his agony he wasn't through fighting. "You can't release that document. It's unpatriotic. General Randolph worshiped FDR. He may have disagreed with this decision to cancel Bloody Sword, but he was loyal. He wanted to protect the president's reputation. He was afraid if the world learned that he reversed himself on a plan to kill Hitler and the war could have been avoided, FDR's name would be mud.

"Without military support, Warren and Myers were left high and dry. They were not aware of the reversal of orders and their fate was sealed. Colonel Randolph went out of his way to recover their bodies after the failed assassination attempt and lay them to rest with respect on the island, far away from inquiring eyes. He did not want to lay blame at the feet of the president. The pirate legend of the island was perfect cover."

"You can't be certain that the assassination attempt would have been successful even if it had U.S. support," Rigby said.

"General Randolph was certain. He drew up the plan. If he was certain then I am certain. The General was afraid those who lost sons during the war years in the service would blame the president if the story came out. He devised a secret operation to retrieve the original order from the *Houston's* safe. When he told me the story he asked me to bury it with him. He wanted to continue protecting the president even in

259

death. I should have destroyed the damn thing."

"What about Paul Mallory. How did he find out?"

"He won a journalistic prize writing about some letter Roosevelt sent to Hitler in 1939. He wasn't part of Europe so he tried to be middleman between Hitler and the rest of the continent. He wrote to Hitler that he would make things better for Germany if Hitler promised twenty years of peace."

"I saw the prize for the article mounted on Mallory's wall," Rigby said.

"He must have learned about Bloody Sword in his research. I learned what Mallory was up to from the Director when I attended the FBI alumni meeting. She told a couple of us about the speaker's plan for Mount Rushmore. But I was the only one who knew Mallory's secret."

Rigby knew the Judge would be embarrassed when she heard about this revelation. That pleased him.

"Mallory wanted to expose Roosevelt as something less than noble. General Randolph would never permit such a thing. It was like I had orders from the grave. I went to Mallory."

"And killed him," Rigby said.

"He refused to cooperate. I was protecting FDR. I was protecting General Randolph. I'd do it again. Now you can destroy it. Do the patriotic thing."

"The president has nothing to fear from this document. He didn't want war. Roosevelt was trying to be a peacemaker. The letter to Hitler proves it. He wanted to keep this country on a moral high ground."

Chapter 59

The Speaker of the House of Representatives, Marshall Gaines, looked up from FDR's order cancelling Operation Bloody Sword. Zane Rigby sat across from the Speaker's desk in an ornate leather chair. The Speaker's aide, Richard Nolan, sat next to Rigby while the Judge paced next to the Speaker's desk.

Days before, Rigby informed Gaines about the results of his investigation. Satisfied, Gaines went public with his Mount Rushmore plans. He had insisted Rigby come by for personal congratulations. He also wanted to see the long-lost document.

The Speaker said. "I just don't understand the damage control in this case."

Rigby said, "General Randolph clearly believed President Roosevelt's reputation would be at risk if word got out that he canceled a plot against Hitler before the war. Much like the bad-mouthing FDR received because it was alleged he knew about the Pearl Harbor attack beforehand but did nothing to stop it. He had his defenders and that theory has been debunked, but this document is proof he canceled a hit on Hitler."

"We weren't at war at the time," Gaines said. "It would have been murder. The president understood that."

"The general didn't see it that way."

"What about the map Mrs. Warren found?"

"Jones said Randolph had it delivered to Alvin Warren. Randolph wanted Robert Warren's brother to know where his remains were. Randolph felt an obligation since he sent Robert Warren to his death with no support team. Jones insisted Randolph kept the document in hopes of honoring Warren and Myers one day, but he could never figure out how to do that without compromising President Roosevelt."

"Harley Jones!" The Judge spat out the name. "One of our own. How could he take the law into his own hands?" She paused her pacing and looked at Rigby. When she spoke her tone was softer. "It was about loyalty. I understand loyalty."

Rigby did not respond. He knew the Judge was looking for a sign, a nod of the head perhaps, to signify his loyalty to her. Rigby let the Judge know Jones began his killing spree in defense of his old boss after learning about Mallory and the Speaker's plan for Mount Rushmore from the Judge. He would let her know that he had no intention of spreading the story—but would wait until after they left the Speaker's office.

"FDR tried to make peace," the Speaker said. "That 1939 letter to Hitler proves it."

Rigby shrugged. "That's for the historians to fight about."

"This revelation won't hurt FDR," Gaines said. "At least by making my Mount Rushmore plan public the other day, it focused the country's attention on the partisan squabbling. It embarrassed the president and the pro tem enough to compromise on the budget."

Nolan laughed. "They're still arguing. Both are trying to take credit for the Mount Rushmore idea."

The Speaker smiled. "I think the only way they'll be happy is if they all get their faces carved in stone on the mountaintop."

"Politics," Rigby muttered. He was the only one that wasn't smiling.

Chapter 60

Rigby finished with the politicians. Let them work out their own problems and play their stupid games. The people noticed. He never understood the political world. Politicians wanted to be liked so that they can get elected, and then they fight all the time so no one likes them.

He had better things to do than deal with politicians. The killer was off the streets. That was what he cared about. He had avenged the death of Pedro Campos. He also found a new girlfriend in the process and he was excited about that. He wanted to get back to her.

A quick visit to the Judge to leave a disturbing hint that he knew how Harley Jones learned about Paul Mallory and he was off to see Danni Warren, who was waiting for him at his place.

When Rigby returned to his apartment he was greeted with a long kiss from Danni, followed by a pouty look as she backed away from him, eyes down.

"What's the matter?" Rigby asked.

"I'll miss you."

"Miss me?" He didn't understand until he looked through the bedroom door at Danni's open suitcase on the bed. He went in to take a closer look. It was filled.

"You're leaving?"

"You mustn't be angry, Zane. I escaped to England to rebuild my career. I was introduced to Alvin Warren at a party. Someone in my family knew—probably it came from Uncle Marvin a long time ago—that Alvin was connected to proof that Marvin Rothman tried to save the world. I was asked to be friendly to Alvin and find out. He started chasing after me. It was unexpected but it wasn't unpleasant. When Alvin appreciated me, shall we say, and wined and dined me—well, I could see he needed companionship and I needed his money. I found out nothing to rescue Marvin's reputation but I gained a husband and a comfortable life."

Rigby nodded and shrugged. He was acknowledging the turn in Danni's life but he couldn't come to terms with it. "Why do you have to go back to England?"

"I'm not going back to England. I'm going *everywhere*. I waited to say goodbye. I didn't run out this time like in Costa Rica."

"But you're leaving." Rigby felt his heart thud as if it dropped in his chest.

"I won the lawsuit, silly. I told you that."

"Right. So?"

"So I'm a rich, young enough lady who can enjoy the world."

Rigby was silent for a moment trying to cope with the change in *his* plans. Finally, he said, "I'm not exciting enough for you."

"Too exciting, actually," she said. "I don't fancy drowning in the Hudson River on my next date. I need time to spend my money."

Rigby sat on the edge of the bed. "Are you going back to the island?"

"Only if I have a real treasure map this time." She smiled. "I don't know where I'm going. But I promise to send postcards. Perhaps we can meet up somewhere."

A car horn rang out from the street.

"My taxi," she said as she closed her suitcase.

"I thought you weren't running away. What if I were late? Were you planning on just leaving a note?"

The bitter sound of his voice matched the bitter taste in his mouth.

"No, sweetie," she said. "I would have sent him away. I wanted to see you. To explain." She kissed him on the forehead. "I must go now. I'll write."

Danni picked up her suitcase and walked from the

apartment, closing the door softly behind her.

Rigby felt dazed, as if a haymaker had laid him out.

The phone rang.

It had to be Smitty, he thought as he fell back onto the bed and covered his face with a pillow.

THE END

HISTORICAL NOTES

The USS *Houston* was Franklin Delano Roosevelt's favorite warship. He traveled on it a number of times, including three trips to Cocos Island off Costa Rica in July 1934, October 1935 and August 1938.

The ship's log reports a meeting and lunch with British treasure hunters in 1935. The men were one team of many expeditions that worked the island looking for buried treasure. A German named August Gissler searched Cocos from 1889 to 1909. At least three treasures were reported buried on the island. One by Edward Davis, a pirate who sailed along the west coast of South America in the late 1600s, the second by Benito Bonito—called "The Bloody Sword" —in around 1819, and the third the treasure from the church in Lima, Peru in 1820.

The 1941 Charlie Chan movie, *Dead Men Tell*, starring Sidney Toler, dealing with four pieces of a treasure map and the ghost of a dead pirate, takes place on a treasure cruise headed for Cocos Island.

Roosevelt did catch a 110-pound sailfish on one of his trips to the island and a plant species on the island is named for him.

He received correspondence and communications while aboard ship and once complained, *Don't send dispatches part in plain language, part in code. Use one or the other.*

On March 1, 1942 the Japanese in the Battle of Sunda Strait sank the USS *Houston* and the HMS *Perth*. Surviving sailors from the *Houston* were used as slave labor to build the Thailand and Burma railroad. William Holden identified himself as a survivor from the *Houston* in *The Bridge on the River Kwai*.

The FBI does have records of an investigation of a plot to assassinate Adolf Hitler in 1933. Agents followed leads but never turned up the mysterious Daniel Stern.

On April 14, 1939 President Roosevelt sent a letter to Adolf Hitler attempting to broker a peace in Europe. Hitler responded weeks later in a two-plus hour speech rejecting FDR's overture.

About the Author

Joel Fox likes to say he has a long rap sheet in California politics. For three decades he has been a taxpayer and small business advocate, served on numerous state commissions, worked on many ballot issue campaigns, and advised a number of candidates. He is an adjunct professor at the Graduate School of Public Policy at Pepperdine University.

Authoring hundreds of opinion pieces, Fox has been published in the Wall Street Journal, USA Today, Los Angeles Times, and San Francisco Chronicle as well as other newspapers and websites.

Fox completed the Los Angeles FBI Citizens Academy program gaining a deeper understanding of the FBI and its mission.

Growing up in Massachusetts, Fox says he got his love of history breathing the air in the Boston area, often driving past the homes of the presidents Adams and visiting many historical sites.

So what did you think?

Please send Joel an email
and let him know what you
thought of
FDR'S TREASURE

He can be reached at:
joel@joelfox.com
Visit his website
www.joelfox.com